"Let me go, Patrick."

"Why are you afraid to be near me, Megan?"

"I'm not!"

"I'm glad to hear that," he said as he drew her against him.

She put out a hand to push him away, but the attempt was feeble. She was melting inside, melting from the ever-growing heat that had been absent for so long, and she wanted so very desperately to look up and see the old Patrick standing there, with that unique mixture of love and amusement in his eyes.

But when she did look up, what she saw was an intensity so powerful that for a few heartbeats she stopped breathing. Patrick had never looked at her that way. She might have forgotten a lot, but she knew she could never have forgotten that. Boyish pleasure had been replaced by a man's demands. And she knew now it was a woman's body that was responding.

ABOUT THE AUTHOR

Saranne Dawson is a voracious reader and has an avid interest in current events, which she says stems from "living in the middle of nowhere" in central Pennsylvania. With a master's degree in public administration, Saranne works as a human services administrator. In her spare time she sews, bikes, plays tennis, gardens and tends three "hopelessly obnoxious and pampered cats."

Intimate Strangers
Saranne Dawson

Harlequin Books

TORONTO • NEW YORK • LONDON
AMSTERDAM • PARIS • SYDNEY • HAMBURG
STOCKHOLM • ATHENS • TOKYO • MILAN

Published December 1986

First printing October 1986

ISBN 0-373-16180-8

Chapter One

"Karen, have the vouchers arrived yet from the Greek tour?"

Megan's tone of voice changed from irritation to uncertainty as she hurried from her office to the front of Touch of Paradise. Several prospective clients were browsing through the racks of travel brochures, but her partner was totally ignoring them. Instead, Karen stood staring out the big front window that faced the main street of Greenwich's elegant shopping district.

"Karen?" Megan said questioningly, after she had paused to greet the couple looking at the brochures. It certainly wasn't like Karen to be ignoring customers.

Karen turned toward her just as Megan herself reached the window. Megan saw the incredulous look on her friend's face—and then saw its cause.

She drew in a sharp, audible breath, then let it out raggedly as her mind began to whirl with the terrifying possibilities. It couldn't be her mother; Megan had spoken with her only the other day and she'd been fine. Could it be Joel, her brother? Germany wasn't exactly a safe duty tour these days; there'd been those recent bombings.

Then the time for anxious speculation ran out. The door opened and was immediately filled with a figure that was no less imposing for being so familiar. Irrationally, Megan's mind chose to fix upon the fact that he was wearing his summer uniform. Warm weather did come far more quickly to Washington than to Connecticut.

The tall man's flinty gaze swept briefly over the two customers, who stood there gaping unabashedly. Even in her confusion, Megan noticed their shock. The clientele of Touch of Paradise was a sophisticated one, but no one could look at a beribboned four-star general without a touch of awe. She actually straightened up a bit herself as his colorless gaze fell on her.

General Mark Daniels never really smiled—at least not in uniform—but his handsome face could go from grim to bland, as it did then. Megan had long since recognized that as a smile.

"Dad! What's wrong? Is it Mother? Joel?" Her voice was breathless and hurried, as if she thought that getting all the questions out quickly could prevent their being true.

Behind her, she heard Karen murmur a greeting. The general favored Karen with a nod, then took Megan's arm and led her toward her office. Her legs were trembling, but somehow she managed to keep up with his long stride.

It had to be her mother—some horrible accident. And she must be dead; otherwise he would have remained with her and called. Megan needed no urging to sink into her desk chair. The general remained standing, filling the cramped space with authority.

"It *is* Mother," Megan said, her voice breaking. "S-something has happened to her. She must be dead or you—"

"Your mother is fine. I came alone because she had a commitment she couldn't break. And under the circumstances, it seemed best that I be the one to come."

Megan stared at him through gathering tears. In or out of uniform, Mark Daniels never completely lost that voice of command—because in or out of uniform he was army all the way. Resentment began to bubble to the surface even as his clipped words of assurance relieved her fears somewhat.

"Joel, then?" she asked in a choked voice. "I've read about those bombings."

General Daniels shook his head impatiently. "No, Meggie. It's Patrick."

"Patrick?" she said, testing the unfamiliar name on her lips. It had been a long time since she'd spoken it.

And then, suddenly, she understood. During the past year or so, the bodies of MIAs had begun to be returned by a Vietnam now eager to make its peace with the U.S. in return for economic aid. American teams were searching the jungles of that ill-fated country for the thousands of men still unaccounted for—men like Patrick.

So his body had been recovered. She was glad, for his parents' sake. They were devout Catholics and deserved a real funeral service with a priest and a grave to visit. For herself, she wanted nothing; she had her memories, locked away in a safe place.

"I'm glad," she finally managed to say. "His parents will be happy."

The silence dragged on until she finally looked up at her father questioningly. Was he expecting her to break down and cry? Surely not, after all these years. He knew that she'd already gone through that particular hell. But then why was he looking at her so uncomfortably? The expression didn't suit him at all.

"He's alive, Meggie. I've talked to him."

"ALIVE." Three hours later, that word was still being turned over and over in her brain. She was alone in the small estate cottage that had been such a lucky find when she moved to Connecticut seven years ago. Outside, the dusk of early spring was falling, bringing with it the chill of winter's last icy breath. She was curled up on her sofa, unmoving. Finally, the dimness in the room registered, and she jerkily reached over to switch on a lamp. But her inner darkness remained.

After escorting her home in his chauffeured limousine and giving her the details of Patrick's homecoming in his brisk tones, her father had departed for Washington. Then her mother called, offering to come up. But Megan brushed aside the offer. Karen had called, too, offering to come over. And Megan had told her that she preferred to be alone just then.

How could she take an indisputable fact, a certainty reached years ago, and thrust it aside? Her life, which had been running smoothly for more than seven years, had just come to a bone-rattling halt, then done an about-face and plunged abruptly into the past.

Patrick Sean O'Donnell had surely been one of the least serious cadets ever to enter the hallowed Gothic halls of West Point. The class clown, the nemesis of the academy's brass, he had nevertheless managed to attain a high academic rank.

Patrick Sean O'Donnell, the tall, flame-haired son of a New York City policeman, had looked upon the staid academy with devilish sky-blue eyes from the very beginning and had tweaked its stuffiness whenever he got the chance.

Nineteen-year-old Megan had fallen in love with this improbable cadet the first time she met him. She'd been visiting the academy with her parents as guests of the superintendent, an old classmate of her father's. Patrick hadn't been her arranged date; his standing with the brass hadn't been high enough for that honor.

But that lack of standing hadn't prevented him from gaining a dance with her and then feigning knee-shaking terror when she told him how she had come to be there. Her father had just acquired his second star, and Megan had been surprised and then amused when this unlikely cadet refused to be impressed. As soon as he learned her name, he had easily slipped into an Irish brogue that reminded her of the delightful maternal grandmother for whom she'd been named.

Even before that first weekend ended she had heard some of the tales of Patrick's nonacademic and definitely non-military activities.

The "Toy Soldier" caper was, according to Patrick's fellow cadets, still being told, even though it had occurred more than three years ago, during those first grueling weeks aptly known as Beast Summer. It seemed that one day Patrick had appeared at morning formation wearing a paper replica of a windup key taped to the back of his shirt. He then inserted himself into the front row, where the key was visible to his fellow sufferers but not to their upper-class tormentors.

And Patrick himself had demonstrated to her his famous talent for talking without moving his lips—a talent that permitted him to make all sorts of outrageous remarks while saluting or standing stone-faced in formation.

He had also admitted that, yes, it *was* true that he had once worn a pearl necklace and earrings with his parade dress uniform. But he had removed them before the actual parade. One had to know the precise moment to quit, he had assured her dryly, and the fact that he was still wearing West Point gray was silent testimony that he did, in fact, know that precise moment.

He was also, she soon learned, the warmest, most affectionate man she'd ever known. His capacity for tenderness and for divining her thoughts astounded a girl who had spent her entire life surrounded by cold, controlled army men.

Eight months later they were one of the many couples who left the academy's chapel under crossed swords to begin married life in the army. General Daniels had beamed at them; his only daughter was marrying a West Pointer. He'd never been quite sure how to take the lanky cadet, but he'd expressed certainty that the new second lieutenant would shape up.

Six months later, Lieutenant Patrick O'Donnell had shipped out to Vietnam, to a war that was a source of violent controversy at home. He told Megan that he agreed with the protestors, but that he had gotten his free education and now he had to pay for it. Seven months later—only two months before the infamous fall of Saigon—Lieutenant Patrick O'Donnell was officially listed as missing in action. The price of that free education had been very high indeed.

That had happened eleven years ago. It had been nearly twelve years since she'd seen him. They'd had only six months together as husband and wife. The numbers bounced around in her head, echoing down the limitless corridors of her mind, alternately making sense and making no sense at all.

A loud buzzing sound shattered the stillness, and Megan started, returning abruptly to the present. She pushed herself up from the sofa, then went to the kitchen to press the button without bothering to turn on the intercom. She knew who was at the gate. She should have called him, but she'd been lost in the past. A few minutes later she heard the car approaching and went to the door, steeling herself in a manner that would have made her father proud.

"Hi, honey. Did you just get home?" the sandy-haired man said, as his gaze swept over her trim business suit.

"No, I've been here for hours," Megan replied, in a voice that must have matched her calm demeanor. It was unbelievable to think that none of her inner turmoil must show.

"Come in, Ted. There's... something I must tell you." She stood aside and motioned him into the small, cozy living room.

He had apparently caught on to something in her voice now, because instead of taking her into his arms he just bent to kiss her lightly.

"What's wrong, Megan? Your voice sounds strange."

She said nothing until he finally seated himself and frowned up at her questioningly. She should have canceled their date to gain some time before she had to face this. It surprised her that she wasn't even tempted to seek the comfort of his arms now. What was that telling her about their relationship?

"My father was here today. Patrick is alive. He's at Clark Air Base in the Philippines at the moment, and he'll be home soon . . . in a few days."

All of this came out very calmly, each word formed distinctly, nothing hurried. She watched as his expression changed from misapprehension to a slowly dawning understanding.

"Patrick?" he echoed uncertainly. "You mean your ex-husband?"

Megan wrapped her arms around herself as a wave of guilt swept over her. "He's not really my *ex*-husband. I mean, I never divorced him, and he wasn't declared legally dead or anything. I don't know what he is." Her final words came out as a strangled plea for understanding—not directed so much at Ted as at herself.

"My God!" was the hushed exclamation from the man who was still seated on the sofa. "I'd wondered about that, but I didn't want to pry. I figured that you'd tell me at some point."

"I never bothered to get a divorce because it seemed pointless. I had no intention of remarrying. I could have gone into court and had him declared legally dead, but I didn't do that, either. Since there was no property—no joint assets or anything—there just was no reason."

She sat down opposite Ted and wished that the numbness would go away. She wanted to feel something, anything. She'd been in this state ever since her father had brought her home—lost in a thick fog. She should be fighting her way out of it.

Megan stared at the man seated across from her. Ted Wayne was a good man—kind, generous, supportive. Also attractive, intelligent and successful. She'd met him about six months before, when he'd come into the travel agency to inquire about spots for a winter vacation. He was thirty-eight, six years older than Megan, and had let it be known in a subtle manner that he was interested in marriage.

During the six months she'd known him, Megan had slowly permitted their relationship to move from a casual to a steady dating basis. Recently, that part of her that had been locked away for twelve years had begun to stir restively. But nothing at all was stirring at this moment.

"He'll be coming home, then? I mean, here to see you?"

"No, not here. He's flying into Andrews—near Washington—in two days. My father spoke with him and told him I'd be there to meet him." She listened to herself for a moment. It sounded as though she didn't *want* to meet him. Did she?

"But how did he survive? All the other MIAs have been coming home in bags."

Megan winced at the harshness of his tone, but she couldn't blame him. He, too, was still fighting this reality.

"It's a rather confusing story. But from what I understand, he and his men and some Vietnamese troops they were training were captured by the Viet Cong in some place whose name I can't remember and couldn't pronounce anyway. It's near the Vietnam-Cambodia border. Some were killed, but those who survived, like Patrick, were put to work in a village. All the village men were either already dead or off at war.

"The Viet Cong apparently kept them there by threatening to destroy the entire village—women, children and all—if they tried to escape."

"But the war has been over for more than ten years," Ted protested.

"Not in that area it hasn't," she replied. "There's been an ongoing war between the Vietnamese and the Cambodians. Apparently, the military governor, or whatever he was, had told no one higher up of his prisoners' existence. They were very useful to him, you see, with all the other men gone. So he just kept them there, doing construction work, agricultural work and so forth.

"Then, about two months ago, the governor died. A new governor came and discovered them there. In the meantime, the political climate had changed, and you know yourself that Vietnam is now trying to normalize relations with us. So they released them, blaming the dead governor for the mess and thereby making themselves look good to the United States."

"So there were others released with him?" Ted asked, his face still registering his shock.

"Yes, there were two others. Three more had died sometime after being captured."

"My God!" Ted said again, shaking his head in disbelief.

Megan was finally beginning to feel a return of something. But it was accompanied by a strange sort of detachment, a surreal sense that all this was happening to someone else. She felt the way one feels when disaster strikes a close friend: she could empathize, but couldn't quite reach her deepest emotions.

"What are you going to do? You said your father told him you would meet him?"

What *was* she going to do? She hadn't really gotten to that question yet, though she knew she should have. *One step at a time,* she counseled herself.

"Yes, well, I'll meet him, of course. He *is* my husband, Ted."

Ted stood up and walked over to her, then cupped her shoulders with his hands and looked at her very seriously.

"Megan, he's *not* your husband. You were married for, what…six months, and he's been gone for twelve years. You were a twenty-year-old kid and now you're a thirty-two-year-old woman."

He paused, then went on in that same somber tone. "And I doubt that you've even begun to consider what's happened to him in those twelve years."

She had in a very vague sort of way. It was impossible to focus on anything just now.

"I have to have some time alone to try to sort all this out, Ted. I'm sorry about our date tonight, but under the circumstances…"

"You still have to eat. Let me take you out to dinner at least. We can skip the film, although a diversion might be just what you need right now."

What she really needed was a respite from well-meaning people telling her what she needed—her father, her mother, Karen, even Patrick's mother, who had called earlier, too.

She stretched up to kiss the corner of his mouth. "Thank you for the offer, Ted. But I'm not hungry and I'd really rather be alone."

He searched her face carefully, then nodded and turned toward the door. But after pulling it open, he paused again.

"I'll be here, Megan. I'm not going anywhere."

She smiled and managed to close the door behind him before the tears began. Worst of all, she wasn't even sure why she was crying. Was it for Patrick and their long-lost love? For Ted and a love that was yet to come? For herself and a contented life that had just blown up in her face?

The phone rang. She considered letting her answering machine take the call, then ran at the last moment to answer it herself.

"Megan O'Donnell, please," said a crisp female voice.

"This is Megan."

"Major Daniels is calling. Please hold."

She heard two clicks and then her brother's deep voice—so much like their father's—beamed through the line. "Meggie? Dad just told me about Patrick."

"Yes," she said for lack of anything better to say.

"Are you all right?"

"I'm fine, Joel." Stiff upper lip. He would expect that. Like their father, Joel was army all the way. A future general.

"You don't sound it, old girl," he said gently. "I don't know what Dad said to you, but you do realize that he's going to be very, ah...different?"

"Yes. It's been twelve years."

"It's not just the years, Meggie. What he went through does something to a man."

For the first time, Megan felt a spark of interest in this conversation. Joel had been two years ahead of Patrick at West Point and had known and liked him.

"What do you think it's done to him, Joel?"

"That's hard to say, Meggie. But I'm reasonably certain that he won't be coming home the same man who left. I hope I'm wrong, though."

She felt as though a shard of ice had pierced her heart. All her memories of Patrick were of a man who laughed at life, whose sense of fun was infectious, whose charm was irresistible. That man might be very different now. That's what Joel meant.

She had a sudden clear memory of that Sunday at West Point when she had announced her intention of spending the day with Cadet O'Donnell. Her father had turned questioningly to his old classmate, the superintendent. She could almost hear the man's chuckle.

"I'm not surprised. O'Donnell seems to be irresistible. I'm afraid the academy won't be quite the same when he's gone."

And neither had she ever been quite the same after that weekend, she thought with a bittersweet smile of remembrance.

"Meggie, are you there?"

She pulled herself back to the present. "I'm here, Joel. I was just . . . remembering."

"He'll need you, Meggie. More than ever."

"Yes. Thank you for calling, Joel. I'll talk to you soon."

She put down the receiver, thinking about her brother's final words. He was wrong. Patrick had never needed her. He had certainly loved her, but he hadn't needed her. Need just hadn't entered into it. She explored that thought for a while, wondering. Was it important?

Then she wandered into the bathroom and switched on the light to peer into the big mirror over the sink. Twelve years. Had she changed much? She didn't think so. Her hair was different, of course—longer and recently restyled into something looser after several years of tangled curliness. But it was as black as ever, with a silvery blue sheen in certain kinds of light.

She wore more makeup now—shadow and a touch of mascara, although her thick-lashed blue eyes required very little adornment. Foundation and blush now covered whatever minor imperfections the years had brought to her normally high-colored, clear complexion. But the heart-shaped face with its big eyes, slightly snubbed nose and full, generous mouth were essentially unchanged.

She lowered her gaze. Not much change in the rest of her, either. She might have gained a pound or two, but that was all. She was five feet four and too curvy for today's standards. Long-legged and lean was the look now.

Then she looked back into her own eyes. There *were* changes; she could see that now. They were all internal, but they leaked out through her eyes. The naive girl of twenty had become the sophisticated woman of thirty-two. Where had she read a description of someone as having "old eyes"? She couldn't recall, but she now knew what it meant.

Megan Daniels O'Donnell had become a very different person during the past twelve years. When the vastness of that change began to dawn on her, she felt herself growing very uneasy. So she left the bathroom and went into the small kitchen, hoping to quell her disturbance with some food.

The refrigerator contained two carefully wrapped slices of pizza, some tuna salad, several kinds of cheese and a bag of apples. She grimaced at the pizza, then dug out the tuna, some cheddar and an apple and put it all on a plate, which she then carried back into the living room.

Megan didn't cook. She ate out or carried home or popped a frozen meal into the microwave. For a time, she had tried her best to ignore housework, too, but that hadn't worked. She was inherently neat—unfortunately, from her point of view.

She also hardly ever entertained at home. When it became necessary to repay social obligations, she generally took the people in question out to dinner. Fortunately, her business had prospered sufficiently to make that possible.

She did no charity work, volunteered for nothing and refused to join any organizations except for professional ones that were business related.

She did none of these things because they were exactly what good military wives were expected to do. Her mother was the very epitome of the officer's wife, and while Megan loved her dearly, she also used her as a guide to what *not* to do.

Megan usually slouched around the cottage and did her weekend shopping in tattered jeans and T-shirts, one of which said "No Nukes" and another of which said "Caution: The Pentagon May Be Dangerous to Your Health." She did this because her mother was always impeccably dressed, even at home, and because it amused her to imagine her father's reaction were he ever to see those T-shirts. But he hadn't as yet, because she hadn't quite worked up the nerve to wear them in his presence.

Megan's relationship with her father was difficult at best. Mark Daniels had never been one to leave his work at the office. He was a general in personality even before he became one in fact. She supposed that she loved him—he was her father, after all. But what she had felt for him through most of her life fell more into the category of respect or awe. What she felt now was that he was the army personified. And Megan hated the army.

Obviously, she had not always been this way. There had been a time when she permitted the army to dictate her life and had truly not known that she had any alternatives. But the seeds of rebellion had probably been there very early on. How else could she explain her instantaneous attraction to a West Point cadet who refused to take the army very seriously? If she hadn't already been harboring thoughts of rebellion, she surely would have married some serious-minded future general instead of a goof-off like Cadet O'Donnell. Not for one minute had she believed her father's expressed opinion that Patrick would shape up into a fine officer.

The Great Change, which she thought of as being her own resignation from the army, had come about gradually, beginning several years after Patrick's disappearance. When the news came, she had been living in Washington with her parents, playing the role of the officer's wife. For a long while after that devastating blow, she had allowed herself to be surrounded and consoled by the army's gigantic extended family.

Ironically enough, her father was the one responsible for setting her on the path that ultimately brought about her severance from the army. He suggested that she take some college courses to get her mind off Patrick, and she had followed the thinly veiled orders with something less than enthusiasm. But a few business courses had led to full-time enrollment, and in the process she met Karen Holland, the outgoing daughter of a Connecticut congressman. Life began to change.

By the time Megan had earned her degree, she and Karen were making their plans to open a travel agency. They were already sharing an apartment, and Megan's life had moved several steps—hesitant steps—away from the army.

The two women took themselves off to Connecticut and opened their business in Greenwich, having borrowed the seed money from their respective parents. The general hadn't exactly been pleased about Megan's departure from Washington, but he had allowed himself to be persuaded by his wife that their daughter needed a fresh start.

All through this time, Patrick had been slowly slipping away. Megan was busy with her classes, then busy building new friendships, and then finally busy building an entirely new life in Connecticut. She could not have said exactly when it was that Patrick went from being "missing" to being "dead," but he had made that move in her mind long before she owned up to it in conversation.

By the time that happened, Megan felt no real guilt about it. Her separation from the army had allowed her life to move on, and Patrick was put permanently into a warm, dark corner of her mind, a memory associated with what she gradually came to think of as her girlhood.

Even their marriage was finally put into that category. They'd spent most of that time at Schofield Barracks in Hawaii, the jumping-off place for officers and troops bound for Vietnam. There had been warm, silvered nights on the beaches, gay luaus, sight-seeing trips—youthful fun made even better by Patrick's laughter and zest for life. Only later would those months seem to have had a fin de siècle flavor to them, an end to childhood.

There had been some serious moments, of course, primarily when they had both realized that the war was not going to end before Patrick would be called to it. But even that unwelcome news could not be taken seriously; they were young and in love and would live forever. Patrick would serve his time and then they would go to New York, where he would set the business world afire while she would find something to do, some sort of job.

That other Megan had never taken herself very seriously, because no one had ever suggested that she should. It was enough that she was pretty and socially poised and handled military life with all the ease of one born into it. The civilian world of the early seventies might have been feeling the effects of the women's movement, but the conservative military world had not yet taken note of it. Officers' wives were...well, officers' wives. Probably they still were; she tried not to think about it now.

Officers' wives kept immaculate homes, always dressed in perfect taste, volunteered endlessly and spent enormous amounts of time trying to further their husbands' careers. She had done all of those things—with the exception of trying to further Patrick's career. First of all, he had no intention of furthering that career himself. Second, if he had, the mere fact that she was a general's daughter would have given him all the assistance he would have required.

Megan bit into her apple and made a disgusted sound. How could she ever have been that way? Surely that silly, worthless girl had died and she had just assumed her body. She became both angry and embarrassed even thinking about it.

The Megan who now sat with her shoes kicked off and her feet propped up on the cocktail table simply refused to claim ownership of that other person. This Megan was a shrewd and successful businesswoman who frequently worked twelve-hour days and managed her finances so well that she was currently considering both the expansion of the business and the purchase of a waterfront condominium. The men she dated were successful and undaunted by her success, and they would have laughed at the simpering idiot she had once been.

How could this Megan be expected to welcome back into her life the man who had married that other Megan? It was patently absurd. He belonged back in that embarrassing extended childhood.

She began to think again about her brother's remark. Patrick couldn't possibly need her. Any man who could have been happily married to that shallow little creature certainly had to be very self-sufficient. What did she have to offer him now—the sympathy of a stranger? He wouldn't need or want that.

But still, she felt uneasy. Was it at all possible that she could slip back into that past? Even as she disparaged it, she could feel it beckoning to her with all its warmth and mindless gaiety. That foolish girl must still be inside her somewhere, despite her denials.

Finally, she reached some sort of compromise with herself. She no longer loved Patrick, but she did cherish the memories of their love. So she owed him something—and besides, he *was* still her husband.

Chapter Two

"When you told me, my first thought was 'How wonderfully romantic.' But that lasted exactly as long as it took me to realize just how long twelve years really is and how much has happened. What on earth are you going to do, Megan?" Karen leaned forward, ignoring her luncheon salad as she frowned at her partner and best friend.

"I have to see him," Megan stated flatly. "I can't even think beyond that."

"But you have to. You can't just go down there without some sort of . . . plan."

Megan nodded slowly. "I know that. But I just have this feeling that it won't be necessary."

"What on earth do you mean by that?"

"Karen, you just said it yourself. It's been twelve years. He married a child, a silly little girl. It surely won't take him long to see that she no longer exists. And as soon as he does, we'll part as friends."

"Do you really think it will be that simple?" Karen asked doubtfully.

"I didn't mean to imply that it'll be easy. Both of us will be tempted to turn back the clock, I suppose. But it won't work. I know that, and I think he'll know it, too."

"But what are you really feeling? I mean, do you love him at all?" Karen peered at her intently.

Megan's answer was slow in coming. It was a simple question—with very complex answers. "I love the memories that we shared, even if I am embarrassed by the person I was then. And he's the only man I've ever...slept with. There are bonds. But that doesn't constitute love."

Megan's voice trailed off toward the end, as she saw Karen's expression. No one who knew Megan would have guessed that this outwardly sophisticated woman was so terribly inexperienced when it came to men. The fact that she'd hidden the truth until now—even from her best friend—said quite a lot about her feelings on the matter.

"So there've been no other men in all this time? I know that you date, of course, and I just assumed..." Karen finished with a shrug, obviously perplexed.

"I know it seems strange," Megan acknowledged, "and I don't know how to explain it, either. I had accepted the apparent fact of Patrick's death, and if I'd been worried about the moral or legal implications I could have had him declared dead and been completely free. But I'm not sure that would have changed anything.

"I've met men I liked a lot over the years, but every time that issue came up it seemed easier to end the relationship than to face up to it. Then the longer I went without facing up to it, the more difficult it became." Megan paused, then grimaced.

"Part of it, I think, is the result of my background—that 'duty, honor, country' thing. Patrick had been serving his country when he disappeared, and even though I thought he was dead, there was still a part of me that felt like a traitor if I even thought about becoming involved with another man. It was that sense of a nonending, too. How can you have a new beginning when there has been no real ending?"

Megan's voice had taken on the quality of a plea for understanding, but she knew that Karen was incapable of giving her that understanding. Other MIA wives would have understood, but she had long since cut herself off from them.

Karen nodded solemnly and began to pick at her salad. Megan knew that Karen was trying her level best to understand, and loved her for that effort. But she also knew that she was alone in this, alone by choice, because continuing with the MIA wives' group would have meant continuing with the army.

Finally, Karen looked up at her with a grin. "You *could* fall in love with him all over again, you know."

Megan was still thinking about that hours later as she tried to tie up some loose ends in preparation for her absence, an absence the duration of which she had no way of knowing, though she didn't intend for it to be long.

Was it possible that she could fall in love with Patrick all over again? There was just no denying the appeal of that idea. But Megan was far too practical to grow starry-eyed at such a prospect. She had undergone a transformation so dramatic that only her outer shell remained more or less intact. Patrick would have changed, too, and perhaps just as dramatically. It seemed to her that the odds in favor of their having changed in complementary ways were very long indeed. It would be useless and even dangerous to let herself hope they could beat those odds.

Besides, how could either of them every truly accept the changes in the other? Wouldn't they always be seeing each other as they had been? Couples who marry as young as they had always change, but the changes are more gradual—or are perceived as being that way. Their six-month marriage had been followed by a hiatus of nearly twelve years. They were strangers—intimate strangers, but still strangers.

The telephone calls began just as she was leaving her office. The news of Patrick's return had been released to the media. Karen stepped in and handled the calls smoothly, saying that Megan was not in the office, which was half true, since she was standing in the doorway at the time, and that she had already left for Washington, which wasn't true, of course—she had a 7:00 a.m. flight from Westchester Airport the next morning. With a grateful smile, Megan escaped, leaving Karen to fend off any other reporters. She marveled at how quickly they'd been able to track her down, then wondered if her father could be behind that.

When she arrived at her cottage, there already were two calls from reporters on her answering machine, and she hadn't even changed clothes before yet another one came in. So she left the machine on, very grateful for modern technology.

The evening news on television was full of the story and showed the formal portrait that had been done of Patrick for his West Point graduation. Megan's own copy of the photograph had long since been packed away and she hadn't see it in years. Bittersweet memories assaulted her as she stared at the screen.

From the news story she learned that neither of the other two men being released with Patrick had been married, and it was this bit of information that brought her, finally, to the consideration of some very practical matters. Where on earth could she and Patrick go that they wouldn't be hounded by the press? Why hadn't she thought about this before?

She considered reserving a hotel suite, either in Washington or in New York. But that seemed so impersonal, and besides, a hotel could offer no real protection from the press. She could bring him here to her home, of course. From a purely practical standpoint, that was an excellent idea; the estate had very tight security. But she dismissed the thought nonetheless. She didn't want to bring him home, and at the moment, she didn't care to examine her reasons, either.

Then the solution came to her. The place was isolated, roomy enough and, perhaps most importantly, it held no memories for them as a couple. Patrick had never been there, although they'd once thought of sneaking out there when he'd visited her in Washington before their marriage. It was perfect.

"I'M NOT GOING!"

"But, Meggie, dear, you must...."

"Don't be ridiculous, Meggie! We can understand that you're nervous, but he's expecting you to be there!" The general's authoritative voice interrupted his wife's softer one.

"He's expecting me to be there because you told him I'd be there," Megan pointed out calmly, meeting her father's determination with her own.

"You're his wife."

Megan heard thirty years of military duty in that statement and it fueled her anger. Her father was reminding her that she was an *officer's* wife, not just an ordinary wife.

"You've turned this thing into a media circus and I am *not* going to appear in the center ring."

Her continued determination must have gotten through to him, because he actually looked and sounded rather defensive.

"I had nothing to do with the arrangements. You know that."

She did know that. Public relations didn't fall within the general's responsibilities. Nevertheless, he could have exercised his influence to stop it.

"By 'you' I meant the Pentagon. As far as I'm concerned, the two are synonymous. I'll wait for him at the cabin. You can see that he has a car and directions and that he gets away without being followed."

Father and daughter glared at each other across the width of the elegant living room. In the middle stood Megan's mother, the general's wife, looking increasingly distraught.

So this is it, Megan thought. How many times had she imagined this confrontation? She'd slipped away from him and from the army so slowly over the years that she knew now he'd been completely unaware of the loss. To him, she was still army—the daughter of a general and the wife of an officer. Yes, the confrontation had been inevitable, but she had never imagined that it would come over Patrick.

There were innumerable speeches in her mind for this occasion, and she felt compelled to use at least some of them, especially since she could feel a slight twinge of guilt over that sense of duty that her father exuded so effortlessly. One could not grow up as Megan had without feeling it, and she blamed him for it—and for everything else at this point.

"I'm not army anymore, Dad, and I haven't been for a very long time. I've resigned. I don't have one single friend who has anything at all to do with the military; I've made very sure of that. So I do not march to that brass band anymore."

The general's expression became even grimmer. Soldiers would quake in their boots at that look, and not so very long ago, Megan would have, too. But not now, not anymore.

"Your husband is an army officer."

"My husband is my husband in name only, and he never considered himself to be anything more than a temporary army officer. He was paying for his education, and that's all." And how he paid, she thought sadly as she felt a pang of guilt that they should be engaging in this petty argument over someone who had suffered as Patrick had. But then, the argument wasn't really over him; he was only the unwitting catalyst.

"Dear, Patrick's parents will be here any minute. What on earth will you tell them?" her mother asked.

"I won't have to tell them anything because I won't be here. I'm leaving for the cabin now, assuming I can dodge those reporters outside. I love the O'Donnells, Mom. They're good people. I'll explain to them later. Goodbye."

"Megan!" Her full name, so seldom used by her father, became a sharp command.

Megan paused at the door and threw him a mock salute. "Permission to leave, General."

She fought down the temptation to run as soon as she had closed the door behind her. He couldn't follow her, of course, because he wouldn't risk a scene with reporters present. There were two of them, a man and a woman, waiting in the tree-shaded Arlington street. As soon as she approached, they hurried up to her.

Megan had already had an opportunity to evaluate them and had decided with considerable relief that they didn't appear to be the obnoxious types who wouldn't take "no comment" for an answer. She held up a hand to ward off their questions.

"I have nothing to say, other than that I'm very happy that Patrick is alive and coming home."

Having said that, she hurried to her rental car and slid in. Just as she'd expected, they looked disappointed, but they showed no intention of following her. She wondered what they might have said or done if they'd known that she was running away from Patrick's welcoming ceremonies. She quickly drove off, before guilt could force her to do an about-face.

THE CABIN WAS LOCATED in the Catoctin Mountains of western Maryland, not far from the presidential retreat at Camp David. Her father had bought the land and had the cabin built as soon as they settled in for his first duty tour at the Pentagon. Megan hadn't been to the cabin in years and had never driven there alone, so she was hoping that she would be able to find it without difficulty. After that little scene with her father, she hadn't wanted to hang around to ask for directions.

For the first half hour or so of her journey, Megan just smiled to herself. Her satisfaction at having stood up to the

general outweighed for the moment her guilt over abandoning Patrick.

Until her arrival in Washington, it hadn't occurred to her
to refuse to meet Patrick's plane. Duty had called and she
had answered—the ingrained habit of a lifetime. But once
she'd listened to her father's description of the welcoming
ceremonies, Megan made her decision not to attend very
quickly.

The vice president would be there, and there was a possibility that the president himself might be coming over from
the White House by helicopter. There would be cabinet officers, congressional delegations and, of course, a plethora
of military brass. Bands would play, speeches would be
made and the Washington press corps would be there in
their usual overabundance.

Something inside her had just snapped when she heard all
this. It wasn't that she didn't want to welcome Patrick
home; she just refused to be a part of this typical army welcome.

Most people who knew of her background might have
assumed that Megan's hatred of the army was the result of
Patrick's loss. But they were wrong. They couldn't begin to
understand that life, that all-encompassing army life into
which she had, quite literally, been born.

Not until she took those first tentative steps away from
that life had Megan discovered that she had a separate
identity, and there remained in her a very deep-seated fear
that she could once more lose it. It had taken years to find
and develop that self, and she wanted to be very sure that the
army didn't get a chance to snatch it away from her.

But her decision to run away now stemmed from far more
than just those fears. At the last moment, Megan had realized that she just could not face Patrick in front of a
crowd. They would be expecting some grand romantic scene
that would make wonderful film for the six o'clock news.
No one would understand that two strangers, not two happy

lovers, would be meeting on that tarmac. She knew she couldn't perform as expected, and she doubted very much that Patrick could, either. She was doing them both a favor.

Megan had managed to glean some further information from her father before her abrupt departure. The general had spoken with the military doctors who had examined Patrick and his companions upon their arrival in the Philippines. Patrick was physically well—"excellent condition," her father had said. And an army psychiatrist had declared him to be "amazingly free from trauma," whatever that meant.

She was very glad that Patrick had survived his long ordeal both physically and mentally intact. Her dreams for the past two nights had been haunted by images she hadn't permitted in her waking moments, images of a physical or emotional cripple, destroyed by his years in captivity.

But still, she was certain that the Patrick she had known and loved had not survived. Halfway across the world, he had been changing even as she herself had been changing. For them both, the long years had worn away all that was recognizable and dear.

She drove on, lost in thought about those changes and trying to guess what he must be like now. Then she frowned as a new thought struck her. At some point during those years, she had given Patrick up for dead, had written him out of everything but her memories. But he, on the other hand, had had every reason to assume that she had gone on living.

She mulled that over with increasing uneasiness. What did it mean, if anything? She had continued to exist for him, while he had ceased to exist for her? She had the unpleasant feeling that this was very important—perhaps the most important point of all.

Her life had stumbled badly, then picked up and moved on, while his had, in effect, remained locked in place. Had he been totally cut off from the world? Had news reached him and enabled him to understand that the world (and by association, she) had moved on?

Twelve years. What had happened in that time? It was surprisingly difficult to recall, but she knew that quite a lot must have happened. Not just political events, but social changes, too. How would Patrick feel about all those things? She was shocked to realize that she couldn't guess, because they had never really discussed such matters.

Instead, they'd talked about army gossip, parties and all the other events in such a shallow existence. Despite what one might think, they'd never even talked that much about the war, and when they had, Megan's only interest in it had been whether or not Patrick would be sent to it.

She knew that Patrick had had a serious side, even if it hadn't been much in evidence, and she wondered now if some of his buddies might not have known him far better than she had. She began to feel again that familiar self-disgust at her old shallowness and once again wondered why on earth he had married her.

Fortunately, she saw her exit approaching just then, and thereafter she was kept too busy trying to find her way to the cabin to engage in any more self-recrimination.

One hour later, Megan was carrying her luggage and bags of groceries into the cabin. A huge steak that she had taken from her mother's freezer was in one of the bags. Anyone who has ever ventured abroad for any length of time invariably returns with steak on his mind, and Patrick had been a steak devotee in any event—he liked them medium rare, done on a grill.

The cabin was musty and dusty, and preparing it for occupancy would keep her busy for a while. After she had put away the groceries and aired and dusted the place, she glanced at her watch. If Patrick's military flight was on time—and considering the exalted status of his welcoming committee, it would be—he was now back on American soil and suffering through the elaborate welcoming ceremonies. She felt another pang of guilt but rid herself of it with the knowledge that her presence would only have made the ordeal worse for him.

After that, he would go to the private luncheon her mother had planned; her parents, Patrick's family, and the chief of staff and his wife would take part. Perhaps she should have stayed for that. She could have waited for him in the relative privacy of her parents' home.

Why hadn't she? Well, partly because she would still have been faced with the unpleasant prospect of playing a role— and before an even more demanding audience. But the real and unpleasant answer to that question was that she had seen the perfect opportunity to make the statement she had been wanting to make for years, and she had seized it without considering the possibility of compromise. That knowledge did very little for her self-esteem at the moment.

She had hung up her clothes in the bedroom that had always been hers, and she went there now to make up the bed. As she worked, her growing uneasiness abruptly gave way to panic. She sank down onto the bed, nearly suffocated by her anxieties. The linens she had gotten out for the other bedroom were lying on a chair, mocking her.

Surely he wouldn't expect to share a bed with her. Surely he would understand that they weren't really husband and wife anymore, that his status was no different from that of a former lover. Of course, since she didn't have any of those, she wasn't too sure just what they considered their status to be. But she knew what *she* believed it to be.

She picked up the other set of linens and hurriedly went off to make up the bed in the room that had been her brother's. The act had a strong symbolic significance that soothed her frazzled nerves to some extent, but she was still trembling and anxious when she returned to the living room.

For twelve years there had been no one else in her life. She began to regret that, because it seemed to lend credibility to their marriage—and she didn't want that.

But what about him? Had there been a woman in his life? He'd apparently spent those same twelve years in a village surrounded by husbandless women, and the Vietnamese were a very attractive people. Did it matter to her if he had taken a lover, perhaps even fathered children? She thought about the possibility of little red-haired, blue-eyed Vietnamese children and dismissed it immediately. Patrick had probably taken a lover, but he would not have fathered children. For all his lack of seriousness, he had never been irresponsible.

Did she care if he had taken a lover? She just wasn't sure. If they'd been together, she certainly would have cared, but... She wondered if she would ask him, if he would volunteer the information, if she even wanted to know.

Then she began to wonder what she would say if he asked her that same question. If she told him the truth, wouldn't that be lending false credence to their nonexistent marriage? But if she lied, wouldn't that be wrong, too?

Why had she allowed this absurd state of affairs to go on after all these years? Would she have spent the remainder of her life waiting for an ending? It was a chilling thought.

She'd eaten no lunch and very little breakfast and decided that the queasiness she was feeling might stem in part from that neglect. The wine she'd bought wasn't yet properly chilled, so she poured some over ice and began to nibble at some cheese. The phone rang just as she was about to cut into the crusty French bread, and its sudden shrill sound shattered her nerves still more.

Patrick? Calling to ask if he should come? What should she say? She licked her lips nervously, cleared her throat and picked up the phone very reluctantly. "Hello?"

"Patrick just left, dear. Your father offered to have him flown out by helicopter, but he said he wanted to drive, so I lent him my car."

Megan wondered why he had turned down the offer of a helicopter. Maybe because he didn't want to arrive too quickly? Might he, too, be nervous about this meeting? It was the first time she had considered that possibility. But she quickly dismissed it. She couldn't imagine Patrick's being anything but his usual buoyantly confident self.

"Thank you, Mom. How... how is he?"

"He's fine, dear. Very healthy and fit."

"I don't mean how he looks. I mean what's he like?" She spoke with a trace of impatience, then almost laughed at the absurdity of having to ask what her own husband was like.

There was a brief, nerve-racking hesitation. "He's different, dear, but then, I'm sure you anticipated that. Your father was quite impressed with him. They had a long talk."

Megan was silent for a moment as she digested that. Her father was impressed? What did that mean? "What did *you* think?"

"You know that I've always been fond of Patrick, and that hasn't changed." She hesitated, then went on rather apologetically. "It's terrible to say this, and I hope you'll understand what I mean. In some ways, I think this horrible experience has done him some good. Your father thinks so, too."

Megan didn't like the sound of that at all. Furthermore, she was tempted to comment on her mother's gift for understatement. "Horrible experience," indeed. "Hell" would be far closer to the truth.

"Meggie, your father is very upset over your behavior. I've convinced him that your decision to meet Patrick at the cabin was probably for the best, but he's still quite shocked at your attitude."

"Toward the army, you mean?"

"Yes. We just had no idea you felt that way. It's ... very hard to take."

"Then we're nearly even, because the army is impossible for me to take. I meant what I said."

"But why? Surely you don't blame the army for what happened to Patrick?"

Megan sighed. "I'm not that naive, Mom. I don't blame the army for anything, really. I just don't want anything to do with it, and, thank heavens, I don't *have* to have anything to do with it anymore."

After yet another pause, her mother murmured a worried "I see," meaning, of course, that she didn't see at all. For a moment, Megan wanted to explain. But how could she? Her mother was as much a part of the army as her father was, and she couldn't begin to understand how Megan felt. So Megan hastily changed the subject.

"Do you think that it was safe for Patrick to drive out here? Has he driven at all?"

"We asked him about that. He's done some driving and he felt confident. Meggie, *do* try to be understanding. I know how difficult all this must be for you, but—"

"I will be, Mom. Don't worry about me." Meggie cut her off without waiting to hear if she had been referring to Patrick or to the general. Then she said a quick goodbye and hung up.

She checked her watch. If Patrick had just left, she had plenty of time. She laughed mirthlessly. Plenty of time indeed. She'd had twelve years to face this possibility, then several days to face the reality. And it had done no good at all.

Carrying her lunch with her, she went out to the screened porch at the rear of the cabin and curled up in one of the chairs. She ate without interest.

What had her mother meant by those remarks about Patrick? Her father had been "impressed" and her mother thought that Patrick's imprisonment had done him "some

good''? Whatever the remarks meant, it didn't sound good
to Megan. She forced down the rest of her lunch and decided that she couldn't spend the next hour or so worrying
about her parents' impressions. She would find out for herself soon enough.

But her anxiety was growing, and the food had done little to settle her stomach. How should she greet him?
Shouldn't she at least have her first words carefully thought
out?

"Hello, Patrick. How are you? Welcome home." She
grimaced. That sounded almost as ludicrous as making
some melodramatic statement about how much she'd missed
him and thought about him.

She *had* missed him terribly and thought about him all the
time for those first few years when she'd still believed him
to be alive. But the intervals between those thoughts had
increased as the years passed and her life changed. Still,
there had been times . . . How could she explain to him that
a sailing excursion on Long Island Sound had brought back
poignant memories of a time when they'd chartered a sailboat with some friends and sailed partway around Oahu?
Could she tell him about that time in a supermarket when
she'd seen a little boy with red hair and bright blue eyes and
had nearly broken into tears? And what about the countless other times, long after she'd given him up for dead,
when some small incident would trigger a flood of memories and aching regrets?

No, they were intensely private things, not to be shared
with anyone. In a way, they embarrassed her, because they
inevitably brought with them painful memories of her earlier, foolish self. Besides, whatever she said to him when he
arrived had to be something that would clearly set the tone
for this reunion. It would be, as they say, counterproductive to fling herself into his arms with some declaration of
love.

She carried the remnants of her lunch to the kitchen, deciding that she would just have to depend on the formidable amount of poise she possessed to see her through those initial moments. She could certainly trust herself to respond properly when the time came.

In the meantime, she thought it would be a good idea to find something to take her mind off all this. It was a warm, gorgeous day—a day that invited a walk in the woods. She knew the area well, and there were numerous paths crisscrossing the forest. So she exchanged her sneakers for sturdy hiking shoes and set out, clad in comfortable if unglamorous hiking shorts and her bright red T-shirt emblazoned with the logo her father had not yet seen: "Caution: The Pentagon May Be Dangerous to Your Health."

She'd brought the shirt along not to shock her father, but to amuse Patrick. He'd always liked her in red, a color she seldom wore anymore, and he would certainly enjoy the slogan. However much he might have changed, Patrick would not have lost his ability to appreciate humor.

She walked along, smiling at a memory. True to his image as a practical jokester, Patrick had worn a T-shirt with the peace symbol beneath his uniform for graduation ceremonies at West Point. When they had a few moments alone together afterward, he'd unbuttoned his jacket and shown the T-shirt to her, grinning broadly.

"No one has more reason to want peace than I do right now."

Megan caught her breath with a choking sound at the horrible irony of those words. Other gung-ho graduates of the academy had gone off to war and returned, while Patrick's life had come to a halt for twelve years.

The forest was returning to life in its uneven fashion. Here and there trees and bushes were in full leaf. Small wildflowers appeared unexpectedly. Lacy dogwoods were scattered around amid barrenness. There was the rush of water in a small brook, and she heard the soft scrabblings of unseen animals celebrating the return of spring.

Her anxiety gradually lessened as she roamed the forest, paying no attention at all to where she was going. She knew the general lay of the land and the general direction of the paths and could always find her way back.

She didn't bother to check the time until she had turned back toward the cabin, and then she stopped in dismay. She'd been gone for nearly an hour, with close to a half hour's walk ahead of her. Patrick could be arriving at any time, and she hadn't even left a note.

Hurrying as much as possible on the rugged trail she had chosen, Megan began to work up an unpleasant lather of sweat. Then she lost her footing and slid partway down a slippery hillside, coating both her legs and the seat of her shorts with mud. Why hadn't she paid attention to the time? Had she subconsciously been trying to do just this: let him arrive and find her gone?

At last she broke out into the clearing where the cabin stood. She was sweating profusely, covered with drying mud and moving at a fast trot as she tried to pick some twigs from her hair. And then she saw her mother's car parked just behind her rental.

If he hadn't blocked her car with his, she might very well have jumped into it and taken off. As it was, she just came to a stop and stared at the cars, then looked wildly around the clearing. Patrick was nowhere to be seen, but she'd left the cabin unlocked, so he was probably inside. She hesitated, imagined how she looked as opposed to how she should look, ran her trembling fingers through her hair again and pushed herself forward.

A man walked out of the front door of the cabin when she was still about thirty feet away, and she came to a stumbling stop in her confusion. Who on earth was this? Her mother had said nothing about anyone else's being with Patrick, and why would he bring someone with him anyway? If it hadn't been for her mother's car sitting there, Megan would have assumed that the man was a traveler who had lost his way.

She anxiously shifted her gaze to the open doorway, expecting Patrick to appear behind him at any moment. But the doorway remained empty and the stranger began to walk toward her.

Recognition came, finally, with an impact so powerful that it forced a sharp, involuntary cry from her. This stranger *was* Patrick! There were small things that made it just barely possible: the cleft chin; the wide, masculine mouth; and those sky-blue eyes that were now staring unabashedly at her.

He raised his hands briefly, then let them drop, and she saw a flash of gold on each hand. That familiar West Point ring—and a wedding band.

She was immediately conscious of her own bare fingers. She had stopped wearing her wedding ring and small diamond years ago. They were locked away in her safety deposit box in Connecticut.

He came to a stop a few feet away from her, having thus far said nothing at all. He was watching her rather warily, as though he weren't quite sure who she was, either.

"Patrick!" His name came out of a terribly constricted throat with an unpleasant, croaking sound.

He gave a half nod as he ran his gaze over her, letting it rest on the left hand she tried too late to hide.

"I . . . I'm sorry I wasn't here, but I went hiking and lost track of the time. Have you been here long?" She was babbling in her confusion and embarrassment, and she still half expected him to say that he wasn't Patrick.

"No, I just arrived."

Even his voice was different, or was her memory of it inaccurate? It seemed deeper and more resonant. But that was probably because it came from a very different body. Patrick had been lean, almost skinny. This man was far more powerfully built. The knit shirt he wore over casual slacks hugged many more muscles than Patrick had ever had.

Then she realized that he was staring at her chest, and a few seconds passed before she understood the reason for that—he was looking at the words on her T-shirt. But he wasn't laughing, not even smiling. Of all the things that were wrong at the moment, nothing struck her as forcefully as that. There was no amusement in his blue eyes and no grin on his wide mouth. The thought of a Patrick without humor chilled her.

When she had waited long enough for him to say something about the T-shirt, she began to babble once again. "I think I need a shower. I fell in the mud and I'm sweating like a pig."

He still said nothing, although he had shifted his gaze to stare at her in a more generalized manner. Megan had the unmistakable impression that he was just as shocked at her appearance as she was at his. She didn't understand it. She didn't exactly look her best at the moment, but she knew she hadn't changed that much.

She gave him a rather tentative smile and started walking toward the cabin. She turned in the doorway to see if he was following. The naked dismay she glimpsed on his face quickly gave way to blandness when he saw that she was watching him. She still didn't understand why, but somehow their meeting had all gone wrong, and she had no idea how to make it right again.

It was too late for any welcome-home speech. The temptation she might have had to fling herself into his arms seemed ridiculous now. She wondered if she should explain why she hadn't shown up at Andrews. She thought about asking him if the president had come.

But most of all she wanted to know why he seemed so shocked. The question was there, poised just behind her lips, but it wouldn't come out. Instead, she babbled again about needing a shower and that there was food and drink in the kitchen. Then she hurried off down the hallway, excusing herself as she went.

She came to an abrupt halt in the doorway to her bedroom. His suitcase was there, sitting just inside the door. Horrified, she stared first at it and then back toward the living room. She could not have been more shocked if a total stranger had shown up and announced his intention of sleeping with her. And she felt that same black fear any woman would feel in such a situation.

He is *Patrick,* she told herself emphatically. *He may look and act like a stranger, but he* is *Patrick. I have nothing at all to fear.*

But in the next ragged breath she reminded herself that there was nothing left of that Patrick—not even a smile.

PATRICK HAD NOT MOVED since she'd hurried out of the room. That look she'd wanted to question was still on his face, a look of dismay and confusion and even outright disbelief.

What had happened? He'd walked into this cabin ten minutes ago expecting to find a dream, then stepped out again into a nightmare. For twelve years he'd lived on the edges of nightmares—and sometimes right in their midst. He'd survived the deaths of comrades, the tauntings and tormentings of his captors, the ever-present dangers of mortar fire or a single shot from a solitary sniper—and perhaps worst of all, the temptation to surrender his will to live.

He'd survived it all by sheer willpower, and by always holding on to his precious dream. A few hours ago he'd taken what he thought was the first step into that dream when he set foot once more on American soil.

He raised a hand and distractedly ran it through his hair. Then he lowered his hand and stared at his wedding ring. Once, not long after his capture, one of the guards had pointed a gun at him and ordered him to surrender that ring.

With no weapon save his bare hands, he would have attacked the man rather than surrender it. Only the timely intervention of the guard's superior officer had prevented Patrick's death then and there.

He didn't understand what was expected of him now, because he hadn't thought that *anything* would be expected. So much had been demanded of him for twelve years. But that had been the nightmare, and this was supposed to be the dream.

Anger and resentment twisted and boiled within him. Why wasn't his dream coming true? Why did the nightmare persist?

Chapter Three

Megan showered quickly and put on a pair of stirrup pants and a light, oversize sweater that was double-belted in narrow leather. She focused all her attention on these activities because she simply did not want to think. She did not want to think about the taciturn man out there who bore only the faintest resemblance to Patrick.

Whatever she might have expected at this point, she had certainly never expected to feel fear. But fear it was—that prickly sensation along her spine, that jumpiness inside. She attempted to soothe herself with the psychiatrist's statement that Patrick displayed no evidence of trauma. But that helped very little. First of all, the psychiatrist hadn't known the old Patrick, and second, she didn't trust psychiatrists anyway, especially not army psychiatrists.

She could still see that look of shock on Patrick's face. Why had it been there? She certainly had every right to be shocked, but he didn't. Was it possible that his memory had played tricks on him, that he'd believed her to be taller or slimmer or some such thing?

She frowned at her reflection in the bedroom mirror, trying in vain to see what he must have seen. Then her mouth twisted into a sad smile. Perhaps it wasn't her appearance, but her disappearance that had shocked him. He had every right to have expected her to be here when he arrived. If things had gotten off to a bad start, it was really her fault. But she still didn't know what to do.

As she left the bedroom, she averted her eyes from his bag and kept her mind resolutely off the intimate time together it implied. Then, after taking a deep, steadying breath, she walked into the living room, only to find it empty.

He was on the sun porch, seated on a chaise. He didn't see her at first because he was looking off toward the woods. Her shock at his appearance hadn't lessened, but it wasn't caused by an overall impression—instead she focused on details. She stared at his sun-bronzed, muscled arms with its bleached hairs, at the large, work-roughened hand wearing a West Point ring that rested on his bent knee, at the taut thigh muscles that pushed against his slacks. Her attention to all this was frightening in itself; she hadn't dwelt on such things in years—maybe never. She was far too aware of him, of the sheer physicality of this familiar stranger.

Her attention must have communicated itself to him, because he turned at that very moment to face her, then ran his eyes slowly over her.

Patrick's shock had subsided somewhat, but his resentment had not. In fact, seeing her as she was now, almost completely unchanged, he could feel that anger beginning to bubble menacingly. She had no right to stand there looking so familiar and acting so strangely. Where was Meggie's warmth, her laughter, her wonderful spontaneity?

Megan knew she looked good; he could certainly have no complaints now. But male appreciation of female attractiveness was completely missing from his face. He might have been an officer making an inspection tour, missing nothing but making no immediate judgments, either.

She stepped forward and tried a smile again, the pleasant, professional smile she used so well in her work. But she found it nearly impossible to maintain eye contact with him. That physical thing again, that heightened awareness. She sat down in a chair opposite him.

"I have a steak for our dinner. You must have missed them." Megan cringed inwardly at such mundane conversation, but did not know how to go beyond it. Her inability to handle this situation was both frustrating and baffling. Where was that matchless poise when she needed it most?

The man who was Patrick smiled at her. It wasn't that wonderful smile of old, but it was a smile. "I did miss them, but I've been making up for it. They served us steaks at Clark and your mother had them for lunch, too."

"Oh," she said stupidly, feeling unaccountably depressed over that. The effect of that smile was very short-lived.

"Thanks for thinking of it. And of this, too." He held up the bottle of his favorite beer that she had remembered to buy that morning.

Megan just couldn't stand this any longer. She had to know why he was behaving this way, and the only way she could think of to draw him out was to explain her own behavior. He deserved an explanation in any event.

"I owe you an explanation for my failure to show up at Andrews. I did intend to be there, but when I found out how much of a media event it was going to be, I just couldn't go through with it. They...the press, that is, would have expected too much. I thought it would be better if we met here, away from everyone."

Patrick stared at her in silence for a moment, and although his expression gave nothing away, she was left with a strong impression of her own selfishness. Didn't he understand what she was trying to say? An image of that suitcase flashed through her mind.

Finally, he nodded briefly. "It *was* a media circus, but we'd been told to expect that."

She decided to ignore the possibility that there was some sort of rebuke there. "Was the president there?"

"Yes. The president, the vice president, the chief of staff and a lot of others."

His tone gave no indication at all of what he thought about that welcome. She kept expecting a joke that never came. The Patrick she had known and loved would have had some choice remark to make about all that attention being paid to a very unwilling officer.

"Your mother tells me that you got a business degree and that you have a travel agency up in Connecticut." He was giving her no indication of what he thought of that, either.

"Yes, I've lived up there for seven years now. In Greenwich. I rent a small cottage on an estate, but I've been considering buying a condo. The business has done very well. I have a partner, and we started it together with money borrowed from our families. But we've paid them back completely and in far less time than we'd expected. We're even thinking of renting a larger space so we can expand, or perhaps opening a second office in Stamford."

She came to a halt rather breathlessly, only then realizing that she had been babbling again. But it was extremely important that he know how well she had done. Was that cruel? She didn't know, and it was too late to think about that now.

"What made you decide to move to Connecticut? I would have thought you'd have stayed in Washington." Those blue eyes were fixed on her with curiosity and nothing more.

Megan wasn't sure that this was the time to bring up the matter of her resignation from the army, so she told a half-truth instead.

"Karen, my partner, is from Greenwich. The area is affluent and growing, and we both decided that it would be easier to become established up there than in Washington."

"I see," he said, and she thought that he sounded just like her mother. Either he didn't see at all, or he suspected what she wasn't saying. The message on that T-shirt had been rather explicit.

He had lapsed into silence once more and was staring out at the woods beyond the screens. Megan began to resent his failure to initiate conversation, but her resentment was superseded by fear, so she spoke into the silence quickly.

"Did you have any contact at all with the outside world while you were there? I mean, did you ever hear any news?"

He turned back to her with that same blandness. "Sporadically. We rigged up antennas on a hillside just outside the village and used a radio we had with us to pick up the BBC from Hong Kong or the Armed Forces Network from the Philippines. But we couldn't always get them and sometimes the Cong tore them down. So there are some gaps in my knowledge. Someone was assigned to fill us in at Clark and on the trip home. That was a help."

"It's hard for me to remember everything that's happened in the past twelve years, but I'll try to help," Megan said brightly. She allowed her voice to trail off because she thought she sounded like some sort of social worker. She also thought that he sounded bored with the whole topic, but of course he'd probably repeated his story many times by now.

"Thank you," he said politely. "The Pentagon is preparing a briefing for us. A sort of crash course in recent history."

Resentment simmered again. Naturally, the Pentagon would do that. They thought of everything and involved themselves in everything. The all-encompassing life. Sell your soul to us and we'll take care of you.

To prevent her resentment from rising all the way to the surface, she decided to pursue the longest statement he'd made so far. It seemed the only safe thing to do at this point.

"If you were able to leave the village to rig up an antenna, you must have had a lot of freedom."

"Oh, we had plenty of freedom, but no place to go. The jungle was impossible as an escape route, and the only roads were always heavily guarded. Then, of course, there was the threat. I guess you know about that."

She was wondering what she could say or do to provoke him in some way. At the moment, she didn't much care what emotion might show up; she just wanted to see or hear anything but that infuriating blandness.

"Yes, Dad told me about it. If that governor, or whatever he was, hadn't died, you might still be there."

"Possibly, but I doubt it. We'd picked up enough on the broadcasts to know that Vietnam was trying to patch things up with the United States. So, sooner or later, they would have let us go."

"But they might just as easily have killed you, rather than admit that you'd been held all those years." It was a cruel point to make, but his coldness was destroying her capacity for concern.

"That didn't seem likely. If they had killed us, there was always the possibility that word could have leaked out about it, and the government would have been in even worse trouble. By returning us and crying 'mea culpa,' they could make themselves look suitably repentant. From what I've seen and heard of the American reaction, it's worked, too."

Megan had little interest in this conversation. She was too busy trying to rationalize his behavior. Was it possible for a man whose emotions had always been open and honest to have built such an impenetrable wall around them? And if so, would that wall crumble at some point?

At the moment, Patrick bore a very unpleasant resemblance to her father; the perfect military officer. She wondered what he'd say if she told him that, and might have done so if he hadn't spoken suddenly and sent her thoughts spinning away.

"Why didn't you divorce me or have me declared legally dead?"

Her body and mind snapped rigidly to attention. The question appeared to be an idle one, asked only out of curiosity, but the result was—for her, at least—a rapid building up of tension that seemed to crackle the very air between them.

She fervently wished that she had a believable answer. But how could she explain such purposeless drift in a life that had become so full of decisiveness in other matters? She shrugged, more to relieve that terrible tension than to deny the importance of the subject.

"I don't know, really. I had no interest in remarriage, and there was no joint property or assets other than military benefits—and I didn't want them." Didn't want them and wouldn't have accepted them. No amount of money could have enticed her into a relationship with the army again.

But even as she spoke, Megan was hearing in her own voice that horrible indifference that had so infuriated her in his. However different this cold, silent man might be from the one she had married, he deserved better than this. She had to try, in any event.

"For the first few years, I believed that you were still alive; it was impossible to think otherwise. It also helped to be around other MIA wives and to be working for your release.

"But then I started college and gradually separated myself from them and from the military in general. The country as a whole—and even the military to some extent—wanted to forget about Vietnam. No one wanted to talk about a war we had lost. Consequently, no one wanted to talk about survivors who might still be there.

"I'd found new friends and developed new interests, and then I moved away from Washington. At some point—I don't really know exactly when—I just ... let go of hope."

Megan's voice had begun firmly, but then it died down to a near whisper. She was staring at her restless hands in her lap and so she didn't see the first sign of real emotion on his face.

"It's impossible to describe how and when it happened. There's no moment of awareness, no time when I told myself that I just couldn't go on hoping any longer. It just . . . happened.''

She continued to stare at her hands, at her naked ring finger. What she couldn't tell him was that now she realized that there really had been such a moment, even if she hadn't recognized it at the time: the day she stopped wearing her rings. She was mortified to think that she couldn't really recall when that had been. It was right after she moved to Connecticut, when she had been excited and happy about starting the business and making new friends.

When she finally raised her eyes, she found him staring at her hands, too, but still without visible emotion. She wanted to talk about the daily agony of waking from dreams of him and having to face the reality of his absence. She wanted to tell him about those times when he'd come back into her thoughts even after she'd given up hope. But the words were simply not there—at any rate, they weren't there to be spoken to a man who was incapable of feeling anything.

''When the United States and Vietnam began speaking to each other again and some bodies were returned, I hoped for a while that yours—'' She stopped abruptly, horrified at her words.

Patrick merely nodded. ''We heard about that. One of my men had some choice things to say about the unfairness of it all.'' A small smile flickered briefly across his wide mouth. ''He kept threatening to sew himself up into a bag and present himself to the authorities.''

Megan smiled, too. His words were a grim echo of the kind of humor she'd occasionally heard at Schofield Barracks as men returned from duty tours in Vietnam. It was gallows humor, the kind used to deny horrors beyond reason. She hadn't really understood it then, not even when Patrick tried to explain it to her.

''Anyway,'' she said, forging on rather desperately, ''when I began to think rationally about the odds, I knew it wasn't likely. Perhaps if I'd still been in Washington, still been part of...that life, I might have been more hopeful.''

''Don't blame yourself, Meggie. You were right. The odds against my coming back dead or alive were very high.''

His voice had softened and he had used her name for the first time. Their eyes caught and held, and something passed between them. She could not have said just what it was, but for a long moment, it was there. An understanding? A sharing of some sort? The door to the past seemed to open just a crack, then closed abruptly as Patrick got up, saying that he wanted another beer.

Her eyes followed him until he disappeared inside. She wanted desperately to cling to that moment, but it was vanishing already. If they had, for just that moment, recaptured something of the past, then he, too, must want to avoid it.

''Did you ever give up hope?'' she asked when he returned. He was as stone-faced as before, but she wanted to keep that conversation going, to find that common ground again.

''No. It was my job to keep hope alive.''

His flat, calm statement had a devastating impact on her. Surely she was misinterpreting his words and his tone of voice. She would have sworn that she'd heard echoes of her father there, and of all the career officers she'd known through the years. That total acceptance of duty, no matter how difficult or unpleasant. She must have misunderstood. However much this man had changed, *that* could not have changed.

She asked him about the others, and he told her about those who had died and those who had returned with him, about the Vietnamese troops they had been training, and about the men who had been executed after their capture. And it was there again—that detachment, the attitude of a soldier, not of a civilian unlucky enough to have been caught up in a war.

He even looks the part now, she thought with mounting dismay. *He has that flinty look, that toughness the military prides itself on.* Even relaxing in the chaise, as he was now, he had something of that power and authority in him. Others might not have seen it, but Megan had lived with this all her life and she knew it when she saw it. A uniform could make it more obvious, but it was there even in civilian clothes.

She'd thought about that often when she first moved to Connecticut. In her business, she often came into contact with rising corporate executives, men with power and authority. But not one of them had ever exuded that same quality that flowed so effortlessly from men like her father, and even her brother.

She broke off these thoughts because she simply could not face the possibility of their being true.

"The country has changed a lot because of that war, Patrick. Vietnam is ancient history to most people now, and that's something you'll have to face. At best, it's used by liberals and conservatives as a rallying point, or by scholars as a fertile field for research. But the general public has put it at almost the same distance as World War II."

"Yes, I've learned that much already. Your father gathered up some of the best books on the subject for me. I appreciated that."

She didn't. How very like the general to have done such a thing. Why hadn't he realized that it was irrelevant to Patrick's future? The best thing Patrick could do was to put the war at the same distance everyone else had and get on with his life. Or did her father still harbor hopes that Patrick would make the army his career? A few moments ago she would have dismissed that possibility out of hand; now she felt just slightly uncertain about it.

Patrick began to question her about old friends, and she fumbled for answers because she hadn't really kept in touch with any of them. This one was in Germany; her brother had mentioned him. That one was in Brussels, at NATO head-quarters. Several had resigned their commissions. Only one had been killed in Vietnam, but his death had occurred before Patrick's capture, so he knew about that. She told Patrick that the man's widow had remarried a year or so later, to another West Pointer.

If Megan had remained in Washington, in the army, that might well have happened to her, too. When a woman married into the army, she tended to stay there. Was there any other profession so restricted, so insular? She doubted it. The military was a world in and of itself, and it was nothing short of a miracle that she had somehow managed to escape it.

The conversation was floundering again. It reminded Megan of other conversations she'd had over the years with former friends—catch up on the news, gossip about mutual friends...and then nothing. Surely there had been more to this relationship than that. This man had been her husband, not just one of the dozens of temporarily close friends of an army brat.

She felt an anguished longing for the old Patrick. Regardless of their present situation, he would have prevented these long silences with his irrepressible humor. When had he lost it, she wondered. When had the agony and hopelessness of captivity stolen from Patrick his most precious asset—the thing she had loved perhaps above all else about him?

With a start, she realized that this must be what her mother—and presumably the general, too—had meant by that remark about the horrors having done him "some good." She hated them for that with a blind, unreasoning hatred. How dare they believe such a thing? Patrick wasn't meant to be serious and solemn. He was meant to stay forever young and filled with life and laughter.

The urge to grab him and shake him until that ugly shell cracked became so strong that she knew she had to get away from him before thought became action. So she got up rather abruptly and announced that she was going to make a marinade for the steak. He merely nodded, giving her a brief, slanting glance before returning his attention to the forest beyond the porch.

Megan went into the kitchen and busied herself with the marinade, wondering how they could possibly survive the next few days, or however long he intended to stay. Perhaps it might be better if she left; he might well be happier here alone. The thought of Patrick as a loner was mind-boggling. He'd been one of the most gregarious people she'd ever known.

The contrasts between the old and the new Patrick were far too sharp, even when one allowed for the passage of twelve years and the way he'd spent them. Her uneasiness was edging closer and closer to outright fear. She just didn't trust that psychiatric report. It was nearly impossible even now to think of Patrick as being dangerous, but until a few hours ago, it would have been ridiculous to think of him as being humorless, either.

As she mixed the marinade, she heard him come into the cabin, then head down the hallway, presumably to the bathroom. Her senses went on full alert, and the sensation was far from being a pleasant one.

She was still in that agitated state when she heard him come into the kitchen behind her. Reason triumphed, at least temporarily, over her fears, and she recalled that she had not asked him about his reunion with his family. The words were about to come out as she turned her head sideways to acknowledge his presence, but they were swept back by a sharply indrawn breath caused by what she glimpsed.

His hand had reached out toward her, and then retreated quickly when she turned her head. Megan went rigid with shock, and her mind spun off in two directions simultaneously. Her fear was magnified, but at the same time, some part of her felt a satisfaction and relief at that halted gesture. It seemed to belie that coldness and rigid self-control she'd seen ever since his arrival.

And as she willed herself to calmness, she knew that something else had happened in that moment, too. Like it or not, she had felt a restive stirring of her own sexuality. She told herself that she'd already felt that with Ted, but she knew that this feeling was very different, however brief its duration. Those bonds she'd spoken of to Karen were still there and far more powerful than she'd believed possible. If he had come back even faintly resembling the man who had left, she would have let loose all that need and desire. She would have once again become his wife—and very quickly after that, the silly, dependent creature she so despised.

The moment had dragged on far too long. He came up beside her as she finished mixing the marinade and began to pour it over the steak. She kept her eyes averted but could still feel him there—far too big and too silent. He seemed too tall by several inches, though she knew he couldn't have grown. It was probably that definitely increased breadth and that essential maleness. She didn't remember ever having thought about that before where Patrick was concerned, and she knew that she'd never thought about it with Ted or any of the other men she'd dated.

Finally, she finished her task, and movement seemed to break the spell and require some conversation. So she asked him about his family in a voice that she hoped sounded more normal to him than it did to her.

"I was surprised at how little they've changed," he said musingly. "A little grayer, a little slower, but still, less change than I'd expected. They told me that you've been visiting them regularly."

"Yes. I think I've seen more of them than I have of my own parents. We've become very close." Her voice softened as she talked and thought about them.

"By the way," Patrick said, "Joel called while we were having lunch. He sounds happy."

Megan wrinkled her nose. "He's got stars in his eyes, I'm afraid, and he'll probably get them. He seems to be on that track."

For anyone as familiar with the military as Megan, it was easy enough to spot the next generation of generals simply by the education and duty tours being offered to them. Of course, having a general for a father helped, too.

"You don't approve of that?" Patrick asked in surprise.

Megan put the mixing bowl and spoon in the sink and then turned to face him squarely. "I wouldn't wish that life on anyone. But he certainly knows what he's in for, and if that's what he wants, I hope he gets it."

Patrick frowned as he peered at her closely. "That T-shirt wasn't a joke, was it? You didn't just leave Washington, you left it all."

Megan thought that he looked even more shocked than he had the first time he'd seen her. But at least this time, she knew why.

"The shirt wasn't a joke; I did leave it all. I resigned from the army when I moved up to Connecticut. Unfortunately, the general didn't seem to notice—until this morning, that is. I've found out that there's a very pleasant life out there for civilians. My only regret is that it took me so long to discover that."

"What brought it up this morning?"

"My refusal to play the expected role," she said, feeling that small twinge of guilt again. "He tried his best to order me out to Andrews."

"I see," Patrick said, and she didn't know if he did or not.

"Don't misunderstand me, Patrick. I didn't resign because of what happened to you. I don't blame the army for that. But when I started college—something the general encouraged, ironically enough—I discovered what the civilian world was like, and then I realized that I could fit into it quite nicely. Now, up in Greenwich, I never even have to see a uniform, let alone an army base, and when I hear the Pentagon mentioned, it's not exactly in the same context I've heard all my life." She gave him a wry smile. "None of this should be coming as too much of a shock to you, since you were the first one to suggest to me that it was all craziness."

Patrick made a sound that might have been a chuckle. "That was a lifetime ago—in another world."

Megan stared at this tall, hard-looking man who had once been a civilian in uniform and now looked shockingly like an officer in civvies. She didn't want to ask the next question, but it came out anyway—with denial behind every word.

"Are you saying that you don't feel that way anymore?"

He held her gaze for a fraction of a second, then let his eyes slide away as he shrugged. "I'm not sure. I . . . haven't really thought about it."

He's lying, she thought incredulously. *Of course he's lying. He's had twelve years to think about his future— twelve years in the back of nowhere. Whatever debt he owed the army was paid in full long ago. Why is he lying?*

She excused herself and went toward the bathroom. It had again reached the point where she was ready to grab him and shake him until the real Patrick O'Donnell came out. Shaking with anger and pain, she had nearly passed the bedroom she intended him to use when she saw the suitcase.

He had moved it. Conflicting emotions washed over her as she stood there staring at it. He understood and accepted the distance between them now, and she was grateful for that. But something had been lost in the process, and that distance now seemed even greater. She supposed that she had thought of Patrick as having stood still, while she herself had moved on. But now she knew that he, too, had moved—in the opposite direction. And he now knew that, too; the suitcase proved it.

When she returned to the living room, he was nowhere to be seen. She found him a few minutes later when she went to the garage to get the gas grill. He was reading the instruction booklet that was kept with it, and she relaxed with a smile. Patrick had always been fascinated by gadgets; he would be the perfect consumer for a high-tech society.

"No fuss, no muss," she said brightly. "You're going to have a field day with all the new gadgets that have come along in the past twelve years."

He turned to look at her and a grin slowly spread across his face. For the first time, he truly looked like Patrick. The years began to melt away. She returned his smile as tears began to sting her eyes and a heavy ache gathered inside her.

What happened next happened without conscious intent and certainly without prior thought. Later, she would realize that it had been the result of that boyish grin. She ran to him and wrapped her arms around him, hugging him as she buried her face in his chest.

"Patrick, I'm so sorry...about everything. That you had to be over there all this time, that so much has changed."

She felt him become very tense, and she backed off quickly, awkwardly. That moved suitcase loomed very large in her mind. He hadn't responded. He didn't even feel like Patrick.

Her cheeks burning with shame, she grabbed the handle of the grill and started to wheel it out of the garage. But before she had gone more than a few steps, he stopped her with a strong hand over hers.

"I'm sorry, too, Meggie. I just need some time to... understand a lot of things, I guess." His voice was uncertain and he paused briefly, then went on in a firmer tone. "I'll take that around back for you."

Cracks. She could almost hear them. Everything was crumbling—the terrifying fragility of their new relationship, Patrick's grip on himself, her self-image and certainty about what she wanted. How much longer could they maintain any of it? What would happen when it fell apart completely?

Megan trailed along after him as he wheeled the grill to the patio. A bubble of hysterical laughter was swelling inside her. Their world was coming apart, but here they were, behaving like any normal couple on a vacation. It was absurd, and yet she could not be the one to bring it to an end.

Neither did she think that Patrick would end this charade. She was certain now that what she saw was a carefully maintained facade. But why? Was it no more than an attempt to adjust to changed circumstances? She could scarcely blame him for that. After all, only a few days ago he had been a prisoner of war in a different country with a different culture.

But if that was the case, then he would get over it in time and might well once more become the man she had loved. And what would happen then? Suddenly, Karen's remark about Megan's falling in love with him all over again didn't seem quite so hopelessly romantic. And it was very scary.

Megan knew that it was irrational to think that she was in any danger of reverting to her old self, but she was finding out that her new self was far more vulnerable than she had believed. The irrational could be very real.

Patrick lit the grill. She went back inside to prepare a salad. They had their dinner and she noted with satisfaction that he seemed to be enjoying his second steak of the day. She'd bought cheesecake for dessert—another favorite of his—and they exchanged smiles as she brought it to the table.

But at some point, Megan began to feel vaguely irritated by all this. She feared that she was catering to him, reprising the role of adoring wife that she was sure she must have played to perfection all those years ago. It helped not at all to tell herself that it was no more than kindness to someone who'd been deprived for a long time. The role just did not suit her now.

Conversation moved along smoothly enough. They talked about political events and social changes of the past twelve years. He asked many questions, but ventured few opinions. She wondered how he really felt about issues that mattered a great deal to her now, and was ashamed to realize that she couldn't even guess. Had they really known so little about each other?

After dinner, he poured himself some cognac and returned to the porch, leaving her to clean up. Her irritation grew to smoldering resentment. On those rare occasions when she'd invited a man into her home for dinner in recent years, he had invariably helped with the cleanup. She expected that.

Patrick obviously didn't understand that things had changed, despite their dinner conversation. She considered explaining all this to him in no uncertain terms, then decided to let it go. Actions speak far louder than words, as he would find out for himself when he had to fix his own breakfast. He'd always expected a big breakfast, while she herself was a coffee-and-toast person.

Just as she had finished the cleanup, he came back inside, commenting that the evening was growing very cool. He went to light a fire in the living room fireplace, and she tried to put out the flames of resentment within her. She was expecting too much too soon. She wanted him to accept the changes, to see her for the person she was now, but it would take time. It was a miracle that he had even survived; she had no right to expect further miracles.

When she went to join him, the living room was lit only by one low lamp and the bright flames. The crackling fire and the darkness gathering outside made her nervous. The scene fairly reeked of intimacy, and yet they were strangers. Still, he *had* moved his suitcase.

She encouraged him to talk about his life in that remote village whose name tripped so easily off his tongue. He made it sound very simple and dull, and she could not help contrasting it with her own exciting, active existence during those years. She was wondering just what he intended to do with the rest of his life, but she didn't ask. The future was forbidden territory.

At some point, she told him about the appearance of the word "yuppie" in contemporary slang, and the life-style that was the subject of so many books and articles. He surprised her by smiling and saying that he was glad he'd gotten back before he was too old to be one. It was another tantalizing glimpse of the old Patrick, but this time she had better control of herself.

She went on to talk about the general acceptance of life-styles that had once existed only on the fringes of society. He said that didn't seem to fit in with what he'd been told was the country's newly conservative mood, and she replied that the new conservatism was no more than a swing back to the middle after the turmoil of the sixties and seventies.

It was his turn to be surprised then, and she guessed that he must be shocked to find that someone whose philosophies had been shaped by an ultraconservative father had become rather liberal.

"Have you ... ah, lived with anyone?"

She stared at him, speechless for a moment. She'd thought about what she would say to this before his arrival, but he still caught her unprepared. It was the second time he'd abruptly switched from general to personal conversation.

"Patrick, we've been apart for twelve years, and we were together for only a short time before that. I really think that it would serve no good purpose for either of us to question the other on that subject. I believed you to be dead and you undoubtedly thought you'd never see me again. Whatever either of us might have done under those circumstances would be perfectly understandable. I think we should just leave it at that."

His shock at her response was very evident and she could easily tune in to his thoughts. He had known she was innocent when he married her, and she really hadn't ventured very far from that näiveté during their brief marriage, either. No wonder he was so shocked—she'd gone from Little Miss Innocence to Woman of the World.

If he only knew, she thought wryly. But he wouldn't because she wouldn't tell him. The truth could create the impression that she was still in love with him, and she wasn't. Besides, she was ashamed of her lack of experience, although she'd never been sufficiently ashamed to do anything about it. She'd just made sex irrelevant to her life.

Then she became aware of his silence. He was staring into the fire and there was tension in his pose. He sat on the other end of the long sofa, leaning slightly forward as he clasped his hands between his knees. While she watched, his gaze dropped to those hands, where his wedding band gleamed softly in the firelight.

Was it possible that he'd been faithful to her all those years? She didn't want to know that any more than she wanted him to know the truth about her. In any event, it wasn't a matter of faithfulness; it was just that she'd never found anyone else. There was a difference, wasn't there?

"Yes," he said finally, still looking down at his hands. "You're right. It would serve no purpose."

He hesitated a moment, still staring at that gold band, then spoke again. "Is…ah, there anyone now? Would you at least tell me that?"

Megan sensed that it was a question he really didn't want to ask, and it made her think of all the ones she hadn't asked. She answered because she thought he had a right to know. After all, she knew there couldn't be anyone for him now.

"Yes. That is, there's someone I've been dating for a while." Ted's image flickered briefly and was gone. Perhaps her hesitance about a deeper involvement had been justified, after all. She could feel him slipping into the past.

"I see," he said in a calm, flat voice. "Does he know about me...about my return, that is?"

"Yes." Megan decided that she would say no more on the subject and conveyed that in her tone of voice.

"Damned inconvenient for him."

Megan drew in a sharp breath. The bitterness in his voice was the first strong emotion she'd heard from him, and it was so totally out of character for Patrick that she couldn't quite believe she'd heard it.

"That isn't fair, Patrick." Her words were actually a denial that he'd even said it.

"You're right," he replied unconvincingly.

Megan was once again uneasy. Those vibes she was getting were telling her that she was hearing male possessiveness. She looked at the man sitting at the other end of the sofa and could not quite repress an inward shiver.

"Patrick," she said carefully, "did you really think we could go back so easily?" She had deliberately selected her words to convey her own feelings on the subject without being too obvious about it.

He finally glanced her way, but his expression was inscrutable. "I don't know what I thought, but I understand now what you were really telling me when you didn't meet my plane. It would have been difficult for you."

"It would have been difficult for *both* of us," she stated unequivocally. It had taken them long enough, but what had to be said was finally coming out. She hurried on.

"If...if you'd rather not stay here, I'll understand. Or if you'd rather be here alone, I'll leave."

He shook his head immediately. "No, I'd like to stay, and I'd like you to stay, too. If you don't mind, that is."

"I don't mind," she replied quickly. But pressure was building again and she sensed that it had, at best, only been temporarily alleviated. Did they need to scream at each other, to vent their rage against the unfairness of it all?

He got up and stretched his long body. "I'm tired. I flew through a lot of time zones in the past twenty-four hours or so, and didn't have much sleep before that at Clark, either. So, if you don't mind, I think I'll try to catch up on some of it now."

"No, of course I don't mind," she said, thinking about a man who had had boundless energy. Or did he just want to get away from her?

"Patrick, are you angry with me?" The words just tumbled out before she could stop them. For the second time this day she had acted without thinking—and acted childishly.

He sat down on the edge of the heavy oak cocktail table, facing her, with his knees brushing against hers. She fought an urge to draw away even as she was still caught in her embarrassment over her outburst.

"No, I'm not angry, Meggie. Or if I am, it's anger with myself. I had no right to expect everything to be the same. Your life has moved on, while mine just . . . stopped. If I'd ever let myself think about it, I would have wanted it that way."

She reached out tentatively and curved her hand over his. He didn't respond, but he didn't move away, either.

"Thank you," she said. But the pressure of the moment became too strong and she withdrew her hand.

He got up then and left the room. Megan stared into the fire. She wasn't sure what it was she had thanked him for. For understanding? For accepting the fact that she had changed? But did he understand, and could he ever truly accept those changes?

For an irrational moment she wanted to believe that he could, just as she wanted to believe that she could accept the changes in him. But she knew that neither of them could manage that, not on the deepest emotional level.

Patrick would continue to want the girl he had left behind, and she would continue to want the old Patrick, even if his return brought fears of her own undoing.

Chapter Four

Patrick squinted in the bright morning sunlight to see the forest beyond the small clearing. How soft it looked, how tentative, with its sporadic bursts of the palest green and the delicate lacy white of the dogwoods. For twelve years he'd seen nothing but the lush jungle that crowded in on the village from every direction. He wondered when it was that he'd started to think of that as being normal, making this landscape now seem alien.

He dwelt on this at some length, because it was easier to think about foliage than it was to confront the real issues of his life just now. It was cowardice, of course, but a man who had gone through what he had should be able to permit himself a moment or two of weakness. The doctors at Clark had told him to expect times like this; still, it didn't sit well with him.

He needed to think about two important things: Meggie and his future. Had he been foolish enough to believe that they would just take care of themselves, that the very act of once more setting foot on American soil would automatically guarantee that his life would run smoothly ever after? No doubt he had; such fairy tales had been necessary.

He was glad that she was still asleep; it was a lot easier to think about her when he didn't have to face the reality of her. Despite what he'd told her about being tired last night, he'd been lying in bed trying to come to terms with that reality when he heard her footsteps in the hallway outside his room. And knowing that he was being a damned fool, he'd still held his breath, waiting to see if she stopped at his door. But her footsteps hadn't even faltered.

He raised his coffee mug to his lips and took a healthy slug. The coffee, the croissants she'd bought, these were the things that felt like "welcome home" to him. He didn't really recall much of his official welcome, at least not after he'd discovered that Meggie wasn't there. He assumed that he'd said and done the right things, and he guessed that he'd been properly awed by the president's presence. But in truth, the only ones he'd cared about had been his parents and General and Mrs. Daniels, the link to Meggie.

Meggie. What had he expected? After he'd talked with the general while still at Clark and found out that she hadn't remarried, he had let his fantasies run amok. And when Mrs. Daniels told him at Andrews that Meggie preferred to meet him privately, he had really gone haywire. By the time he arrived at the cabin, he was expecting to find her waiting for him in some sexy gown, with the bed covers already turned down. He was embarrassed now to think that he could have allowed himself to stray so far from reality. Just how damned ridiculous could a man get?

Well, he'd certainly received his answer to that when she'd come running out of the woods wearing baggy shorts, that T-shirt, and mud. He still wasn't sure that she hadn't deliberately staged that little scene. If she had, it had worked, all right. He'd known then and there that he wasn't coming home to the marriage he had left twelve years ago.

Physically she'd changed very little, less than he might have guessed if he'd been dealing in realities. Certainly far less than he himself had changed. But the soft girlishness was gone, replaced by a hard-edged womanliness. Even her voice was different, more confident and authoritative.

And the love was gone. He could see that in her eyes. There was only regret and sadness, and even some fear. When he saw that fear he realized just how much he'd changed, but he didn't yet know what to do about it.

At some point, while he'd been comforting himself with her love, it had slipped away. He'd become part of her past. Now she just felt responsible for him. Despite her statement about being out of the army now, that sense of duty remained. She would probably stay with him as long as she felt that duty.

A muscle twitched along his jawline, betraying that coiled inner tension that he couldn't quite conceal. Should he tell her to get the hell out, absolve her of all her responsibilities toward him? He thought that, if he did, she would probably go with great relief. Wouldn't he be guilty of terrible selfishness if he kept her here now?

Yes, he would be, but he was going to do it anyway. He was going to hold on to her as long as he could. He needed her just now, even though admitting that hurt badly.

He heard sounds behind him just then and went back into the cabin to find Megan pouring herself a cup of coffee. She was wearing a long, sweatshirt robe that covered her from neck to ankles, a far cry from the cute fuzzy pink robe she used to wear. She looked up at him warily and he felt that hurt again. Her big, dark-fringed blue eyes looked as if they had spent much of the night open. He felt a sudden surge of pity for her, coupled with his first real awareness of how difficult all this must be for her. But he was also thinking about how they should have spent last night, and what he should be seeing on her face this morning.

Patrick didn't look any different—and she had so hoped that he would. Sometime during her largely sleepless night, Megan had decided that she'd been wrong, that he hadn't really changed so much. She'd halfway convinced herself that she'd overreacted to what were probably only small changes.

But there he stood—too big and too male and too impassive—and probably waiting for her to fix his breakfast. She couldn't look at him without seeing the ghost of the real Patrick hovering just behind those broad shoulders and grinning that wonderful old grin.

"Good morning," she said brightly. "Did you catch up on your sleep?"

There was a momentary hesitation before he nodded, and in that moment, she again felt that terrible tension caused by his maleness and her femaleness. It made her angry. If he had come back unchanged, she could have understood those feelings. But how could she be feeling this toward a stranger, this officer temporarily disguised as a civilian?

"Didn't you have breakfast yet?" she asked innocently, having just recalled her decision of last night. "Or did you just get up, too?"

There was another hesitation, but this time she could have sworn that she saw the ghost of a smile and a brief twinkle in his eyes. "No, I've been up for a while, but I haven't eaten yet. Would you like me to fix something for you, too?"

It irritated her that she couldn't be sure about that smile or about the slight mockery she thought she heard in his last words. But then she dismissed both. Humor and this man did not go together. She'd just been indulging in some wishful thinking.

"No, thanks. I'm still a coffee-and-toast person. Half a cup and I'm off for my morning run."

"Run?" He repeated in surprise.

She hid her amusement at his shock. "Yes, I usually run a mile or so each morning...that is, when I don't play squash."

And then he did smile. It wasn't quite the devilish grin of the old Patrick, but it *was* a smile. And there were even little hints of light in those blue eyes that ran slowly over her.

"Is that the latest in running wear?"

"No, it's the latest in comfortable at-home wear. I'm going to change now." She set down her unfinished coffee and hurried back to the bedroom. It was back again, that awareness. How could a silly remark about her robe have brought it on?

She quickly changed into her running shorts and a T-shirt, then put on her running shoes. She needed her morning run badly before she faced the day. If it could relax her for the normal tensions of her business life, surely it could do something for this situation.

She came out of her bedroom and started down the hallway past his open door. He called out to her to wait and she stopped reluctantly in the doorway. He was wearing a pair of army shorts and a T-shirt and was lacing up a brand-new pair of sneakers. Then he stood up and bounced on the balls of his feet a few times, testing the fit of the new shoes.

Megan felt a nearly irresistible urge to run right then, as far from him as she possibly could. Clad as he was, he looked even bigger and more alien. The hard muscularity of his long body was accented beneath the flimsy clothes, and his bare legs were long lengths of ropy muscles sprinkled with bleached hairs.

"We ran every morning, too," he said as he came toward her. She took a few quick steps backward.

"W-we?" she stammered, irrationally thinking that he was referring to some woman.

"My men and I. We had to keep in shape."

She recovered quickly from her absurd thought. "But I thought you did all sorts of work over there. Dad said . . ."

"We did, but most of it was just back-breaking, not muscle-toning. So we ran and did calisthenics, too."

This was definitely not welcome news to Megan. She knew that she was in serious danger of being caught in a lie, or at best a half-truth. She *did* run nearly every morning, but she just wasn't that serious about it. She'd bragged about it to him only because she remembered how he'd often teased her about her lack of athletic prowess. When the fitness craze had begun to sweep the country, Megan was among the first enrollees, but she'd never become a fanatic.

They left the cabin and jogged down the steep driveway to the rural road in front of the cabin. She was overly conscious of each step, and of the big man moving easily beside her. There was something very menacing about all those muscles, although "menacing" was the last word she would ever have associated with Patrick.

During her long and very nearly sleepless night, Megan had been haunted by such thoughts. No matter how many times she told herself she was being ridiculous, she could not quite rid herself of the fear that he might be dangerous. If a man could lose something as important as his sense of humor, couldn't he also change in even more unpleasant ways? And hadn't she once read somewhere that loss of a sense of humor almost invariably accompanied mental illness?

Her feet pounded the pavement rhythmically as she chanced a cautious sideways glance at him. How absurd it was to be concerned for her safety with Patrick. Besides, he *had* smiled this morning. And, of course, there'd been that incident with the grill which had precipitated her embarrassing behavior. Weren't they good signs? Or was she seeking too desperately for good signs?

Lost in her thoughts, Megan ignored the first warning signs that under ordinary circumstances would have made her turn back. Besides, she was running in unfamiliar territory this morning. Even the effortless running of the man beside her might have contributed to her negligence. A sudden stitch in her side sharply reminded her that she wasn't exactly in contention for any marathon. She glanced his way again and caught him staring at her. He slowed down immediately.

"Hadn't we better turn back now?" he asked.

Oh, how she wanted to say no. It was obvious that he had
no need to turn back and equally obvious that there was
some sort of rebuke implied in his question. He was pa-
tronizing her, implying that she didn't know when to quit.
Had he always been that way, or had her perspective simply
changed? She'd probably thought that he was being wonderfully protective back then.

She stifled her anger and nodded, then crossed the road
and started back. He trailed slightly behind. She was very
careful not to slacken her pace, as she surely would have
done if she'd been alone. Far from easing her tension, this
morning's run was only adding to it.

By the time they reached the bottom of the driveway,
Megan had pushed herself to her limit and then some, but
there was no way she was going to admit it. If he decided to
jog up that driveway, she would, too. Even if it killed her.

He did, and she followed gamely, knowing full well that
she was asking too much of an already exhausted body. But
at least pain had taken the place of tension. He continued
to move effortlessly beside her, obviously holding himself
back to her slower pace. And to add insult to injury, she
knew he was watching her. She kept her own eyes resolutely
on the top of the hill, a goal that seemed incredibly distant
just now.

Suddenly, her foot slipped on the loose gravel and her
ankle turned painfully. Off balance, she started to fall forward—only to be caught quickly by a strong arm.

They came to a stop. Megan was mercifully still on her
feet, but her ankle was throbbing in protest. Patrick was far
too close as he continued to hold her lightly. His bare leg
brushed against her own as his fingers curved into the hollow of her waist. She moved slightly, trying to take herself
out of his reach, but the pain reasserted itself and she cried
out involuntarily.

The sound she heard then shocked her. Laughter. For a
brief moment, she just stared at him in openmouthed

amazement, and she was still staring dumbly as he scooped her up into his arms and started up the driveway again.

"You haven't changed at all," he said when his laughter had subsided into a chuckle.

"Wh-what do you mean?" she sputtered angrily as she twitched with indignation. Of all the things he might have said, that statement was by far the worst.

He shifted her easily in his arms, cradling her against his body and forcing her to wrap her arms around his neck.

"You still throw yourself into things for all you're worth," he replied in an amused tone, bending his head to stare down at her before returning his attention to the driveway.

"Put me down, Patrick. I just turned my ankle. I've done it before. The pain is gone now." She struggled for a moment, then gave up when it only increased that awareness of him.

"We're almost there," he said, merely tightening his grip on her.

Megan felt his every movement, was completely aware of the scent of him, of the mingled heat of both their bodies. She tried her best to ignore it all.

Was he right? Had she always been that way? It didn't fit at all with her own memories of that earlier self, so she chose to dismiss it as a figment of his imagination.

He set her on her feet at the front door, but still kept an arm around her waist as he pushed the door open. As soon as they were inside, she moved as far away from his as possible. There was still some tenderness in her injured ankle, but she walked with a conscious effort to demonstrate its wholeness.

"Sit down and let me check it."

That sounded entirely too much like an order to her, so she shook her head emphatically. "I told you it's okay. I've done this before."

He stared at her for a moment, then gave up with a shrug that she welcomed as a victory.

"I'm going to shower," she stated as she headed for the hallway.

"Fine. I'll get some breakfast for us."

She tried to hear mockery or reproof in his words, but was forced to conclude that neither was present. He must simply be humoring her—for whatever reason.

BREAKFAST WAS VERY GOOD, although Megan had some difficulty persuading herself that she was hungry. Patrick obviously had no such problem, she noticed. She asked him about his diet during his prolonged captivity, and he answered her as briefly as possible. She had the unmistakable impression that he just didn't want to talk about those years.

But she wanted to talk about them. She wanted to make him understand how much had changed and how there could be no future for them now. She was still worrying about that remark he'd made after her mishap. Whatever he might have thought initially, she was sure that he was now in the process of convincing himself that she hadn't changed at all. Somehow, she had to reverse that process.

The best way to do that, she thought, was to get him to talk about his future plans. She was nearly certain that he intended to remain in the army, and the terrible irony of that was not lost on her. Patrick was the one who had encouraged her own break with the army through his refusal to take it seriously. And now that she had made that break, he himself appeared likely to make the army his career.

After she cleared away the breakfast dishes—"Fair is fair," she had told herself, even if he hadn't done his share the previous night—Patrick suggested they go for a walk in the woods. She agreed quickly, even as she wondered what on earth they were going to do with their time. Obviously, she hadn't thought too clearly before she decided to bring him here.

That question about his future remained in her mind and eventually came out as they crested a small hill and paused to enjoy the view.

He didn't answer immediately but continued to stare out into the forest. Then, when she had just about decided that she wasn't going to get an answer, he turned to her.

"I don't know. There's no need for me to make a hasty decision."

"Hasty?" she echoed, certain that he had already decided but just didn't want to admit it. "But you've had years to decide what you would do when you came home."

He drew in a deep breath, then let it out slowly. "First of all, I was never all that sure that I would be coming home. And second, I spent most of that time thinking about...the things I missed."

She felt properly chastened. She still tended to disregard the very real danger he had been in during those years, perhaps because she just couldn't bear to think about it. And she'd heard that tiny but all-important pause before his final words. He was letting her know exactly what he'd been thinking about. Was he also suggesting that she might have spent more of those years thinking about him than rebuilding her life without him?

"Well, you're right, of course," she said quickly. "They won't push you to make any decisions in a hurry, will they?"

"You mean the army?" he asked. Then he chuckled. "If they do, I'll just remind them of twelve years of accumulated leave."

Megan's mouth curved into a smile as she felt a bittersweet tug at her heart. Something of the old Patrick was still there, however small and however infrequently it revealed itself. But her next question was her way of reminding herself that it still could not work.

"But you are considering staying in, aren't you?"

He stared at her for a very long moment, then nodded. "Yes, I am."

"How can you?" she shouted, forgetting all about her careful self-control. "You never wanted that life. How can you possibly want it now?"

"I'm not sure that I do," he said calmly. "I only said that I was considering it. Besides, your father said that a lot has changed in recent years."

"He's lying. Nothing has changed and nothing ever will change for the army. They still uproot your life every few years and they still demand too much."

"Duty tours are necessary for anyone headed for the top, Meggie. You know that as well as I do. And of course they demand a lot; it's an important job. The army is more important now than at any time since World War II. With the current worldwide political climate, the best thinking seems to be that—"

"You *have* decided," she cut him off angrily. She'd already heard it all many times from her father—the army's increased importance in what was expected to be a series of limited actions, like Grenada. "Why don't you just admit it?"

"And why wouldn't I be willing to admit it?" he asked in that infuriatingly calm way.

"Because you think—" She stopped, then went on before she could lose her courage. "Because you think that you can persuade me to accept that life again."

"And you won't?"

"No, I won't. But it doesn't matter anyway." She took a few steps away from him and stared down into the gully. Tears she simply refused to shed were stinging her eyes.

"I see," he said quietly.

She whirled around to face him, caught in the grip of emotions too powerful to control. "Don't say that. I hate it when people say that, because it usually means that they don't see at all but don't want to talk about it, either."

A ghost of a smile flickered across his face. "Do you want to talk about it?"

Yes, she did, but she was too afraid. "No!"

"That's what I thought."

"Patrick, you've been gone for nearly twelve years. We'd known each other for only a year when you...disappeared. We were kids; now we're adults. We've both changed beyond recognition. We're...strangers."

He nodded. She didn't know whether or not to consider that a victory, so she forged on.

"There's something else, too. Something I thought about yesterday while I was driving out here. For most of that time, I believed you to be dead. But you must have known that I was still alive. Can you see the difference that makes?"

"You're telling me that you've found someone else," he said bluntly.

"I'm not telling you anything of the sort. That has nothing to do with it." She thought he was missing the point altogether.

"It seems to me," he said with a hint of dry humor in his voice, "that that has everything to do with it."

"I don't understand," she replied with a shrug. They were supposed to be talking about changes, not about other lovers. They'd already agreed that that subject was forbidden.

"This man you've been seeing...is it serious?"

She thought about saying yes, knowing that it might be the easiest way out. Then she thought about asking him if what he really wanted to know was whether or not she was sleeping with Ted. But she ignored both possibilities and simply shrugged again.

"It depends on what you mean by 'serious.' We've been dating for about six months, rather steadily for the past month or so." As she spoke, she was trying again to conjure up Ted's image, with even less success this time.

"Then is it fair to say that you have no immediate interest in marrying him?"

"Yes...I mean, no, I'm not interested in marrying him. Or anyone else for that matter."

"That's all I wanted to know."

"You were never possessive before, Patrick," she commented, feeling that it might be wise to point out a few of the changes in him.

"A man can become damned possessive when he's had everything taken away from him," he responded in a sudden burst of bitterness that reminded her of the night before, when they'd discussed this same subject.

Megan didn't know what to say to that. She'd managed thus far not to show any pity for him. If he'd come home a broken man, she might well have done so. But regardless of what he'd been through, it was very difficult to feel pity for this hard, controlled man who stood before her now.

"I'm sorry," she said after a pause. "I know I've been very selfish."

Although she'd given what she thought was the expected response, she knew how true it was as soon as she said it. She'd spent far too much time feeling sorry for herself and thinking about her own situation, and too little time trying to understand him. He deserved better than that, no matter how much he'd changed. Tears of self-condemnation filled her eyes and began to spill over. She swiped angrily at them with the back of her hand as she kept her face turned away from him.

He reached out to take her hand, surrounding it with a big, callused palm that felt very alien.

"So have I, Meggie. I knew I'd be coming home to so many changes, and I selfishly wanted one thing to be exactly the same. It was pretty damned stupid of me."

Then he gently squeezed the hand he held. "Neither one of us has to make any decisions quickly. We have time."

She nodded, but she knew he was wrong. They didn't have time. Or at least she didn't. More of the old Patrick seemed to be coming out all the time now, and if she didn't get away soon, she would be trapped forever. She knew it, and she thought that maybe he knew it, too.

They walked on, reverting to safe, casual conversation that consisted mostly of her attempts to fill in the vast gaps in his knowledge. He listened, nodded, interjected comments or questions and otherwise gave every indication of being very interested.

She chattered on, unwilling to let silence fall between them. But her words were no more than noise overlying the tension that seemed to get worse after each outburst between them. It was like a huge dam, springing small leaks one after the other until it would all let go.

By the time they returned to the cabin, Megan was once more worrying about the immediate future. She could sense that they wouldn't be staying here very long. They couldn't. It had been a mistake to come here in the first place.

"Have you thought about how you're going to hold the press at bay when you leave here?" she asked, wanting to find out what his plans were. "I think you're safe here, but you won't be when you leave."

"That's already been taken care of," he said unconcernedly. "I'll be billeted at Fort Meade, where they can keep things under control."

She was greatly relieved to hear that, both because she knew that he'd be safe at the sprawling base in suburban Maryland and because she knew now that he didn't intend to follow her back to Connecticut.

"The others will be there, too," he went on. "One of them has some health problems that need attention and the other one . . . needs help, too."

"What do you mean?" she asked curiously, having forgotten all about the other two men.

"He, uh, has some mental problems. He tried to commit suicide several times and he had a Vietnamese girlfriend he had to leave behind, along with a baby."

Megan stiffened at those words, once again wondering if Patrick had left anyone behind. Why did it seem so difficult for them to stay away from that subject? And why did she feel so sick when she thought about it? She knew she had to be practical and rational.

They were on the screened porch behind the cabin. Patrick was seated on a chaise with a beer in his hand; she sat on a chair across from him, sipping a soda. He began to talk about his busy schedule of debriefings and press conferences, his crash course in recent history and some dental work he required after his long ordeal.

Megan was only half listening, but she thought it was good that he'd have so much to occupy his time. She would be very busy herself when she returned to Connecticut. Poor Karen would be swamped. Perhaps it was for the best that they would both be too busy to dwell on their situation, even if she did hate to prolong the inevitable break.

Then, once again, he made an abrupt shift from general to personal conversation.

"I still don't understand your changed attitude toward the army."

Megan was annoyed. She thought she'd explained all that before. Obviously, he hadn't been listening.

"It was your attitude once, too, Patrick, so I don't see why you find it so hard to understand."

She waited for him to say something; when he didn't, she finally continued, uncomfortably aware of his eyes on her.

"From the time I was born, the army was my life. It just never occurred to me that it could be otherwise. Everyone I knew was army. Joel was headed for West Point from the time he could walk. Then I married you and I was still in the army.

"But after you disappeared, Dad virtually ordered me to college—and that was where it began. I made my first real friends who were civilians, and I met women who were career-oriented. Gradually, I became one of them.

"The travel agency was a natural for me, because I'd traveled all my life. Karen, my partner, had done a lot of traveling, too.

"When I made these new friends, I began dropping my old ones, especially the MIA wives' group. They were living in the past. Then we moved to Connecticut and that ended all of it and gave me a new beginning. I loved my new life, and the more I grew to love it, the more I realized just how terrible the old one had been.

"I think I told you that I'm considering buying a condo up there. It's the realization of a dream, a place of my own where I can stay the rest of my life if I want to. No one can come along and tell me that I have to go to Germany or Kansas or Panama. It's mine—and so is my life."

Patrick sat silently through all this, his expression giving nothing away. She couldn't be sure that he had understood anything she'd said, but she hoped that he had—because this was the key to his understanding that it couldn't work between them.

"Patrick," she said when the silence lengthened, "I can't go back to that kind of life. Not now, not ever."

He finally nodded slowly and, she thought, reluctantly. "So that's what it's all about . . . freedom?" he asked.

"Yes." She supposed that was as good a word as any for it, although there was far more to it than that.

"And there's no place in your life now for anyone who could restrict that freedom?" His question was asked in that annoyingly bland tone that never failed to irritate her.

"No, there isn't. I'm not saying that I wouldn't like to find someone eventually, but it will have to be on *my* terms." *And not on the army's terms,* she added to herself.

Belatedly, she realized the strangeness of this conversation. She was still married to this man, even if she didn't feel married. On the other hand, she truly didn't feel unmarried, either.

He stood up suddenly, unfolding his long frame from the chaise with muscular grace. As he stood with his back to her and his hands jammed into the rear pockets of his jeans, staring out at the woods, she felt that rippling sensation again. It could be provoked so easily and seemingly for no reason.

"Freedom apparently means different things to different people," he said suddenly.

His bursts of bitterness didn't affect her quite so strongly now, but she still felt selfish—and that made her defensive this time.

"I'm not trying to pretend that I've suffered what you've suffered, Patrick, but I went through my own version of hell. Did I have a husband or didn't I? Was he alive and being tortured or locked in some windowless cell? Would he come home someday in a body bag, a casualty of a pointless war?"

"It wasn't pointless."

She took a deep, calming breath. "Patrick, I simply refuse to debate that issue with you. I've listened to my father's opinions often enough, including the 'we weren't allowed to win it' theory prevalent in the army. If the army knew that and still sent men over there to die, then the army was just as much at fault as the politicians."

"It's called duty, Meggie. There was a time when you would have understood that."

Her anger was bubbling ever closer to the surface. "And there was a time when you would have agreed that it was pointless—and wrong."

"I've done some growing up. I agree with your father."

She got up, unable to listen to this any longer. The worst had happened: she was married to a carbon copy of her father. That realization made her sick and sad—and even angrier.

"Of course you agree with him, with all of them. You're one of them."

Her disgust dripped from every syllable. She whirled around and left the porch quickly, before matters could become even worse.

Chapter Five

Megan peered hurriedly into her mother's car, hoping that Patrick might have left the keys in the ignition. When she saw that he hadn't, she backed off and considered the possibility of maneuvering her rental car around it. There wasn't much space, but she was desperate.

She had to get away from him for a while, away from the crushing burden of their shared past, away from the unbearable tension of the present. In truth, what she wanted to do was to get into her car and not stop until she was back in Connecticut. But that was clearly out of the question; she couldn't just go off and leave him here. So she had decided to do the next best thing: go into town for a few hours, and perhaps call Karen to pour out her fears and pain.

With a nervous glance back at the front door of the cabin, she slid into the driver's seat and inserted the key in the ignition with a shaking hand, irrationally certain that the car wouldn't start. But the engine caught immediately and she began to inch forward cautiously, bringing the front bumper as close as possible to the nearest tree. Then she swiveled around to see how much clearance she had gained, and jumped with a startled cry as a hand brushed against her arm.

Before she could even realize what had happened, Patrick had switched off the ignition and withdrawn his hand with the keys firmly in his grasp. Those earlier fears about him roared through her brain—irrational, absurd, but very much there. She stared at the empty ignition as though willpower alone could start the car again, then finally jerked her head toward him as she heard the click of the door opening.

"I'm going into town for a while," she said in a voice that was half command and half plea. By now, her fear had been replaced by embarrassment.

Patrick made no immediate response as he carefully searched her face. She began to wonder if perhaps *he* thought *she* was insane. At the moment, she might have found that difficult to dispute.

"I'll go with you. We might as well take your mother's car."

He had already opened the door, and now he reached in to help her out without waiting for her response. His voice had been quiet, rational, calm—the exact opposite of her own state at the moment. It was an echo of other times, of quarrels and flares of temper on her part. But the hand that grasped her arm lightly was callused and strange. She didn't know how much more of this volatile mixture of familiarity and strangeness she could take.

Then she let him help her out of the car, because she had no choice and because she was feeling increasingly foolish. He'd always been able to do that, she recalled. His laid-back, easygoing nature had always made her sometimes volatile one seem childish and foolish.

She thought about explaining to him that she hadn't really intended to run away, but any explanation would only exacerbate her feeling of foolishness. Besides, she was half afraid that he knew that running away was exactly what she had been thinking of doing.

In a tense silence, she let him lead her to her mother's car and hand her in on the passenger's side. Then he walked around to the driver's side, and she followed his movement with her eyes. The plethora of emotions assaulting her coalesced for one terrible moment into a kind of hatred—blind, unreasoning hatred.

She didn't dare examine that hatred too closely and, in any event, had little opportunity to do so, because he quickly slid into the driver's seat of the Cadillac, filling the space menacingly. She stared straight ahead, unwilling to look at him as she pushed that ugliness from her mind.

Then, when the moment had lasted too long and she became aware of his silence and stillness, she finally did turn to look at him and found, unbelievably, that he was smiling at her. She just stared in dumb amazement at that easy grin on this very different face.

"The last time you did something like that, you wrecked the car... and could have hurt yourself."

She had forgotten all about that incident, which was certainly understandable under the circumstances. And she wasn't exactly pleased to be reminded about it now, either. No wonder there were so many things she seemed to have forgotten; her mind had obviously drawn a protective cover over them.

At twenty, Megan had been something less than a good driver. She had been prone to drifting off into her thoughts and assuming that other drivers would have the good sense to give her a wide berth. The incident to which he referred had occurred at Schofield Barracks, when she had run out and driven away after their first serious argument, the cause of which she couldn't even recall now. He was right; she could have been seriously injured, considering the damage she'd done to their trusty old Chevy. Patrick's reaction, she remembered, had been one of worry, not anger, despite her foolishness.

"I'm a much better driver now," she stated firmly.

He chuckled as he started the car. "I assume you must be, or you wouldn't be here."

She turned away to hide her smile. Why was he doing this to her, taunting her with glimpses of a man who didn't really exist anymore? It hurt, with a pain that was very nearly physical.

Except for the directions she had to give him, their trip into town was made in silence, a silence no more or less comfortable than earlier ones had been. It was a toss-up with them, she thought, between tense silences and conversations that could produce sparks or even full-scale conflagrations.

It wasn't until they had entered the downtown business district and she saw other people that his celebrity status came to mind. She wondered if he had thought about that or even understood it.

"Patrick, you're bound to be recognized." She looked nervously around as he searched for a parking space. Although she hadn't watched television herself since the original announcement of his return, she was certain that TV coverage of the welcoming ceremonies must have turned him into an instant celebrity.

"Possibly, but I doubt it," he replied with nonchalance. "No one has any reason to expect me to be here, and people tend to forget the six o'clock news pretty fast."

"But if you are recognized, there will be reporters hounding us within hours," she persisted, imagining the press laying siege to the cabin and forcing her to play the role she'd thus far avoided.

"I'll deal with that if it happens," he said confidently.

They found a parking space and left the car, with Megan searching each and every face for a sign of recognition. But the glances they received appeared to be no more than polite curiosity about strangers in town, and she finally began to relax. That is, until Patrick's hand curved familiarly around hers.

Each time he touched her, no matter how innocently, she was jolted back to that moment in the kitchen of the cabin when she'd seen him reach for her and then retreat. It had been such a tentative move, so very unlike the self-confident man Patrick had always been—and even more unlike the man he appeared to be now.

"Where do you want to go?" she asked him, wondering if she could manage to break free long enough to call Karen. Just the sound of her friend's voice would be a welcome link with her real life, a life that was seeming more and more unreal.

"Oh, nowhere in particular," he replied. "It's just nice to walk around among people and look into stores. It's been a long time."

She felt yet another wave of crushing guilt and rather resented his honesty. He'd been deprived of so much that what was to her a mundane activity was to him a source of pleasure. Surely she had no right to be thinking only of herself at a time like this. And yet, if she didn't . . .

He stopped suddenly and then began to draw her to the curb. She looked across the street, following his gaze, and then broke into spontaneous laughter.

"There goes your twelve years of back pay," she said, laughing, as he hurried her across the street. Heath, the do-it-yourself electronic gadgets chain, had always been a favorite of his. He'd built parts of the stereo system they had owned and countless other gadgets whose purposes had seemed improbable or remained unknown to her.

She watched with amusement as he bounded into the store and totally ignored her as he moved through the various displays. Seeing such boyish pleasure on the face of this harsh man drew emotions from within her that were far more powerful than anything she had yet felt. She'd occasionally passed these stores over the years, and once, for some reason, she had received one of their advertising circulars in the mail. On all of those occasions she had thought of Patrick with the sharp pain of remembrance. Now he was here and thought had become reality.

An aching hope was rising within her, feeding on these moments, a hope that the old Patrick might really be there. Not just the bits and pieces she'd been seeing, but all of him, whole and real. But then she thought about the decision she was sure he had already made, and the hope shuddered and died. He had made his choice—and she had made hers.

Patrick was enjoying himself. Little by little, he thought, he was recapturing old pleasures, the small things that others couldn't understand. He enjoyed just being with people, seeing familiar signs, hearing English spoken all around him.

Yet he couldn't quite bring himself to communicate all that to Meggie, and he felt foolish when he tried. Her silence after that brief statement about what this meant to him had troubled him. Was the fault his or hers?

He glanced over at her and wondered if she wanted to be here with him and why he couldn't bring himself to ask her that. Should he have admitted how very much he needed her with him now? Was the price of that need too high? Could she really understand what it would mean to admit that need?

He realized that neither of them had ever made demands on the other. There'd never been any necessity. He guessed, though, that he'd always believed she needed him in some undefined way. Typical male arrogance.

At that moment the clerk interrupted his thoughts to inquire if he would be paying in cash or by credit card. Patrick started to reach for his wallet, then stopped in confusion.

"Uh, I don't have any..." His voice trailed off in irritation over this renewed evidence of his helplessness. It was inconsequential, he tried to tell himself, but that inner voice mocked the attempt.

"Meggie, do you have any credit cards?"

She was already digging in her purse as she nodded. It was ridiculous that such a minor thing could raise a lump in her throat. But that confused look on his face and the irritability in his voice when he'd asked her to pay betrayed things she didn't want to see in Patrick, more things she'd never seen before. She handed the clerk a credit card, then saw the young man look from it to Patrick with that expression she'd been fearing earlier.

"You're Lieutenant O'Donnell...the one who just came back from Vietnam. I thought you looked familiar." The clerk's face wore an expression of mingled awe and respect.

Megan expected Patrick's discomfort to increase, but just the opposite happened. Before her disbelieving eyes he was transformed back into the epitome of an army officer.

"Yes, I am. But I'd appreciate it very much if you wouldn't let this get out. We'd like some time alone."

His voice was pleasant enough, but Megan heard—and guessed that the young clerk heard, too—the underlying command in it. When, she wondered, had that begun to come so easily, so effortlessly, to him?

"Oh, yes, sir. I understand." The young man's reply proved to Megan that she had been correct.

Still, the clerk could not refrain from asking questions, which Patrick answered with polite formality. She'd heard that tone of voice all her life, the tone officers use on civilians that never fails to set them apart. In any civilian gathering, she could spot a career officer in less than five minutes' conversation, no matter how he tried to blend with his surroundings.

That memory-sparked warmth had already begun to evaporate by the time they left the store. Patrick spotted a hardware store and indicated an interest in it. Megan saw her chance to escape temporarily and told him that she needed to find a drugstore. He nodded agreeably, his mind obviously already on the treasures to be found in the hardware store, and she hurried off down the street, searching for a pay phone.

Luck was on her side, because she found a convenient phone just outside a drugstore. She punched in her credit card number and dialed Touch of Paradise. Her receptionist-secretary answered and immediately began bombarding Megan with questions and comments about seeing Patrick on TV but not seeing her.

Megan gently put off the questions and asked to be put through to Karen, who, of course, came on the line with the same question. Megan told her the truth, feeling much better just for having a dear and familiar voice on the other end of the line. But after a lengthy conversation, she was forced to conclude that the feeling was very short-lived. As soon as she hung up, she felt as alone as she had before. Connecticut still seemed so very far away.

Perhaps that was why she decided to make the other call. She got out her address book and found Ted's office number, then dialed it before she could change her mind. She was still having difficulty conjuring up his image clearly when he answered.

His surprise at her call was obvious, and his question was just the same as Karen's. So she told him what she had told Karen—that she had decided it would be better all around if she and Patrick met in private.

That statement was followed by a strained silence, during which Megan wondered why on earth she had decided to call him. She certainly didn't need any more tension-filled silences, and talking with Ted didn't bring him any closer, either. In fact, he already seemed to be very far in the past.

She finally told him that she would be back in Connecticut in a few days.

"Alone?" he asked hesitantly but, she thought, hopefully.

"Yes," she answered firmly, thinking that life could be a lot simpler if she had lied to Patrick and could now lie to Ted.

"Does that mean what I think it means?" he asked with still more hope in his voice.

She cringed, then managed to make a noncommittal response about Patrick's remaining in Washington for debriefings, while she had to get back to work.

As she fumbled her way through this half-truth, she turned away from the phone to face the street. She was paying no real attention to the pedestrian traffic as she concentrated on sounding plausible. Then, just as Ted was telling her how much he missed her and was asking when they could see each other, her unfocused gaze cleared.

Ted's voice became an annoying buzz in her ear as she stared at the tall figure coming toward her. He had already spotted her and his boyish grin was back. She watched him move toward her with that confident, easy stride and felt again the shivery consciousness of his attractiveness.

She mumbled a quick goodbye and hung up, only vaguely aware of having cut Ted off in midsentence. He was already slipping from her mind by the time she replaced the receiver.

Patrick stopped in front of her and extended the small paper-wrapped package he'd been carrying. "I didn't have time before to get you anything."

"I didn't expect . . ." Her voice trailed off with a choking sound as she realized what the package contained.

Violets. Deep purple violets. Megan had always loved them, more than roses or orchids or any of the more extravagant flowers. When she'd managed to come down with a bad cold just after their arrival at Schofield Barracks, Patrick had searched the island of Oahu from one end to the other to find them for her—and had come close to being put on report for showing up late to a staff meeting.

"Thank you," she whispered, her voice embarrassingly husky and her eyes threatening to flood with tears.

He, too, seemed to be slightly embarrassed, and as he took her arm to guide her back to the car, she became angry that they had to be so ill at ease with these emotions. They'd lost so very much, but the loss of their spontaneity, their former openness, was the worst loss of all. It was, she thought, the one thing they could never recapture now.

"Oh," she said brightly into the silence, "did you find anything you wanted at the hardware store? You can use one of my charge cards if you want."

"Thanks, but I'll wait," he replied. And then, as though he, too, found the silence unbearable, he began to talk about new tools that interested him. When he had exhausted that subject, he switched to the matter of purchasing a car. Tinkering with cars had been another favorite pastime.

"Your father was going to arrange for a rental, so I'll have something available when I get back to Washington," he finished.

Megan said nothing, thinking that the general was being entirely too helpful and hoping that she would have the opportunity to tell him that in person. She knew exactly what was going on. The general was trying to overwhelm Patrick just the way he had always overwhelmed her. She thought about saying just that, but decided to remain silent. Patrick, for reasons that eluded her, had always liked her father; it seemed apparent from both his comments and her mother's that that hadn't changed. Besides, she had no desire to provoke another argument just now.

Megan hadn't thought that the presence of others would help their relationship much, but as soon as they were alone in the car and leaving the town behind, she knew she had been wrong. The world had once more contracted to two people, and the atmosphere grew ever more taut.

En route back to the cabin, they passed a charming old inn that she recalled from past visits to the area, and it suddenly occurred to her that they could escape their isolation for the evening. But before she could make the suggestion, Patrick glanced at the inn and then turned to her.

"I wonder if their restaurant is any good. We could have dinner there tonight if you like."

She definitely did like. It was exactly what she had in mind, and she guessed that he, too, was seeking an escape. "It was very good years ago. I used to come here often. Unless it's changed, it's Southern cuisine."

"Sounds good to me," he replied, then turned to her with a grin. "Did you ever learn how to cook?"

She bristled at that. She hadn't done so badly, all things considered. And even if she had, she didn't want to be reminded about it now.

"I didn't think I was all that bad, but no, I haven't improved. I never cook." She made the last statement with a degree of perverse pride. It was time to start reminding him that she was not a good candidate for an officer's wife—or anyone's wife, for that matter.

"You weren't that bad," he said reassuringly, to her annoyance. "Just a bit limited, that's all."

"So were our living quarters," she rejoined stiffly.

"Tell me about your present living quarters," he said with that infuriatingly amused tone.

"They're very nice. I told you it's a small cottage on an estate. The owner of the estate is a corporate chief executive officer who uses it only on occasional weekends, so the caretaker and I have it all to ourselves most of the time. It was a very lucky find." She didn't bother to add that she'd gotten it only after the owner had learned who her father was. His company had some large defense contracts.

"Who were you talking to on the phone?" he asked suddenly, once again catching her off guard. She suspected that he'd deliberately waited for just such a moment to ask.

"Karen. My partner," she answered, glad to be able to tell a half-truth, since she didn't dare tell a whole one. "I did run away at a very busy time. This is when most people begin to plan their summer vacations."

She didn't look at him, since she didn't want to risk the possibility that he might see the rest of the truth, and she prayed that he wouldn't ask why she hadn't just called from the cabin. She was also chafing over what she saw as a resurgence of his possessiveness, although she could scarcely say anything about it after his earlier statement on the subject.

"I'm looking forward to meeting her," he said as they pulled into the driveway.

"Yes, she's looking forward to meeting you, too," Megan replied stiltedly.

Their conversation was making her very nervous. She had come here with every intention of ending it all, and she was becoming increasingly certain that it wouldn't be that easy or that fast. Those ever-increasing glimpses of the man she had loved, and the moments of confusion, bitterness and vulnerability were all conspiring against that decision. She stared down at the bunch of violets she still clutched in her hands and felt herself wavering still more.

But she didn't want him to come into her life in Connecticut, either. He didn't belong there.

They got out of the car, and Patrick picked up the kits and tools he had purchased. "I guess you won't mind if I work on one of them a bit."

Megan said nothing. She didn't mind but she knew she should. They had things to talk about, decisions to make. He had no business playing with his toys at a time like this. But she seemed unable to force the discussion they must have, so it wasn't his fault, really. And she knew she'd been cold and sometimes even cruel, too, but she didn't know what else to be.

They went into the cabin and she just stood there, staring down at the bunch of violets. He set down his packages and came over to her. When she didn't look up at him, he reached out to hook a finger beneath her chin and tilt her face up to meet his gaze.

"Meggie, we have to take this slowly. You understand that, don't you?"

She just nodded, caught by the gentleness of his tone and the warmth of his touch.

Only when he had settled down at the table with his kit and she had curled up on the sofa with a novel did she realize that his words could have provided the opening she needed. They had to talk, and not in fits and starts as they'd done so far. They had to sit down and let it all out. But she was afraid of what might or might not be there when they had finished.

THE DINING ROOM of the inn was quiet on a midweek evening, with only about a third of the tables occupied. No one seemed to be paying them any undue attention, although some heads did turn to watch them as the hostess led them to their table.

Megan knew they made a striking couple, even more so now with the changes in Patrick's appearance. She had always been (unfortunately, from her point of view) very petite and feminine in a wide-eyed, innocent sort of way. The old Patrick had once drawn attention because of his red hair and his charmingly insouciant manner. But the man with her now commanded, rather than attracted, attention. He was hard, tough, authoritative—the perfect antithesis of the impression she created.

She wondered if the others in the dining room saw what she saw: an officer in civilian clothes. Like most military men she'd known, Patrick had little or no interest in civilian clothes and had relied on her to take care of that unimportant part of his wardrobe when they were married. But before they left the cabin, he'd apologized for his tweed jacket and casual slacks, saying that they were the best he could come up with during his brief stopover in the Philippines.

The jacket was obviously of inferior quality and the slacks were just a bit too short, but they did not in any way detract from the essence of the man. She couldn't look at him without feeling that faint stirring inside. It was absurd; if there was one woman in this world who could be expected not to respond to such a man, it was Megan. He just wasn't her type; in fact, he was the apotheosis of everything she had avoided for the past seven years. Did she feel what she felt only because they had once been intimate? Did people always feel that way toward past lovers? She had no way of knowing.

Stranger still, she could recall very little about their love-making. There were vague impressions of love and tenderness and laughter and teasing, but nothing was clear. The memory was there—it had to be—but it was apparently sealed off in some place she couldn't reach. Anyway, she should be grateful for that, considering their present situation.

She wondered how much Patrick remembered. That hand reaching out toward her came back to haunt her again. Had he been remembering at that moment what she could not now recall, or did he just want a woman—any woman?

Their dinner arrived then, breaking her thoughts, and she realized that he had let her silence run on without any attempts at conversation. She wondered if he might have been off in the same thoughts she was having.

This was just no good. They had to talk, no matter what the outcome. But once again, she felt that reluctance. He had said they must take it slowly—but why? Wouldn't it be far better to get their feelings out and have done with it?

"Tell me more about Touch of Paradise," Patrick suggested. They had begun to eat and conversation seemed to be required.

She was flattered that he'd even remembered the name of her business; she'd mentioned it only once that she could recall. Although she was certain that he was only trying to make safe conversation, she was very willing to oblige. It was far better than those silences, and besides, she loved to talk about her work.

So she did just that. She told him about how she and Karen presently catered only to nonbusiness trade but were considering opening a second office in Stamford, where a recent influx of corporate headquarters would give them the opportunity to expand into the corporate travel business. She explained that many corporations, especially smaller ones, preferred to contract for travel services for their executives rather than hire staff to handle it.

It was a big step, she explained, a gamble. And while both she and Karen believed it would pay off, they were hesitant about what would amount to doubling their present business. Also, they would no longer be working together—one of them would have to go to Stamford.

"You're very close, aren't you?" he asked.

She nodded. "Karen is the first true friend I've ever had. I'd always moved around so much that I never really had the opportunity to get that close to anyone before. Subconsciously, I guess I knew that it just wasn't worth the effort, because we'd soon be separated. But Karen and I have known each other for over ten years and it's a wonderful feeling. We're different in a lot of ways, but we understand each other."

"Is she married?"

"No. She lived with someone briefly, but it didn't work. We're alike in that respect. Very independent."

The words were scarcely out of her mouth when she realized her error. She had made it sound as though she, too, wasn't married. But it was a natural mistake; she still didn't feel married.

So she hurried on, talking still more about the business. But she began to suspect that his attention had wandered, so she stopped as quickly as she could, then reacted with surprise when he asked yet another question.

"How do you work the partnership? Does she handle the business end?"

She refused to see that as an innocent question. She knew exactly what he was getting at. "No, we both do. We have an outside accountant, of course, and our receptionist does some of the bookkeeping. But I actually do most of it. Karen isn't all that fond of computers."

"And you are?" Patrick didn't even try to hide his incredulity.

"Yes, I've taken courses. In fact, we've just upgraded our hardware and I was the one who made the decision." She leaned back in her chair and narrowed her eyes dangerously. "I know just what you're thinking, Patrick. The girl you knew wouldn't have been able to turn on a computer, let alone communicate with it. But at the risk of sounding terribly immodest, I'll tell you that I'm a very good businesswoman. And to be that these days, you have to be computer literate."

He continued to stare at her in amazement for a few more seconds, then shook his head in mingled disbelief and amusement.

"You don't believe me, do you?" she asked defensively.

"Oh, I believe you. Your father said that your business was doing very well."

How nice, she thought. Her father he believed, but without that authority backing her up, she'd still be trying to convince him.

"But you just assumed that Karen was the one carrying the business and that I was just...window dressing," she finished scornfully, suspecting that her father had implied just that.

Patrick didn't answer right away because he had resumed eating his dinner, but she saw the guilty look on his face. At least she was reasonably sure that he believed her now, and there was some satisfaction to be had in that.

The silence dragged on for a few more moments as he ate and she glared at him. Finally, he looked up at her apologetically.

"You have to give me some time to get used to these changes, Meggie. Besides, I never meant to imply that you couldn't be successful."

"Well, I am. I've worked very hard. I often put in ten- or twelve-hour days, and I've even been taking some graduate-level business courses. I'm not the same, Patrick. Not at all. And I'd have thought you would have seen that by now." She didn't bother to keep the irritation out of her voice.

"I *can* see that," he said with quiet insistence.

But you don't like it and you'll never really accept it, she said to herself. *You want a wife just like my mother. Well, go find one, Patrick. There must be plenty of them left.*

Dinner continued mostly in silence, partly with safe observations about the weather, the food and the inn's decor. But neither of them seemed inclined to hurry as they lingered over coffee and liqueur. However uncomfortable the present situation might be, it would only get worse when they were once more alone at the cabin.

When the bill was presented Megan reached for it, and then started to pick up her purse. But he took the bill away from her and drew out his wallet.

"I'll get it," she offered. "I know you haven't had time yet to make financial arrangements."

"I'll take care of it. Your father gave me some pocket money."

That did it. She'd already been feeling brittle, but now something snapped completely. She'd heard one too many references to the general. Patrick had mentioned him more than he'd mentioned his own family, and she knew it had nothing at all to do with the fact that the general was her father. It was a perfect example of what she hated most—

that all-male fraternity that shut out even wives and children.

"How very thoughtful of him," she said sarcastically. "No doubt he figured that I wouldn't have enough sense to plan for such a situation."

A small, charged silence followed while the waitress came to take the money. Megan glared at him.

"Or maybe he just thought you might have had other things on your mind and had forgotten about it," Patrick remarked with a hint of the sarcasm she had flung at him.

She looked away quickly. She knew exactly what he was implying, that she might have been so ecstatic about seeing him again that such mundane details could easily have slipped her mind. It was a cruel blow—and the first he had struck against her.

She got up to leave without waiting to see if he was following. It was all so stupid. Why were they arguing over such unimportant things as who would pay for dinner and whether or not her father should be helping him out?

Too many emotions were too close to the surface, and each flare-up seemed to presage even larger explosions. Megan felt as though every square inch of her flesh had been flayed until it was raw and irritated. She wanted nothing more than to be able to curl up in a corner somewhere to wait until it healed.

Chapter Six

They returned to the cabin in what might have been called a state of undeclared war. Megan was angry with Patrick for his failure to accept her, or probably even to *see* her, as she was now. She was angry with her father for his meddling, which she knew perfectly well was calculated to persuade Patrick to remain in the army. And most of all, she was angry with herself for allowing petty bickering to sidetrack them from the far more important issues.

Patrick had remained silent, and she had no idea what he might be thinking. That brief burst of sarcasm on his part had shocked her. He'd never been like that; on the other hand, neither had she.

During her first hours at the cabin, before his arrival, Megan had discovered a closet shelf full of games, among them Trivial Pursuit. Fortunately, she remembered that now as she wondered how on earth they were going to spend the remainder of the evening. She got out the game and showed it to Patrick almost as a peace offering. He seemed to like the idea, though she suspected that he, too, viewed it as a safe way to pass some time.

So they spread the game out on the dining room table, seated themselves across from each other and confined their conversation to the game. He won both games, although he did so more by the luck of the dice than by knowing the answers. This did little to improve Megan's state of mind, even though she was not normally the competitive type who would chafe over such matters.

When they both reluctantly admitted that they had tired of the game, the hour was still too early to make excuses about being tired. So he built a fire in the big stone fireplace while she made some coffee.

She brought in the coffee and seated herself on the opposite end of the long sofa on which he sat, then began to cast about rather desperately for a suitably safe topic of conversation. Normally rather outspoken, she was beginning to feel that she had become a stranger to herself. But before she had come up with something, Patrick took the lead, fixing her with those blue eyes in which she now saw no trace of amusement.

"Meggie, it isn't fair for you to be blaming your father for anything and everything."

"Why not?" she asked somewhat flippantly. It seemed very logical to her, and furthermore, she was determined not to lose her temper this time.

"Because he's a good man and he loves you very much," Patrick replied, obviously caught off balance by her tone of voice.

"Wrong! He's undoubtedly very good at his work, and I don't doubt that, in his fashion, he loves me. But he's *not* a good man, and he loves me best when I do exactly as I'm told, which he discovered yesterday that I don't always do."

"You're blaming him for a life that you've decided was miserable."

She thought that his phrasing was a bit strange and wondered why he found it necessary to repeat that obvious fact. For that matter, she wondered why they were even having this pointless conversation.

"I don't see your point, Patrick. It *was* a miserable life, one I wouldn't wish on any child."

He settled more deeply into the corner of the sofa, but his gaze never wavered and his expression didn't change. "You gave every impression of being a very happy girl when I met you."

"And that's exactly what I was . . . a girl. I was a brainwashed army brat who didn't even know that any other kind of life existed." She paused and drew a deep breath as she wondered why she seemed to have to explain what was very obvious to her, and should be to him, too. "Can't you understand what it's like to pick up and move every year or so, to make friends only to lose them? Or to be told that you can't have a pet because pets can't be dragged all around the world with you? Or to go to a new school where the other kids and even the teachers dismiss you immediately as 'one of those kids from the base?' "

That shut him up for all of ten seconds, and just for a moment, she thought she might have made her point at last. But then he spoke again, rather defensively, she thought.

"You had opportunities most kids only dream of."

"And they're better off only dreaming of them," she retorted angrily. "Of course my life would sound glamorous and exciting to those who'd lived all their childhood in one place."

"And of course their lives sounded wonderful to you because you didn't live them." He gave her a half smile. "It's the old grass-is-always-greener theory."

"Spare me the quaint homilies, Patrick," she said in disgust. "Who appointed you to defend my father, anyway? It's none of your business what I think of him."

"No, maybe not," he admitted quietly. "Maybe it's myself that I'm really trying to defend."

"Because you intend to follow in his footsteps," she said in that same disgusted tone. "Wonderful! Soon I'll have three generals in the family: my father, my brother and you."

"I told you that I haven't decided yet," he reminded her with a trace of impatience.

"If you haven't decided, it's only because you haven't figured out yet how to have your cake and eat it, too. That's all." She flung the words at him without pausing to consider them first. But now she was committed to a course of action with which she was surprisingly uncomfortable. "Don't worry, Patrick. A divorce won't cost you your stars. Even the army has gotten around to accepting divorce, and the general will probably applaud your good judgment."

The silence that followed that outburst was thunderous, to say the least. In it, Megan heard unpleasant echoes of her viciousness and, most of all, that word divorce. It shouldn't be upsetting her so much. She'd known it would come to that.

There was absolutely no change in Patrick's demeanor. He continued to look at her calmly, and no rigidity or sudden shift of position betrayed any tension in that long, hard body. She might have been commenting on the weather for all the reaction her statement had produced.

Instead, she was the one who was uncomfortable. She looked away from him and felt a drawing-back sensation, the kind of feeling one might have if one had just leaned out to peer into a dark, yawning chasm.

Finally, he took a deep breath and released it slowly, a gesture she'd seen him use often since his return. "I tried to tell you that I think we need to take this slowly, Meggie."

But she was there again, drawn back to that black pit. "Slowly?" she scoffed. "We've had twelve years, Patrick. Twelve years to accept the fact that we were kids then and now we're adults. I've accepted who and what I am. Why can't you?"

"But for most of those twelve years, you also thought I was dead," he said in a voice devoid of any emotion.

That stopped her with about the same degree of effectiveness as a pail of cold water. She could not refute what he said; neither could she deny its importance, since she herself had said the same thing. Angry tears pricked at her eyes, and she blinked them away as she kept her face carefully lowered.

Then she jumped with a startled sound of protest as he moved to her. His action was so swift and so unexpected that she had no time to move away before he seized both her hands in his. She could feel him willing her to look at him, and finally, reluctantly, she did.

She could see it immediately. This man had a claim on her. This hard man could summon back at will the husband she had loved. His claim might be no more than a piece of paper locked away in a box and photographs and a long-ago ceremony, but that could not detract from its importance.

"Meggie," he said softly, still holding her hands in his much larger ones, "maybe the bald truth needs to be said. Although you'll never admit it, you would have preferred that I stay where I was—dead, to all intents and purposes."

His calm, unemotional words crashed down on her, then left in their wake a bleakness and desolation unlike anything she had ever known. She started to protest, then stopped. That blind, irrational hatred reared its ugly head again, and she knew he was right. The mind has an ugly, dark side, a side that, fortunately, few of us are ever forced to acknowledge. But Megan was compelled to do that now.

In those dark, barely remembered hours after her father's devastating announcement, she knew she must have thought just that. And again, in those rushes of blind hatred, that hideous thought had been there. In a strange, convoluted way, she was grateful to Patrick for having spoken those terrible words. She herself could never, never have spoken them, or even have allowed them into the conscious part of her brain.

But they were there. She could admit that now, if only to herself. Patrick had long ago been put into a deep, safe place in her memory—a warm, glowing kind of place where he remained forever unchanged—and she had not wanted to be forced to bring him out once more into the light of day. If he had come back unchanged, the resistance might not have been there, or at least not have been so strong. But she saw that a part of her must have known from the moment she learned that he was still alive that the reality would destroy that memory.

"I . . . I could never wish you dead, Patrick," she finally managed to say, certain that, in spite of his words, he understood that.

"I didn't say that you did," he replied gently. "But you had every reason to believe that I was, and your whole life since you gave up hope has been based on that assumption. Obviously, from what you've told me, you've built a life you enjoy very much. Then, suddenly, here I come, turning it upside down."

He *did* understand, she thought. He understood it too well. She was filled with self-loathing now. She twisted her hands within his grasp, trying to free them, thinking that perhaps the physical contact was responsible for his horribly accurate reading of her. But he continued to hold them, refusing to break that contact and forcing her self-disgust to the surface.

"I'm being so selfish," she blurted out, wanting to say it before he could, as though that would somehow make it easier to bear.

"We're all selfish when we're backed against a wall, Meggie. It's that natural instinct for survival. I've been selfish, too, and probably with less reason. Not until I was actually on my way to Clark did I allow myself to consider the possibility that you might not be waiting for me, that you might have found someone else.

"Then, when the general told me that you hadn't remarried, I didn't give any further thought to the havoc I would be causing in your life. I just went right back to believing that you were still waiting for me. It was unbelievable self-ishness on my part."

He paused for a second, then went on. "And that self-ishness hadn't stopped by the time I reached here, either."

Megan was silent as the honesty of his words washed over her and began to cleanse her of her terrible guilt and shame. She was beginning to understand the reason for his shock and strangely silent behavior when she'd first seen him. If she hadn't been so self-involved at that time, she would have known. But, as he had just said, it was that instinct for survival.

"By the time I got here, I'd, uh, let my fantasies get way out of hand. I wanted the kind of reunion I'd been dreaming about for years, and I just never stopped to consider it from your point of view."

Megan stared off into space until she knew she had to look at him. The pain that was so obvious in eyes that had once held only laughter twisted inside her like a knife. She wanted to go back—if not to the very beginning, then at least to the first moment they'd seen each other outside the cabin. If willpower alone could turn back the clock, hers would have done so in that moment. Instead of presenting him with the mud-spattered apparition that had greeted him, she would have given him his fantasy.

"Patrick," she cried in anguish, "I wish—"

He cut her off in midsentence. "We can't afford to wish, Meggie. Wishing won't take us back."

She felt a brief burst of anger at his harsh insistence on reality, but it subsided quickly. He was right. The damage done by the years of separation and by the selfishness of their reunion could not be wished away. But still, she could not quite face the consequences of those past events and, instead, drifted into a dreamscape of what might have been.

When he moved, she was lost somewhere in her memories of that flame-haired cadet and junior officer, and they were all jumbled up with the dreams she, too, had once had of a perfect, beautiful reunion, dreams she'd set aside so long ago that they hadn't come back when the reunion had become reality.

So she offered no resistance at all as he curved one arm around her and slid the other beneath her to draw her onto his lap. Still lost in what couldn't be, she let reality slip so far away that this all seemed natural and so very right. The unfamiliarity of this very different man slipped away, too. Her hand came up to touch his thick, wavy hair and it felt wonderfully familiar. As long as she held that other Patrick firmly in her mind, she was all right. So, knowing that it was the wrong thing to do, she did just that.

He lowered his face to hers and brushed his mouth against her temple. Then he began to trail his lips slowly down along her cheek until she moved slightly and their mouths met.

It was all so careful, so tentative, on both their parts. Their mouths clung together with the softest of pressures, as though unleashing more might somehow destroy them. They were both exploring new and fragile territory against the seductive background of past love. He held her as though she were made of glass, and she touched him with a constant need to remind herself that he was real.

Megan was only barely aware of exercising any self-control, but she was powerfully aware of his doing just that. He had meant it when he said they must take this slowly.

She was feeling those old, achingly familiar stirrings again, but they were still deep within her and not threatening. Too much time had passed for such passions to be quickly aroused. That unconscious self-discipline had become far too deeply ingrained.

The slow withdrawal was a mutual one, making it both easier and more difficult. His hand remained entangled in her hair and her hand still touched his face.

"There's one other thing we can't afford right now, Meggie, and that is to say no."

MEGAN CAME UP out of her sleep very slowly, perhaps because she knew even unconsciously that she didn't want to face this day. She wished herself back in her Connecticut cottage, then opened her eyes to see that her wish had not been granted.

So she lay completely still in the bed, listening for sounds in the cabin. Nothing. The faintest aroma of coffee managed to penetrate her closed bedroom door. Staying in bed became even more appealing because she knew she wouldn't have those first few moments of the day to herself.

She thought about all the years of mornings when she had been able to get up and go about her routine without the distracting and demanding presence of another person.

Had there ever been a time when she'd enjoyed waking up with another person in the house? Surely there must have been. Of course there had been. She had loved Patrick, and those waking moments of their married days had been the highlight of her day. Of course, when one considered the meaningless drift of those days, it was no wonder.

She made a disgusted sound and sat up in bed. She didn't want to think about her old life now. She didn't want to wake up with all these negative thoughts. But then, she didn't want to think about last night, either.

Absentmindedly, she reached up to touch her lips, then withdrew her fingers quickly when she realized what she'd done. Fear and disgust vied with each other in her waking brain. She simply refused to believe that she might be in danger of reverting to that mindless girl she had once been, just because of last night.

That man out there wasn't Patrick, however much he might be able to imitate him at times. He was a stranger who had once been Patrick. Last night, for a few dangerous moments, she had allowed him to be the man she had loved. It wouldn't happen again. She knew exactly how to deal with strangers who had overstepped their bounds; she'd been doing that for years, and very effectively, too.

''There's one other thing we can't afford right now, Meggie, and that is to say no.''

His words came back to her now, in that voice that wasn't quite right. When he'd said it, she feared for a moment that he meant they couldn't say no to lovemaking. But that wasn't what he meant at all. Instead, he meant that they couldn't afford to write each other off at this point.

But that was precisely what she thought they should be doing, and the sooner the better, too. They simply could not allow this to go on, when it could only end in pain for them both. Patrick had made his choice, whether or not he cared to admit it, and she had made hers. Stalemate. No room for compromise.

As she reluctantly got out of bed, she toyed with the notion of telling him that she must return immediately to Connecticut. She'd already laid the groundwork for that when she explained that this was the agency's busy season. It was true, but it was also true that Karen could manage without her for a few more days.

She grimaced as she pulled on her robe. Why did that little voice inside keep whispering that she couldn't just walk out on him now? He didn't really need her, as he might have if he'd come home an emotional cripple. He didn't need her at all; he had the army. Duty. That was the word that explained it. She hated the very sound of it, but, or so it seemed, she could not escape it.

Opening her bedroom door as quietly as possible, Megan poked her head out into the hallway and listened. No sound anywhere. Could he have gone out running? She hoped so. Finally, she stepped out into the hallway, drawn by the enticing aroma of coffee and pushed along by the thought of how absurd her behavior was. She'd have to face him sooner or later, but later sounded distinctly better. Facing anything was much easier after that first cup of coffee.

So she silently made her way to the kitchen and quickly poured herself a cup of the fragrant, steaming coffee. Then she tried to peer out onto the screened porch, but the angle was wrong and she couldn't tell if he might be there.

She picked up one of the sticky buns they'd bought at a bakery in town and noticed that none had as yet been eaten. That drew her attention back to the coffee maker and she realized that she had taken the first cup.

He'd obviously made the coffee for her. He knew that she had to have her coffee first thing. His thoughtfulness warmed her and she let the gesture become blown up out of all proportion for a few seconds before firmly putting it aside.

Carrying her coffee and sticky bun, she padded into the dining area and peered cautiously out to the porch. Still no sign of him. So he must have gone running. She relaxed and sank down gratefully at the table.

He'd be back soon, of course, and then they'd have to face yet another day of this wary circling of each other, of this polite conversation that inevitably seemed to turn personal and at some point produce sparks. Not for one minute did she believe that last night had changed that. Still, it did seem that they'd moved across some threshold, although she couldn't have said from what into what.

Was he really suffering as much as she was? She thought about that look of pain in his eyes when he'd said they couldn't afford to wish themselves into the past. Yes, he, too, was suffering. And for what? For a past they couldn't recapture and a future they didn't have? They were both fools.

The telephone rang, so startling her that she nearly dropped her mug. Then, as she set it down, she realized exactly who it must be. Who but her father would call at half past eight in the morning? The general rose at six and was at his Pentagon desk by seven-thirty. She supposed she should count herself lucky that he'd waited until now; he'd been known to call even earlier.

Even as she hurried to the kitchen, she was considering ignoring the call. But she knew the general. He'd just have his secretary continue to dial every ten minutes or so until the call was answered. And if Patrick was the one who answered, it would undoubtedly set off another argument about her father.

"Hello, Dad," she said dryly as soon as she lifted the receiver.

There was a brief silence, during which she feared that she might have been wrong. But then the general's unmistakable voice came out of the receiver.

"Did I wake you?" He always asked that, especially when he called early on weekends. She'd said yes a few times, but it hadn't done any good.

"No, I've been up for all of ten minutes."

"Is everything all right?" Another standard opening, to which she always replied in the affirmative, regardless of whether or not it was true.

"At the moment, yes," she said, especially since Patrick wasn't around.

"What do you mean?"

Aha! she thought with amusement. *The general is just the slightest bit concerned. Fancy that!*

"Nothing." Let him worry. She was beginning to enjoy this.

"Meggie, this conversation isn't very productive. Is Patrick there?"

"No."

A slightly longer hesitation, then a quick show of concern. "Where is he?"

"Probably out running," she said offhandedly. "He was gone when I woke up."

"But he hasn't left?"

That possibility just hadn't occurred to her, and the idea disconcerted her. Would he do a thing like that? She could hardly blame him, since she'd thought about absconding herself. Then she wondered why the thought should have occurred to her father. Well, for one thing, there had been her antiarmy statements the other day, she thought.

"Just a minute, Dad."

She dropped the phone, letting the receiver bang against the wall as she ran into the living room. When she saw her mother's car still parked in the driveway, she didn't know whether to be relieved or disappointed.

Then, just as she was about to turn away again, she saw Patrick jogging up the driveway, and there was no mistaking the relief she felt. She watched the big, rugged-looking man as he moved up the driveway—with his sinewy, bare legs pumping effortlessly and his broad, T-shirted chest rising and falling regularly. Hovering behind him still was the ghost of the young second lieutenant, but the ghost was fading fast.

She roused herself as she remembered that her none-too-patient father was still on the phone, probably nursing a bruised eardrum.

"He's coming up the driveway now, Dad. He was out running."

"Meggie, about the other morning..."

"I don't want to discuss it, Dad. I said what I should have said a long time ago, and if you'd been paying any attention at all to me, it wouldn't have come as such a shock to you. I resigned from the army long ago. You just didn't notice, that's all."

Halfway through all this, she heard the front door open and close. Without turning around, she knew that Patrick had come into the kitchen behind her.

"Meggie, you're making things very difficult for Patrick. You must know that."

"I don't know that at all," she replied in a saccharine tone. "Would you like to talk to him? He's here now."

As soon as the general answered in the affirmative, she turned around and held out the receiver to the man who stood in the kitchen doorway, exuding far too much maleness.

"The general wishes to speak with you."

Patrick gave her what she interpreted as a reproachful look and took the receiver, greeting her father with a "Good morning, sir." Megan walked away with a sound of disgust. Patrick's voice followed her as she picked up her coffee and the sticky bun and went outside. She had no desire to hear any part of a conversation the contents of which she could easily guess in any event.

Her father would be trying in a discreet manner—or what he considered to be a discreet manner—to determine the status of their relationship. If Patrick hinted at all about problems, the general would remind him of the shock "little Meggie" had suffered and would probably also remind him of the inherent weaknesses of females. The general was most definitely not a liberated male.

She walked over to the edge of the woods where a large boulder provided a convenient perch and a wonderful view of the glorious spring morning. Sitting cross-legged atop the boulder, she finished off the sticky bun, licked her fingers and then sipped at the coffee.

The rest of the conversation inside would be subtle and perhaps not-so-subtle attempts to persuade Patrick not to resign his commission. In Megan's opinion that persuasion was unnecessary; Patrick had already decided to stay. Everything about him now spelled army; they had won and she had lost.

No. She hadn't lost at all. It was really better this way. Now there was no chance that they would resume their marriage. She wouldn't have to worry about the seductive pull of the past. They could part as friends, just as she had planned. Then Patrick could find himself an appropriate wife. He certainly wouldn't lack for candidates.

Was that what she really wanted? How could it be, when the very thought of Patrick with someone else made her ache? Was that ache caused by real emotion, or was she acting like the dog in that old fable about the dog in the manger, who couldn't eat the hay but didn't want the other animals to have it, either?

Her thoughts had just begun to drift back to the previous night when she saw Patrick emerge from the cabin and start toward her. That all-too-familiar sensation rippled through her again, leaving her trembly. He stopped beside the rock and she gave him a rueful smile.

"I can think of better ways to wake up than to the sound of the general's voice."

Patrick ignored her attempt at humor. "Meggie, he's very upset."

"Tough," she said nonchalantly as she drained her mug. "His life has been one long run of well-ordered smoothness. A few bumps once in a while won't hurt. It might show him that he's human, though I doubt that."

"I just don't understand your attitude," he said with mild exasperation.

"My attitude is caused by his attitude. It's very simple, really."

"And what do you think his attitude is?" Patrick asked.

"Whatever the army says it should be. Duty... honor... country. You do remember those words, don't you?" she taunted.

"Of course I do. What I don't understand is why you find that so offensive."

She affected a careless shrug. "Maybe I find it offensive because I've become a hedonist."

His jaw tightened. "Someone has to pay the price so that you can pursue your pleasures."

She rolled her eyes. "Spare me all that, Patrick. This is an army brat you're talking to, remember? I've already paid more than my share. I'm entitled to be selfish."

Then she glared at him. "You sound just like him, do you know that? You're even beginning to look a little like him."

"Is that what's really behind this—the fact that I'm staying in the army?"

"Are you?" She already knew the answer to that, but she wanted to hear him admit it.

His gaze slid away from her, just as it had done before. "I don't know."

"You do so know, and I don't understand why you won't admit it."

"It isn't an easy decision to make, Meggie."

"Well," she said as she started to climb down from the boulder, "if it will make it any easier for you, I approve."

"You approve?" he asked in astonishment as he reached out for her and lifted her down, allowing his arms to continue to circle her waist after he set her on her feet.

"Yes," she said, forcing herself to ignore his closeness. "I approve because you obviously fit the role. If it looks like a soldier, walks like a soldier and talks like a soldier, it's obviously meant to *be* a soldier."

"You dislike what you see now, don't you?" he asked, still holding her.

She tried to back out of his arms, felt the slight increase in pressure and gave up. This was not a question she wanted to answer at such close quarters, so she temporized.

"You must be aware of how much you've changed, Patrick."

"I guess I wasn't, really, until you made your feelings plain."

She looked at him nervously and licked at her sticky mouth. "Well, you should have known. I know how much I've changed."

"And you've taken every opportunity to let me know that," he finished for her in a dry tone.

She had no response to that, since she knew he was right. She brought up her hands to grip his wrists and push him away, expecting that he would let her go immediately. But he didn't move. He just ignored her attempts to free herself and continued to watch her intently. Fear skittered up and down her spine. It wasn't a revival of that earlier fear of him, though. Instead, it was a new fear that the rules might have changed.

"Let me go, Patrick."

"Why?"

"Because I said so, that's why." She was beginning to get angry. At him and at a body that was making far too much of this.

"Why are you afraid to be near me now, Meggie? You weren't afraid last night."

"Don't call me Meggie. No one calls me that now, except for the general."

"All right. Why are you afraid to be near me, Megan?"

"I'm not!"

"I'm glad to hear that, even if I'm not sure I believe it," he said in a much softer tone, as he took half a step toward her and drew her against his body at the same time.

She put out a hand to protest or to push him away, but the attempt was feeble. She was melting inside, melting from the ever-growing heat that had been absent for so long, and she wanted so very desperately to look up and see the old Patrick standing there, with that unique mixture of love and amusement in his eyes.

But when she did look up, what she saw was an intensity so powerful that she stopped breathing for a few heartbeats. Patrick had never looked at her that way. She might have forgotten a lot, but she knew she could never have forgotten that. Boyish pleasure had been replaced by a man's demands. And she knew now that it was a woman's body that was responding.

He lowered his face to hers slowly, stretching out that moment to give the inevitability of his kiss a mesmerizing sensuality. And then he was teasing her lips softly, sending his tongue on little forays into her mouth, caressing her pliant flesh with strong, sure fingers.

She could feel the hard planes of his body pressing against her and was excitingly aware of her own nakedness beneath the robe and his near-nakedness in his running clothes. Her heated skin chafed against the soft fleece lining of her robe and tingled with a total desire for him.

Patrick continued to caress her, lifting her off the ground as he drew her face up to his. The teasing subtlety of his kisses began to change slowly, growing into a demand. Driving need flowed from his body to hers. Twelve years of denial began to melt away, only to be halted in confusion as he separated them abruptly.

If he'd let her go entirely, she thought she might have crumbled to the ground; in fact, she was sure of it. But he had gone back to holding her lightly, and she stared up at him in confusion.

"So now we both know why you're afraid," he said in a voice that managed to register satisfaction even through its huskiness.

She pushed at his encircling arms as she had done before, and this time he let her go. She took a few shaky steps backward as she tried to understand his cruelty, because that was exactly how she thought of his behavior at that moment.

"How many men did it take to make you forget that, Megan?" he asked sharply, with a sarcastic emphasis on her name.

She cowered inwardly at that ugly tone of voice and the even uglier implication of those words. But as he waited for an answer, she began to stiffen in defiance.

"That's none of your business. We agreed not to talk about that."

There were subtle changes in his expression that might or might not have been regret. She had no time to consider it.

"You're right. It's none of my business."

None! There had been none! She wanted to shout it at him, to see his reaction. But she was afraid he wouldn't believe her, not after his cruel words. And warning lights began to flash: tell him that now and you're finished. So instead, she turned her back and started to walk away, then paused and half turned toward him.

"I didn't forget anything. You're not the same."

Patrick stood stock-still, watching her walk away, her body held with unnatural rigidity beneath the long robe. His fists balled helplessly at his sides as he tried to forget that body he knew to be naked beneath the robe.

Damn! He'd really blown it now. If she didn't actually hate him, she was very close to it. He continued to clench his fists until veins stood out against the ropy muscles of his arms.

All the years of carefully reining in his emotions, of learning a degree of self-control he would never have believed possible, were unraveling before his eyes. In all that time, he'd never reached his limit, and so he had foolishly believed that he had none.

But she was doing the one thing he now knew could push him beyond that limit—comparing him to the kid he'd been. He could fight another man, he could even fight indifference on her part, but he couldn't fight his lost self, that self that had died in the jungles of Vietnam.

He willed his body to relax and then set off on the path that led into the woods. It didn't take much perception on his part to guess that he wouldn't be welcome in the cabin just now. Then he stopped, wondering if she might take off. The keys to both cars were back there. He hesitated, then went on. No, she might think about it, but he didn't think she'd actually do it.

What had happened to her during the years he'd been over there, foolishly believing that she was waiting for him, eternal and unchanged? What forces had shaped her, molded her into the woman she was today? And what kind of woman was she now, anyway?

Outwardly, there was a coldness, a total lack of emotion except for her irrational hatred of the army and of her father. The only other times he'd seen any emotion in her was when she talked about that damned travel agency.

Well, not only then. But they'd been brief moments, and he knew damned well that if he hadn't stopped it, she would have. He also knew that both last night and a few minutes ago, she'd been pretending, pretending that he was the kid she had married.

Had there been other men? He didn't want to think about it, but he couldn't get it out of his mind. Surely there must have been. But she was right when she said that it was none of his business. His rights had been forfeited a long time ago, through no fault of his own. And it wasn't really important, anyway, except down deep in that primitive part of his nature that he hadn't realized even existed before.

What was very important to him was whether or not there was anyone now. Could he believe her when she said that she wasn't serious about this other guy? He thought he could. If she were having an affair with him, she would surely have chosen a more public place for the reunion, something like a hotel. They would have made polite conversation, she would have told him that she'd found someone else, and he would have managed somehow to sound pleased. Perhaps it would have been better that way.

But as it was, the atmosphere between them vibrated with tension and unanswerable questions, with clashes between the past and the present, with fears about the future. He didn't really know what to think about the woman currently inhabiting the body that had anchored his dreams for twelve years. And he suspected that she felt just the same about him.

That's what he'd meant when he told her that they had to take it slowly and could not afford to say no at this point. Both of them had to get free of the past. He couldn't be the kid she remembered, and she couldn't be the girl he had held in his dreams. Still, that past provided something, something that shouldn't be let go too quickly or too thoughtlessly.

At the moment, however, he doubted very much that she would agree with him.

Chapter Seven

Megan stomped into the cabin and slammed the door behind her. Then she stopped uncertainly as her anger-driven adrenaline began to taper off. Few times are worse than those moments when anger gives way to self-examination, so she postponed that moment as long as possible. While she nervously awaited the return of calmness and reason, she stared at the door, expecting it to open at any moment and wondering what either of them could say. Would they both try to repair the damage by ignoring this episode, as they had done before?

But the door did not open, and she finally went to the window, reaching it just in time to see him disappearing into the woods. Body language had never spoken more plainly. He even had his fists clenched at his sides. She watched until he was hidden from view by the trees, then sank onto the sofa. A small smile of slightly guilty satisfaction came to her face. At least she was finally seeing some breaks in that carefully controlled facade of his. Both last night and just now, some emotion had finally leaked through.

Then, abruptly, she was ashamed of herself. What had she wanted from him? And what right did she have to demand anything at all from a man who had suffered as he had? Once again, she was reminded of her selfishness, and his earlier explanation of that selfishness did little to ease her conscience. He deserved better than this. They both deserved better than this. They had loved each other once; surely that should count for something.

Little curls of pleasurable warmth began to unfold within her as she relived his kiss. He wanted her; she had no doubt at all about that now. In spite of the many reasons why that should not have pleased her, it did—at least until she began to consider the possible reasons for that desire.

He might simply be sex-starved, or, perhaps even worse, he might have been guilty of the same self-deception she had been practicing. He might have been pretending that she was still the same girl he had loved and married.

That would be a lot easier for him, she thought, since she'd changed so little outwardly. If he closed his eyes and she shut her mouth, he could very easily have conjured up that girl. In all likelihood, that was just what had happened, both last night and just now. And it certainly explained his drawing away.

It was bad enough that she couldn't seem to shake free of that past, but if he, too, were caught in the seductive grip of memories... Feeling helplessly and hopelessly caught in the grip of forces neither of them could control, Megan flung herself off the sofa and started toward the shower. Then she stopped. She hadn't gone running this morning, and with him off roaming around in the woods, she could run in solitary peace.

So a short while later, she was at the bottom of the driveway, setting off at a comfortable pace in the bright spring morning. A moment or so later, the total absurdity of their situation struck her and she faltered briefly, caught between laughter and tears. Would anyone believe this? Here they were, presumed by everyone to be having some sort of second honeymoon, and he was stalking through the woods while she was running down the road, each of them consciously avoiding the other and both of them unwilling or unable to face reality?

As the last remnants of anger and tension drained away, that nagging guilt moved back in to take its place. She *had* been cruel, especially with that comparison to her father. On the other hand, there was truth in what she'd said.

Then there was that parting remark about how he'd changed. Implicit in that statement had been the disapproval he'd accused her of—another truth that shouldn't have been spoken. In fact, the entire day thus far was filled with things that shouldn't have been said or shouldn't have happened, beginning with the fact that the general shouldn't have called.

Her father was weighing far too heavily in all this, when he didn't belong in it at all. But the general was the army personified to her, and for good reason. His quick rise to multiple stars proved that. Some made it to brigadier who really weren't army all the way, but when a man made it to full general, he was very definitely army. And now, with Patrick, as with her brother Joel, she could see the ghosts of those stars hovering above broad shoulders. So there was really no way she could extricate her father from all this, even if he weren't making himself very evident. He was what Patrick would one day become. And she was most definitely not on her way to becoming like her mother, the perfect general's wife.

Then, wanting to return to the cabin with a cleared mind, she deliberately turned her thoughts to pleasant things—her business, the lovely condo she planned to buy, the pleasant weekends she would spend poking around in antique shops or taking the train down to New York. These were the pleasures of her life that were not going to change, because she would not permit them to change. There had been too many changes for too long, all courtesy of the army.

This time, because she had not run so far or so fast, she jogged all the way up to the cabin, not stopping until she burst through the front door. There was no sign of Patrick, and she assumed that he must still be off somewhere in the woods.

She hoped he wouldn't get lost. He didn't know the area and there were many paths, some of them endless meanderings that resulted from foraging herds of deer. Then she shrugged off that concern. Of course he wouldn't get lost. He'd been trained for combat in unfamiliar terrain. He knew how to spot the landmarks that would give him the lay of the land.

Her mind balked, as it always did, at the thought of a soldier's ultimate purpose. It had been easy enough to ignore, at least until Patrick shipped out to Vietnam. By the time she was old enough to consider her father's occupation, he had already risen to a rank that kept him deskbound. Then, when Patrick underwent combat training, he made light of it, spinning humorous tales about drill sergeants and crawling on his belly through a mile of mud.

Only after Patrick was gone had the full impact hit her. For the first time she watched on TV the actual horrors of war. The army was no longer merely something that moved her around and filled her life with uniforms and pomp and circumstance.

She thought despairingly now of that part of Patrick's life and how it could never be shared with her or with any civilian. He didn't seem to want to talk to her about it, and in truth, she didn't want to hear about it, either. But it was one more wedge that had been driven between them by the army.

She had started toward the bathroom, intending to take her shower, but a sudden sound brought her to a halt in the hallway just as Patrick walked out of the bathroom.

He was stark naked, the hair on his head and chest still damp from the shower. The scent of steam and soap and an unfamiliar cologne wafted toward her. She was both poised for flight and rooted to the spot.

"I, uh, didn't hear you come in," he said somewhat uncertainly, though he made no move to hurry away.

"I didn't know you were back, either," she replied, compounding the foolishness and trying at the same time to find a safe resting place for her eyes.

A few more seconds ticked past, each of which seemed to last forever, and then he moved on to his bedroom and she managed to remember how to walk.

She hurried on shaky legs into her bedroom, expelling the breath she'd unconsciously held. Their ridiculous dialogue replayed itself in her mind.

How totally absurd, she thought now from the safety of her room. They were married; they had once known each other's bodies well. This scene must have occurred on a regular basis twelve years ago, without the apologies and excuses.

She began to undress in preparation for her shower, and the simple act of stripping off her own clothes felt strange. From a shocking awareness of him, she was now coming to an equally terrifying awareness of herself.

She donned her robe, but the strangeness was still there. *Admit it,* she told herself angrily. *That man turned you on. However much he doesn't look or act like Patrick anymore, and however much you dislike what he's become, you are attracted to him.*

Attracted to him. What did it mean, really? Some sort of chemistry? What were those things called? Pheromones, those invisible signals people send out for which other people might or might not be receptors? She tried to draw some comfort from such pseudoscientific thoughts, but there was very little to be found. She could make all the excuses she wanted: they were isolated here and they had both lived without sex for a very long time—though she really didn't know for sure about him. But the fact remained that he turned her on.

Why couldn't it have happened with Ted or with any of the other men she'd known over the years? They were men whose natures and careers made them acceptable in every way. And yet nothing had happened. If Ted or any of them had been in Patrick's place a few minutes ago, there would have been a brief embarrassment and nothing more. No electricity in the atmosphere, no rubbery legs, no time distortion. And she hadn't spent any time at all reliving Ted's kisses, either.

A FEW YARDS and a solid wall away, Patrick pulled on his jeans with a smile of grim satisfaction. He'd heard her come into the cabin, all right, and his timing couldn't have been better. Furthermore, there was only one way the results could have been better, and he hadn't been foolish enough to have hoped for that.

It irritated him that he'd had to provoke such a confrontation. But he knew that she was trying to deny the differences in him, including the physical ones. If he couldn't get her to accept the other differences, he was damned well going to be sure that she saw he was no longer that gangly kid she'd married. The rest would have to come later.

He finished dressing and went outside, heading for the boulder where she'd been sitting earlier. Then he set about convincing himself that progress was being made, to use one of the army's favorite phrases. It wasn't easy.

It wasn't going to happen here and now. Something was wrong and had been from the beginning. He'd been expecting too much, and as long as they stayed here, he'd continue to do so.

But on the other hand, as soon as they left she might go running back to that other guy.

By the time she showered and changed, Megan had reached a decision. She was going to leave this very day, drive back to Washington, and catch the first shuttle to New York. By evening, she would be back in Connecticut and the reality of her life.

She knew she was running away, but that knowledge troubled her far less than the thought of remaining here.

They were not going to resolve anything here; that had become obvious. How and when they would resolve matters between them, she didn't know, and at the moment, she just didn't care. All she wanted was to be away from this place where everything was so very wrong.

Objectivity, she thought. *That's what I need right now, and I'm certainly not going to gain it here, with this stranger from my past staring at me and turning me into a bowl of Jell-O.*

She found him outside, sitting on the same rock where he'd earlier found her. He didn't see her approach because his face was turned in the other direction. He was squatting on his heels, a strange and unnatural position, although she'd seen photos of various Asian peoples who sat that way.

He must have heard her approach because he turned sharply to face her, settling back into a more normal position at the same time. She tried on a smile.

"Did you learn to sit that way over there? It looks uncomfortable."

"It can be, at first. But we all picked up the habit without even realizing it. I guess I'd better try to give it up." He appeared relaxed and his rueful grin looked far more natural than she suspected her own smile did.

She tried again. "I think you'd better. You might draw some strange looks at the Pentagon or at Fort Meade if you do that."

"Are you going to invite me up to Connecticut?"

He had done it again. A few moments of safe conversation and then, without warning, he'd abruptly shifted gears.

"Of course. You're welcome to come up anytime. You'll be going to New York to see your family, won't you? You couldn't have had much time with your parents."

Megan did not want him to come to Connecticut. Connecticut was hers—her life, her place. She tried to let him know that by making the invitation as casual as possible, since she could think of no way to get out of it altogether.

"I didn't, but I'm planning to go up to see them late next week, so I'll come on up for the weekend. What about your boyfriend? How's he going to react to my visit?"

For the briefest moment, her mind went blank. Boyfriend? Oh, yes, Ted. She wondered uneasily if her temporary confusion had showed.

"He's aware of your existence but I'm not accountable to him for anything in any event." She knew that she sounded defensive and that this conversation was veering off into the danger zone again.

"Does he know that?"

"Know what?" she asked.

"Know that you're not accountable to him."

"I assume so," she said offhandedly, sending the strongest possible signal that she wanted to change the conversation.

"So you've made no commitments to each other?"

"I told you that before, Patrick. How many times do you need to hear it?"

"What does he do?"

She stopped being subtle about her desire to end the conversation and gave him an exasperated look, followed by a disgusted sigh. "He's a computer software consultant, in business for himself."

"How old is he?"

"Thirty-eight," she answered, wondering when she'd find the courage to tell him outright to knock it off.

"Isn't that a little old for you?"

"Hardly," she replied sarcastically. "I'm thirty-two, in case you'd forgotten."

He stared at her for a moment, then looked away. His voice grew more tentative. "I *had* forgotten. I guess I'd even forgotten that I'm thirty-five."

Megan's irritation was swept away as she heard that bleakness in his voice. Twelve years of his life had simply vanished. Twelve years ripped away and gone forever. Without thinking, she reached out and touched his hand, which rested against his thigh.

She wanted to say that she was sorry, but she knew instinctively that this was not something he would want to hear. With no other words available, she simply left her hand there. Then, when she would have withdrawn it, he grasped it and held it, still not looking at her.

"I knew you would have changed, Patrick," she said in a choked voice. "But I never expected it to be so much, I guess."

He turned to look at her then and she could see the unnatural brightness in his eyes. She knew it must be in hers, too, since she could feel the tears forming.

"At least you were better prepared than I was," he said sadly. "I just hadn't thought about you changing. I guess that was because it was so important to me to think that you were still there, just the same, waiting for me."

Neither of them said anything more for a long time. Their feelings were too strong for words, and perhaps too strong for tears, too, because that didn't happen, either. It was a time for staying just where they were: close to each other, but still apart.

"What happens now, Meggie?" he asked in that same sad, quiet tone.

It was her chance to tell him that they must end it and that it would be better to do it now than later. Better for them both. There was no anger in either of them at the moment, and she thought that if she said it now he would accept it, as he might not have done earlier. But what she could have said earlier in anger, she simply could not say at all now.

"I . . . don't know. I came out to tell you that I'm going back to Connecticut today."

"Could you wait until tomorrow? I told your father that I'd be back then."

So he, too, had made the decision to part. She didn't know what to think about that. She nodded; staying until the next day seemed little enough to ask.

As soon as she agreed, his mood changed dramatically. He gave her that old-Patrick grin and twisted around to gesture behind them. "How do you feel about some serious hiking? That mountain looks interesting."

She followed his pointing finger and smiled. She'd climbed it several times with Joel when they were younger. Even her father had come along once.

"It's not a bad climb," she said, "and my old hiking boots are still here. But you don't have any boots, do you?"

He shook his head and his eyes glinted mischievously. "No, but if my successful wife would care to finance the expedition, there's a place in town where I can get them."

She laughed in pure delight, only too happy to throw off that dark cloud that had hovered over them.

"I'll make it a present. After all, I've missed a few birthdays and Christmases."

He got down from the rock. "Ah, well, in that case, maybe I'll see if there's a Porsche dealer in town."

"I own a travel agency, not a bank."

HOW COULD A MOUNTAIN GROW in only fifteen years? Megan had always thought that it took far longer than that—centuries, millennia even. She was sweating and gasping for air.

"Are we high enough for the oxygen to have disappeared?" she groaned as she scrambled up to meet him.

"What's disappeared is your youth, old lady," Patrick replied smugly as he helped her up the last few feet.

"I resent that. Besides, if my youth is gone, yours went even before that."

She flopped down exhaustedly and tried to decide if the view was worth it. Smaller mountains marched off to a hazy, gray-blue horizon, and the tentative greens of early spring filled the valleys in between. Joel had once estimated the vista at about seventy miles, and she had accepted that because she was a very poor judge of such things herself.

Despite the strenuous effort required to reach this peak, the day seemed to possess a languorous quality, certainly a far cry from its tumultuous beginning. Megan wasn't quite sure just how or why they'd reached this present, calmer state, but she wasn't inclined to examine it too closely, either. For now, the emotional seesaw was in perfect balance.

Patrick sank down beside her, then reached around to his newly purchased backpack for the small canteen it held. He opened the canteen and offered it to her. She had already taken a grateful swallow when she realized that it wasn't water she was drinking.

"Beer?" she spluttered.

"Isn't that what canteens are for?" he asked as he took a healthy slug himself.

"I should think that at some point during your training it might have been pointed out to you that canteens are supposed to carry water," she replied dryly, amused at the way he could still manage to project a certain blue-eyed innocence even in this far less innocent face.

"I was probably asleep that day," he said, shrugging as he withdrew a packet of trail mix. He sniffed at the food and then tossed a handful into his mouth.

"This stuff isn't bad. It goes well with beer, too."

She lay back on the long, soft grass and laughed again. This couldn't last. Their moods shifted too rapidly. At any moment he might return to being the army officer, or she might become the cold, unpleasant person she'd been earlier. These moments were gifts, offered to each of them by the other. She was sure that he was deliberately resurrecting the old Patrick for her, and she knew she was pretending to a peace between them that didn't exist.

He settled back, too, bracing himself on his elbows as he stared at the view. In profile, he looked more like his old self. She remembered the rather long nose with its small bump from a childhood break, the aggressive cleft chin, and the tousled curls that always fell across his brow. But there were big, ropy muscles in his arms now, and the color of those curls was wrong.

She stared at him, wondering how she'd be reacting if she were meeting this man for the first time. His old boyish charm and exuberance weren't much in evidence anymore, and even his wry humor appeared only occasionally. Still, she thought gratefully, it wasn't gone altogether.

Would he have changed like this if he'd spent the past twelve years differently? Or would time alone have eroded those things she had loved best about him? And if that had happened, would she have adjusted to it, learned to love him for other reasons and been willing to see those cherished traits go?

She again felt the enormity of those missing years and wondered if she would ever truly grasp the extent of them. But she had little time to ponder the question, because he shattered the silence just then by turning to stare at her and speaking in a quiet, serious voice.

"There weren't any other women, Meggie. I want you to know that. But I also want you to know that there might have been if there'd been any opportunity."

There was simply no way to explain what Megan felt in that moment. It was pain and pride and respect and perhaps, finally, a reason for her own behavior during those years. She hadn't permitted herself to dwell on that subject, but she knew from her own reaction that she had, nevertheless, assumed there'd been other women. Even now, in the face of his confession, that assumption died slowly.

"I . . . I don't understand. I thought you were in a village filled with women."

"I was. But they didn't know the meaning of birth control and I had no way of getting anything." He looked away from her and his voice became slightly harsher.

"Mixed-race children aren't treated very well over there. Far worse than here, actually. I know it's not something you wanted to talk about, and you're probably right. But I had to say it anyway. I didn't want you to think that I had a mistress or even a wife over there that I'd abandoned."

"I never thought that," she said almost to herself, remembering that she had briefly considered, then dismissed that thought.

His statement was incredibly honest; he made no attempt to pretend that love alone had kept him faithful when he had every reason to believe that he might never see her again. Such things made wonderful copy for romantic novels, but she knew them for just that—the stuff of fantasy. She also knew that, at least in part, his honesty was meant to exonerate her from any affairs she might have had.

The silence was pressing heavily upon her. The only real response to his words was the truth from her, too. But she didn't know how to explain. His reasons could not be her reasons, too.

He was watching her again, his expression one of concern. "Meggie, I didn't tell you that to force you to make any sort of confession. I said that if the opportunity had been there—"

"There hasn't been anyone for me, either, Patrick." She cut him off in midsentence before she could think of all the reasons why she shouldn't be saying this.

So there it was, out at last, hanging in the warm spring air. She saw her own slight doubts mirrored in his face, and she knew that she somehow had to make him understand what she didn't fully understand herself.

"I really don't know why there wasn't anyone…I mean, after I'd given up hope for your return. I've dated a lot over the years, but it just never went beyond that. Somehow it seemed easier to give them up than to face…"

Her voice trailed off. To face what? Was the simple truth that she had never really faced up to the fact of his death? That even though she told people she was a widow, and even though she spoke of Patrick as though he were dead, she still had never accepted it down in that deepest core of her being?

They were sitting side by side, their arms touching lightly. She was afraid to look at him, afraid she might not have convinced him she was telling the truth. But then his arm settled across her shoulders and his fingers caressed her bare arm.

"There are different kinds of prisoners, Meggie. I was one kind and you were another. My prison was physical and yours was emotional."

She knew then that he believed her and that he was right. They had both been prisoners. She also knew that her own sexuality had just been confirmed, that after years of denying its existence without fully understanding why, she was now ready to welcome back that part of her.

It was a quietly dangerous moment, filled with a very different kind of tension that was more seductive than charged. Both of them had just acknowledged needs unmet for twelve years. But once again, fantasy and reality were poles apart. It could not be said that they weren't thinking about it, but long years of denial could not be tossed aside so quickly. Through those years, they had both set a very high premium on intimacy. And the future could not be ignored, either.

At last he got to his feet and reached down to help her up. "We'd better be starting back."

As she accepted his hand, she wondered if they might be doing just that.

MEGAN'S GAZE kept straying to the rearview mirror as her rental car cruised along the interstate, heading east into the morning sun. The view never changed. Her mother's gray Cadillac stayed right there, a safe distance behind her, changing lanes whenever she did.

She might as well have gone along with his suggestion that they leave her car behind and send someone for it. But she'd insisted on driving herself, because she couldn't bear the thought of being locked in a car with him for what would have become an extended farewell. As it turned out, she felt just as edgy as she would have if they'd been in the same car.

Ever mindful of what he thought about her driving, she was forced to pay too much attention to it herself. She was also unhappy about his insistence that he accompany her to the airport, because it made it seem all the more as though she were deserting him. But after their minor disagreement over her refusal to stop first at her parents' home, she just hadn't felt like protesting anymore.

It was a Saturday, and even though there was an excellent chance that the general would be either at the Pentagon or out on the golf course, Megan just hadn't wanted to risk running into him. Whatever confrontations lay ahead for her and her father, she did not want them to take place in Patrick's presence. Besides, her feelings toward both men were far too explosive at the moment for her to risk seeing them together.

She saw the speedometer creep past sixty and eased off the gas slightly, feeling guilty over her urge to get back to Connecticut as quickly as possible. Another hour or so and she would be on her way, hurtling through the skies to the safety of her own life. But she already had the unsettling feeling that that life would not be the same. She was merely running away from a problem that had yet to be resolved.

Their final evening at the cabin had been spent in a kind of bittersweetness, where small slices of the past were served up by both of them. She discovered that Patrick's memo-

ries were far sharper than hers, something she knew was the
result of his being forced to live in those memories while she
had been busy creating new ones.

But there had been laughter and smiles and almost-tears,
and she thought that it had been good for them both. At one
point, she had shamefacedly confessed to feeling guilty over
her inability to recall things as clearly as he could, and he
had merely smiled that sad, gentle smile and told her she had
nothing to feel guilty about; she had given him those memories—and without them he might not have survived.

But despite all the remembrances, all the "remember
whens," their old intimacy had not returned. It had hovered there, not quite out of sight, crooning its seductive
song. However, the resistance to it on her part—and, she
thought, on his as well—was still very powerful, strong
enough to ignore the urgings of the body. They wanted, but
they resisted that wanting. The why of it really didn't matter.

He had kissed her good-night in the living room, not in
the hallway near their separate bedrooms. She thought that
that had been significant, too, though she couldn't really
explain why she felt that way. She had lain awake for a long
time, half willing him to come to her and take the decision
out of her hands. Then, finally, she had fallen asleep, wondering if he was waiting for her to go to him.

And so she was able for the moment to maintain her be-
lief that they were two formerly married people who had
been torn apart through no fault of their own and who were
now doing no more than brushing against some fond memories as they pursued their separate lives. It was absolutely
essential to her at this point to believe that.

The traffic began to pick up noticeably as they neared
Washington, but the gray Cadillac remained locked in her
rearview mirror. They had left behind the isolation of the
mountains and were reentering the fast-paced, real world.
But Patrick was still there, even if she couldn't actually see

him at the moment because of windshield glare. He'd be there when she went back to Connecticut, too.

She changed lanes, moving onto the Beltway, heading for the airport. For a moment the Cadillac was lost to view, and she felt a totally irrational and profound sense of loss. She laughed aloud at her foolish overreaction when it reappeared.

She still wished that he weren't coming to the terminal with her, and she further wished that she had the courage to confront her father and tell him to butt out of their lives, especially out of Patrick's life.

But what difference would it make, really? Patrick's mind was made up, despite his persistent refusal to admit it—and hers was certainly made up. Not even the almighty general could alter the paths they had chosen.

As she drew closer to the airport, a sense of impending loss became stronger and stronger. After twelve years, a few days together seemed so pitifully inadequate. When she saw him again, everything would be different, because they would no longer be on neutral territory. What hadn't been resolved at the cabin would have to be resolved in her home. Perhaps, after all, it was better this way. She would be herself again, out of this volatile mixture of pain and guilt and remembrance, and he would be himself, too—his new self, that is—after some time spent in the bosom of the army. The time for regretting and remembering would be over, and the time for reality would be upon them.

It wouldn't be fair to either of them to prolong it after next weekend. He would surely have realized that by then. The final break had to be mutually acknowledged, accepted, formalized.

Her mind wanted to dwell on all this, but the traffic was heavy and she reluctantly gave it all her attention. A short time later she was pulling into the airport, still trailed by Patrick. He found public parking while she turned in her rental car, and they met in silence to head for the New York shuttle departure area. If she'd been willing to wait another hour, she could have gotten a more convenient flight to Westchester Airport, but she had wanted to get away, and not even the discomforts of the "cattle car" and the long, unpleasant ride in the so-called limo could dissuade her.

When she saw that there was a shuttle boarding within a few minutes, she very nearly sighed aloud with relief. Patrick saw it, too, and set down her bags near the ever-present metal detectors.

They stood close together, a tiny island amid bustling activity. Both of them were oblivious of the occasional stares they received. Washingtonians paid far more attention to the news than did inhabitants of towns like the small rural one near the cabin.

She looked up at Patrick, and it seemed to her that he had changed. Perhaps, she thought, it was only the close proximity of the Pentagon, but he looked now as he had when she'd first seen him at the cabin. That flinty look was back and he seemed to be standing taller, more erect. All this made their parting easier, even if it still hurt.

"I'll see you next weekend, then." Even his voice sounded different, more formal.

She nodded. "You have my home and office numbers." What an absurd thing to say. Of course he had them; she'd given them to him before they left the cabin.

He nodded, still standing ramrod straight, but now looking as though the facade might crumble at any moment. She felt rather crumbly herself. She almost asked him if he wanted her to stay, but the words thankfully stuck in her throat.

Their little island had grown ominously silent when the announcement came that the shuttle was boarding.

"Take care, Meggie." His voice was slightly husky as he bent awkwardly to kiss her. She felt unspoken words in him, too, and wondered what they might be. She started to reach up to touch his face, but then quickly withdrew her hand when it was only halfway through its journey and reached instead for her bags.

She turned back once, just as she entered the passageway to the plane. His tall, erect form was moving quickly in the opposite direction, striding through the crowd with that purposefulness and near-arrogance that reminded her of her father. It was nearly impossible to believe that that huskiness and awkwardness had been there at all.

Chapter Eight

The uniform felt very constricting. He hadn't worn one in years. As he sat listening to Sergeant Jackson explaining the routine of their lives in captivity to the reporters, Patrick was astonished at how very distant in time that all seemed, when in fact it had been less than two weeks.

The army was responsible for that, he thought without rancor. From the moment he presented himself at Fort Meade four days ago, the army had drawn him into its familiar routines: meetings, debriefings, crash courses on recent history. He'd resented all of it at first, but now it occurred to him that, consciously or unconsciously, the army had done it right.

He glanced surreptitiously at his watch. The press conference was more than half over. The assembled reporters had been told they had one hour, and no more. They'd also been told what areas were off-limits for questioning, and for that Patrick was very grateful. The only thing that had bothered him thus far was a tendency on the part of the two men who had returned with him to make him sound like a candidate for sainthood.

Beside him, Corporal Carson shifted nervously in his chair, and Patrick had to restrain himself from putting a steadying hand on the man's shoulder. His problems were serious, Patrick knew, although he thought that even in

Carson's case the army's routine had had a beneficial effect.

Then he abruptly came out of his reverie as the questioning shifted once more to him.

"Lieutenant O'Donnell, was there any time when you actually considered trying to escape, regardless of the consequences to the villagers?"

Patrick had expected this question. He grinned ruefully. "Only about once a day...and that was on the good days."

When the sympathetic laughter subsided, he turned serious. "Of course we thought about it, and sometimes we even tried to convince ourselves that they'd never carry out their threat if we did escape. But it was a chance we just couldn't take. We'd have spent the rest of our lives wondering if the price of our freedom had been the lives of over a hundred people. Freedom is very precious, believe me, but not at that price."

Then, as the reporters began to question Sergeant Jackson, who was black, about whether or not he had suffered racial discrimination at the hands of their captors, Patrick's mind drifted back to that village. There were people he cared about there, still surrounded by war and death, still struggling to stay alive. If it ever ended and he had the chance to go back to see how they'd fared, would he take it? He wasn't sure. Maybe, if he ever reached a point when he could put those years at a long, painless distance.

Finally the press conference was over. The lights on the TV cameras winked out and the flashbulbs ceased their glaring bursts. Fodder for the six o'clock news. Would Meggie see it? He should call her; in fact, he should have called her before this. But he just didn't know what he could say to her.

He followed the others out of the room, one uniform among many. She certainly wouldn't be happy seeing him in that uniform. Maybe that's why wearing it bothered him.

He was still hearing regular echoes of her cutting remarks about his having become an army officer.

Well, dammit, that's what he was. And that's what he'd been when she married him, too—even if he hadn't exactly been the finest of the lot.

He was having dinner that evening with Meggie's father. He'd always admired the general, maybe even idolized him a bit. Mark Daniels was the epitome of an officer, just as Meggie had said. The difference was that Patrick didn't think that was bad, while Meggie obviously did.

Patrick thought about his own father, recently retired from the New York City Police Department. Only during the past few days, when he'd been trying to come to terms with who he was now and where he wanted to go, had he finally understood the parallels between his father and General Daniels. Their professions were not dissimilar. Both required self-sacrifice, willingness to accept heavy responsibility and acknowledgment that danger of one sort or another constantly lay in wait.

Both men, he thought, exemplified the finest of their professions, although they were completely opposite in temperament. His own father was an easygoing man of good humor and with an uncanny ability to defuse a potentially dangerous situation. General Daniels, on the other hand, was the kind of man who used his formidable presence and innate power to command a situation. And both, in their own ways, were very successful.

Patrick thought that these revelations were very important, even if he didn't yet see why, or how they pertained to his own situation. He had a decision to make—and soon. No one was pushing him yet, at least not overtly, but he was pushing himself, simply because he hated indecision.

If it weren't for Meggie, the decision would have been made. He knew that, even if he didn't want to know it.

"I NEVER EXPECTED to see the day when I'd be unhappy about free publicity," Karen said ruefully as she watched the latest reporter leave Touch of Paradise.

Megan made a sympathetic sound, but her mind was elsewhere. How could she have been so naive as to have believed that she could return to find her life unchanged? Perhaps she was beginning to understand just how easily Patrick had fallen into that same trap.

"It's my own fault, I suppose," she said to Karen. "I should have foreseen this and gone into hiding at the cottage."

"You're lucky they can't get at you there," Karen replied. "If you'd already bought your condo, they'd be camping on your doorstep."

Megan nodded. Her cottage was wonderfully safe, and her landlord had called her personally to offer even more security. Megan had politely declined the offer with grim amusement. His company was a major defense contractor and she could detect the long arm of the Pentagon in that offer.

Karen's mention of the condo made her uneasy. The agent had called her only this morning to press for a decision. Even though she'd been certain that she wanted to buy, and had even gotten her mortgage, she was now hesitating. She hated herself for this sudden indecision, but not even self-hatred could produce an answer.

The small stream of reporters was another irritant. The first question was always the same, allowing for varying degrees of rudeness. Why was she here instead of with her husband? Megan's answer was always the same, delivered with a polite smile. She was here because her business was here and this was the busy season. That fact was borne out by a steady stream of customers even as she talked to the reporters. The publicity, in the form of a lengthy article with pictures in the local paper, had definitely brought them business.

Each day she found herself hoping that some crisis or another would grab the fickle press's attention and she would be left alone. But the world appeared to be in one of those no-news periods when reporters are forced to scrounge for stories to justify their existence. Still, she thought that the worst was probably over. There'd been only this one reporter today, and no more calls.

Patrick and his fellow returnees had held their press conference, well covered by television and well orchestrated by the Pentagon's public relations apparatus. She had watched it on the evening news. He was in uniform, which didn't surprise her. But what did shock her was that he still wore a lieutenant's bars. It seemed to her that if he had decided to stay in he would have been promoted immediately. That fact had given rise to her first serious consideration of what she would do if he did resign his commission. But as she watched him deftly answering questions, what she saw was an officer.

The conference excerpt she saw was limited, and there had been no questions about his plans or about his marriage, either. The Pentagon had obviously handed out their "Thou Shalt Nots" before the conference. It never ceased to amaze her how an essentially unruly bunch of reporters could become almost docile, and even respectful, when they were confronted with uniforms. One journalist of her acquaintance had told her that not even the president was accorded the respect given to military brass. She could believe it; she'd seen ample evidence all her life of that "apartness" of the military. It grew even worse when officers attained the rank of her father and his friends.

Patrick hadn't called, but her mother had. Megan had been expecting that. She knew that her father would send in his loyal assistant rather than risk her wrath by calling himself. So the call gave her some small satisfaction, but it also brought on yet another attack of the guilts.

Her mother loved her and loved the general. Her pain at being caught between them was obvious. So, too, was her inability to see a way of life different from her own. Of course, she said, it was marvelous that Megan had made such a success of herself. But now that Patrick had returned, she had more important matters to consider. Patrick needed her.

Megan had listened to all this with her teeth clenched to prevent an outburst she knew she would regret. If her mother had been living all these years in the real world instead of the army world, she would have understood that Megan's business was far more than just something to occupy her time, which is all her mother's charities were. Karen's mother understood that; other women her mother's age could understand. But the army had blinded and brainwashed her mother. Megan wanted to scream, "Patrick doesn't need me and the general doesn't need you, either. There's nothing there to be needed. The army has taken it all."

But she had remained calm and noncommittal, and the call had ended pleasantly enough. Megan guessed that her mother, like the general, didn't want to upset her at this point. They undoubtedly believed that she would eventually come to her senses and leap back into the army's steel embrace. Or perhaps they were planning to send the MPs after her at some point. After all, she'd been AWOL for more than seven years now.

The matter of Ted was resolved on her third evening home. She called him and invited him over, with no really clear cut notion of what the result of their encounter would be. But, almost from the moment he stepped through the doorway, she knew. Perhaps she had been hoping to put their relationship on hold until matters could be settled with Patrick. She suspected that Ted would have accepted that, and he proved it by stating so himself.

He hugged her briefly—and a bit self-consciously, she thought—then looked at her levelly.

"You look like you've been through hell, honey, and before you say anything I want you to know that I'm prepared to wait this out. It can't be easy to end things with him, especially now. I want you to know that I understand that and accept it."

His kindness and intuitive understanding made what was to come all the more difficult but could not change things. Megan knew with total certainty that there was nothing left of her feelings for Ted. She had probably been kidding herself all along. It had happened before over the years, and possibly the only difference this time was that Ted had been extraordinarily patient.

So she tried to end it as gently as possible, explaining about the still-powerful bonds between her and Patrick, despite the impossibility of a future for them.

"I can't ask you to wait, Ted, because there's nothing for you to wait for, regardless of what happens between Patrick and me."

Ted had apparently heard the certainty in her voice, because he accepted her decision and left, after wishing her well. As soon as he had gone, Megan shook her head in grim amusement.

She might have played each of them off against the other: told Patrick that she finally realized that she was in love with Ted, and told Ted that she was still in love with Patrick. That would surely have been the easy way out.

But even as she toyed with that scenario, she saw the problem with it. Patrick would never have accepted such a statement from her. He knew what she knew: that despite the years and the changes and the impossibility of a future, something was still there. She refused, however, to give that something a name.

For the remainder of the week, Megan worked long hours instead of efficient ones, then retreated to her cottage and her thoughts, except for one evening when she let Karen persuade her to go out to dinner. And that evening was no help at all.

To her amazement, Karen seemed to expect that Megan and Patrick would resume their marriage. Megan poured out her concerns at length to someone she thought was a sympathetic listener who could be counted upon to be levelheaded instead of hopelessly romantic, but she was left with the very strong impression that Karen believed these were only minor problems, to be followed in short order by "happily ever after." Surely, Megan thought, Karen, of all people, could see the impossibility of that. Karen had had a front-row seat at the transformation of Megan Daniels O'Donnell.

Such was Megan's state of mind that she was thoroughly unsettled by the fact that Karen apparently agreed with her mother and the general.

On Friday morning, Megan awoke to the immediate thought of the weekend looming before her. She'd still heard nothing from Patrick and didn't know what to think about that. If he wasn't coming to see her, he would surely have called. She wanted him to come; she didn't want him to come.

The only good thing that had happened was that the reporters had ceased to trouble her. In that sense, at least, life had returned to normal. Then she arrived at Touch of Paradise only to have Karen thrust a copy of the *New York Times* in her face.

"You've seen it, haven't you? I think I'm still kind of awestruck."

With a sinking feeling, Megan took the proffered paper. She usually picked up her copy from her mailbox during her morning run, but after another restless night, she just hadn't felt like running. She scanned the front page quickly and had no trouble finding the source of her partner's awe. The headline said: "O'Donnell to Get Medal of Honor."

Megan sank into the nearest chair as she read the article. What Patrick hadn't told her was now there for the world to see, most of it apparently having come from the other two returnees.

When they had come under heavy fire, and might well have left the Vietnamese troops they were training to their own resources, Patrick and his men had stayed. One of the returnees stated that the lieutenant had told his men they could leave, but when they knew he was staying, they chose to stay, too.

After their capture, one of Patrick's men had attempted to escape, and when he was brought back to be punished, Patrick had offered himself instead, saying that he was responsible for his men.

Both of the other returnees had admitted that there had been later opportunities to escape, and that they might have seized those opportunities if it hadn't been for Lieutenant O'Donnell's example. He had placed the lives of the villagers above his own freedom. He was, one returnee said, the one who "kept us going, and reminded us of who and what we were."

The congressman from Patrick's home district of Brooklyn, who had introduced a resolution to award Patrick the Medal of Honor, called Patrick the "quintessential military officer" and "proof positive that West Point continues to instill the finest values."

Finally, Patrick was described by another congressman as being a man who had sustained heroism for not just a few, dramatic moments but for twelve long years.

Megan finally dragged her eyes from the newsprint and looked up at Karen through a blur of tears.

"You didn't know about all this, did you?" Karen asked quietly.

Megan shook her head. "He didn't talk very much about it." But she was remembering that at one point he had said that his job had been to "keep up hope." She should have known. She should have asked questions, instead of considering that statement to be just another example of the unwelcome changes in him.

"Megan, he's really and truly a hero. The paper is right: true heroism comes over the long haul, not just from some impetuous charge up a hill or something." Karen's voice was filled with wonder, and beyond her, Megan could see their receptionist nodding in agreement and wearing a similar expression.

Megan got up and walked unsteadily to her office, hearing the echoes of Karen's words.

A hero? Not just a lucky survivor as she had assumed, but an undeniable hero? How and when had that lanky, carefree, irreverent cadet who poked fun at the army transformed himself into the "quintessential military officer" and a genuine hero? He'd been captured only a few months after she'd said goodbye to him in Hawaii. She just didn't understand it, and her failure to do so was frightening. What had she missed? Whatever was in him after his capture must have been there before they parted—or, perhaps, even from the beginning. But she hadn't seen it, because she'd never really known him.

But the general had, hadn't he? Megan's mouth tightened grimly. Her father had liked Patrick almost from the beginning. How many times had she heard her father say that Patrick would "shape up into a fine officer," while she had privately smiled in the absolute certainty that the general, for once, was wrong. But he hadn't been wrong; she had. Patrick had belonged to the army from the very beginning.

Everything was so terribly confusing. She had fallen in love with and married a man she'd never really known. Even the wonderful memories of him that she had cherished over the years now seemed suspect. She remembered the funny, gentle man who never took anything too seriously—except for her—and all the while he had been someone else entirely. And worst of all, the army had owned him from the beginning.

So now the army—or the country, really—was about to bestow its highest military honor on him. Over the years, Megan had seen that medal a few times, and she knew how it set apart the few who wore it. Doubly apart, actually, since that apartness was already there by virtue of their profession.

She felt as though the last little bit of Patrick that she might have claimed for herself had just been snatched from her. Then she was promptly ashamed of her selfishness once again.

The telephone on her desk rang and she fumbled for it, still lost in her desolate thoughts.

"General Daniels is calling," the crisp female voice said when Megan identified herself.

Megan reached for the button to cut off the call, but she wasn't quite quick enough.

"Meggie?"

"Yes."

"Have you heard the news?"

"Yes."

"I don't know what went on between you two at the cabin because Patrick won't talk about it. But regardless of what happened, you belong here with him."

"I have a business to run. It's our busy season."

"Nothing can be more important than Patrick right now."

"Don't try to give me orders, General. I resigned, remember?"

"Meggie, you have no right to allow your private war with the army to affect Patrick."

"I doubt that it will. As far as I know, he's fine."

"He needs you. Maybe he hasn't been able to say that, but he does."

"If he isn't able to say it, then he probably doesn't feel it.
I grew up with a man who could never say what he felt, if he
felt anything at all, that is. And I'm not going to spend the
rest of my life that way. He's yours, Dad. Yours and the
army's. You told me once that he had the makings of a fine
officer and obviously you were right. But fine officers do
not make fine husbands."

"Meggie—"

She slammed down the receiver, at the same time pictur-
ing the dismay on her father's face. She doubted that anyone had ever had the nerve to hang up on the general. Then
she jumped up and ran out to the front office.

"Suzie, if my father calls back, please tell him that I've
gone out."

The receptionist gave her a look that mirrored the one
she'd just imagined on her father's face. Megan didn't really
hold out much hope that the girl could lie to the general if
he called back, but she was counting on the fact that he
wouldn't want to risk another dismissal and so wouldn't call
again. No doubt he'd order her mother to give it another try.
Troublesome women were not his line of work.

Megan returned to her own office and stared without enthusiasm at her day's work. A trap was closing slowly but
surely around her. She could see it coming but didn't know
how to avoid it. Besides being a celebrity, Patrick was now
a hero. After more than ten years of peace, the nation was
eagerly awaiting a genuine hero—even one from a lost war.
And the nation liked its heroes to be idyllic, which included
having an adoring wife.

That, of course, had been the real reason for her father's
call. The army didn't want any unpleasantness to detract
from its shining hero. A wife who refused to be one could
cause a scandal. The fact that this particular wife was also
the daughter of one of its highest-ranking officers would
make it even worse.

First, she cried. Then she berated herself for her weakness. After that, she shed more tears—of frustration this time. She wanted it to be over, wanted her life to return to normal again. Then she thought about Patrick's understanding of that dark side of her that had resented his return, and that brought on still more tears.

Somehow, she got through the morning. Letters were signed, calls were made and received, even a recalcitrant computer was dealt with. She allowed Karen to persuade her to go out to lunch, if only because she thought that the lightheadedness she was feeling, that out-of-sync-with-the-world sensation, might be the result of too much coffee and too little food.

"Tell me about the medal," Karen said as soon as they had ordered.

Megan didn't want to talk about it, but she understood Karen's interest. "I don't know all that much about it, except that it has to be voted by Congress and it's usually presented by the president."

Karen was usually sensitive to her friend's moods, but this time she ignored everything in her excitement. "Does that mean you'll be going to the White House?"

"I suppose so," Megan said without enthusiasm. "The president seems to like that sort of thing."

"Megan, you will go, won't you?" Karen's tone had changed, and she was now staring at Megan with mounting dismay.

"Yes, I guess so." That was far from certain, as far as Megan was concerned, but she could hear duty calling insistently in the background.

Fortunately for the sake of their friendship, Karen let the matter drop.

Back in the office, Megan struggled once more to get some work accomplished. Gradually, the guilt came sneaking back in. She should be proud of Patrick. She should enjoy basking in reflected honor. As a daughter of the army, this should be one of the highlights of her life. And maybe Patrick really did need her.

She *was* proud of Patrick, and always had been. Of course, that pride had always been tangled up with love, but it was certainly nothing new. As for his heroism, well, the truth was that once she had gotten over her shock, it became just one more thing separating them now. Maybe she was just a bit awestruck herself.

Reflected honor, in her opinion, meant less than nothing. And the highlight of her life thus far had been the day she and Karen opened Touch of Paradise, and she had thereby established her own identity.

And Patrick most certainly did not need her. He'd always been one of the most self-sufficient men she'd ever known, and that hadn't changed. His heroism alone proved that he didn't need her. Now as then, need just didn't enter into the equation, from her point of view.

But not one of these thoughts helped at all. Guilt had settled in for a long stay.

By late afternoon, Megan was longing to escape to her cottage, even though she assumed that Patrick would show up there at some point. All she dared to hope for was a few hours or perhaps an evening to herself, to try to sort through all this.

Karen was standing in the doorway of Megan's office as they discussed a particular tour about which they had doubts. The company in question had proved to be rather unreliable in the past, but now had new management.

Suddenly, Megan saw that Karen's attention had wandered out to the front office. Megan had heard the buzzer that announced customers, but her partner's expression indicated that this might not be an ordinary client. Before Megan could say anything, Karen turned back to her with a stunned look on her face.

"He's here!"

Megan immediately knew just who "he" was, and in the next instant she knew that she should have expected this. No wonder he hadn't called, since he'd planned all along to spring himself on her like this.

By this time, Karen had stepped out into the front office, and Megan heard her surprised greeting, followed by that familiar voice. So by the time she herself reached the door, she was fully prepared to see him there. But she was not at all prepared to see him in uniform. There was a fleeting moment when she thought how very well he wore it—and then she saw the gold oak leaf of a major on his broad shoulders.

His gaze moved away from the animated Karen to rest on Megan as she halted in dismay and shock. But she shouldn't be shocked, she told herself sternly. She had known what his decision would be. She had known he belonged to the army. And yet it hurt.

In the next moment, as she walked toward him, she was glad that he had come here, that he was seeing her in her own milieu, surrounded by her own success. She was every inch the successful businesswoman in an expensive light wool suit and silk blouse, and the recent refurbishing of their office created a strong impression of success, too.

Then she stopped rather awkwardly as she realized that she had no way to greet him. A handshake was obviously too formal, and a kiss—well, she just couldn't do it. Nor did he seem to expect it. This meeting was far worse than their initial reunion, to her way of thinking.

It was all somewhat of a haze after that. She said some silly, forgettable things, and he responded, appearing to be very relaxed and yet every inch the officer and gentleman.

"You've been promoted," she said, trying to sound impressed, but not exactly succeeding.

He nodded, not taking his eyes off her. "Retroactively, too. I may get that Porsche yet."

Karen laughed and so did their receptionist, and Megan noticed them both for the first time since Patrick's arrival. Both women wore the look one might expect if a Greek god had just descended from the heights of Mount Olympus. Irritation surfaced for the first time. What right did he have to come here like this, flaunting the army in her territory?

"I want to know about the medal," Karen said quickly into the small silence. "Will it be presented at the White House?"

"So I'm told," Patrick replied with an indulgent smile. "It was voted this afternoon."

"Congratulations, Patrick," Megan managed to say, feeling very silly at her formality.

There was a flurry of comments from the others, and then Patrick spotted their computer and began to move in that direction, already asking questions.

Karen, who was standing near it, laughed. "Megan's the expert on that. I don't speak its language."

Megan could have hugged Karen as she followed Patrick and began to explain the computer's features. She felt back in control, at least temporarily. So she showed off shamelessly and didn't even question why she felt the need to do so.

An important call drew her back into her office at that point, and she left Patrick to the other two women. Sitting down gratefully at her desk, she forced her mind to deal with a troublesome charter service. But her body remained tense, singing with electricity, prickly. Patrick's voice drifted into the office, providing a constant reminder of his presence. By the time she hung up, she wasn't at all sure just what it was that she and the service had agreed upon.

She paused in the doorway of her office, staring at Patrick. She wanted to ask why he'd shown up unannounced like this, and in uniform. But she thought she already knew the answer. He had arrived unannounced because he probably feared she would disappear if he gave her the opportunity, and he had shown up in uniform because he wanted to show her in the clearest possible manner that he had made his decision.

The late afternoon sunlight was slanting through the front windows, and its rays glittered off the oak leaf. She blinked a few times, trying to ignore it, wanting to protest, and then stopped as an ugly lump of despair caught in her throat. Slowly and carefully, as though she wasn't quite sure how to walk, she made her way toward him.

But Patrick turned and saw her then, and he crossed the small distance between them quickly, sliding an arm around her waist and drawing her back into her office. Megan started to protest, then stopped. Her small office was totally filled by his presence. She felt awkward and edgy and devastatingly aware of every square inch of him.

A ghost of a smile hovered around his mouth as he carelessly swept off his cap and tossed it onto her desk. She stared at it dumbly, but her attention quickly turned back to him when he caught her by the waist and murmured her name softly.

Her name was a caress, maybe even a plea. But it was gentleness followed by possessiveness; he lowered his mouth to hers and drew her into his arms. There was a brittleness to them both, a tautness, a sense of something about to let go, though not just now. His kiss was far from gentle and his arms had tightened around her almost painfully, forcing her against the hard angles of his body.

Then Megan was reliving the one other time he'd kissed her and held her like this: the day he'd left for Vietnam. She was slipping away from herself, spinning off into a different plane, and all the while melting beneath his touch.

Reality came hurtling back the moment her fingertips touched the cool metal on his shoulders, and she recoiled at the very instant he lifted his mouth from hers to rain kisses across her neck. But her skin no longer felt heated and her body no longer begged for release. She stared at the oak leaves and wanted to rip them away, along with the whole hated uniform. Beneath that uniform must surely be her Patrick, the man whose kisses could reach into her deepest core as no others had every done.

Belatedly, he sensed her withdrawal and lifted his head to frown down at her. "What is it, honey?"

She did not look up at him because her gaze was still fixed on that uniform. But she did hear the gentleness in his tone, and she knew that he must still be there, beneath all that.

"Why did you wear that uniform?"

He moved slightly away from her, sliding his hands around until they were once more resting lightly against her waist. Then he gave a sigh of resignation.

"I wore it because the New York newspapers sent photographers to the house, and because I knew Mom and Dad would be expecting to see me in uniform."

But you could have changed! she screamed silently. *You could have changed before you came up here!*

Perhaps he read her mind. It wasn't an unreasonable assumption when he could see the expression on her face quite clearly.

"And I guess I wanted you to see it, too," he said with that same air of resignation.

She said nothing. He finally dropped his hands and backed toward the doorway. For a moment she thought he might be leaving, and her heart skipped a few beats. But he stopped, obviously waiting for her. She moved to her desk, straightening some papers, folding a computer printout and putting it away, then retrieving her purse from a desk drawer. She wondered if she would ever sit in this office again without being reminded of his presence here this day, and of what he had come to tell her.

For days after her father had stood in her office, telling her about Patrick, there had been a faint impression of him here, hovering around the soft blue walls and pastel prints and flowering plants. Now it would be Patrick who remained, somehow mocking her, whispering that it was all so trivial, a meaningless bit of fluff as opposed to the harsh reality he and the general represented—uniforms and orders and weapons systems with unpronounceable names and multibillion-dollar price tags and dangerous places far away. She hated it all. And she very nearly hated Patrick, too.

She was almost to the outside door when she realized that she hadn't said good-night to Karen. Her partner came hurrying out of her own office at that moment.

"Megan, I'll work tomorrow."

Megan had completely forgotten about that. They worked alternate Saturdays, with the additional assistance of a retired agent. But Karen had already worked the past two Saturdays. Besides, the weekend was looming up as unpleasantly as the days at the cabin had.

"No, I'll work. It's my turn."

Patrick's hand touched her back lightly as he turned to Karen. "Thanks, Karen. I appreciate it. I'll see you again soon."

He had opened the door and was urging her through. Megan considered digging in her heels and venting her anger, but there were several people outside looking at their window display, and their attention immediately turned to the man in uniform. So, fuming inwardly, she allowed him to usher her outside, and even managed a pleasant smile for the older couple who stared at them.

She heard the couple congratulating Patrick, heard his polite thank-you, and managed to move beyond his reach. But not for long. As she hesitated at the curb, he was there again, his hand back in place against her spine.

"My car's just across the street in the lot. Is yours there?"

She nodded, not trusting herself to speak just then.

They reached her Subaru first, and he looked it over as she dug through her purse for her keys, then dropped them through uncoordinated fingers. He bent quickly to pick them up.

"Why don't you leave your car here and we'll pick it up later?"

She grabbed the keys from him and unlocked the door in a frozen silence. He hesitated, then closed the door behind her as she slid into the driver's seat. When he then strode off to his car, she felt as though she might have won some sort of victory, but hardly an important one.

Without waiting to see if he was following her, she pulled out into traffic. But when she finally did look, he was there, right behind her. Momentarily distracted, she had to brake hard for the traffic ahead, and she could just imagine his reaction.

A temper tantrum will get you nowhere, she told herself as she took some deep, steadying breaths. No matter how satisfying it might be to explode, the result would certainly be counterproductive.

She crept through another few blocks of rush-hour traffic as she thought about all the other times when her temper had flared and Patrick had responded with that same quiet calm. Despite his red hair, he was one of the least temperamental people she'd ever known. She, on the other hand, was the kind of person who was inclined to let minor irritations pile up until she exploded with what was often unwarranted anger. The end result was that she would invariably begin to feel ridiculous and silly, just as she did right now.

All week long she had been determined that she would end it as soon as he arrived. She had planned to explain calmly and rationally that they had no future, that it was pointless to go on as they were now, tormenting themselves with a dead past they could never hope to recapture because they were two different people.

Then he had shown up in uniform, letting her know that he had made his decision, too, and now she was uncertain. Maybe what she'd subconsciously wanted to happen this weekend had been something entirely different. Maybe she had wanted to make her little speech and have him declare his love and say that he would give up the army for her.

But it wasn't going to happen that way. He had made his decision; she had made hers. It all could end now, and she could go back to the life that she'd built so carefully and enjoyed so much. Or could she?

Fortunately, the route home was so well known to her that she could more or less put the car on automatic pilot. From time to time, she glanced in the mirror and saw that Patrick was still there. She could even make out the brass buttons and the ribbons and the shiny major's insignia. The U.S. Army was in full pursuit. He might as well have been driving one of those new tanks her father loved so dearly.

Major. Joel's rank—and Joel had been two years ahead of Patrick at the academy. The medal undoubtedly had something to do with that decision, but it couldn't have been the only reason. Patrick had jumped from the jungles of Vietnam straight onto the fast track to the stars. Her mind began to speculate on possible education and duty tours before she brought it to a halt with a disgusted sound. After all this time, she could slip right back into it, couldn't she? It must be in her genes.

She reached the gates of the estate more quickly than she'd expected and began to worry that she might have been driving recklessly. She also realized that she should have been using that driving time to decide what to do about him now, this evening.

The gate operated on an automated system that required the insertion of a card into a box standing alongside the driveway. She slid her card into the slot, then drove through as soon as the gate opened, knowing that the system was set to permit only one car to enter. She had forgotten to mention that to Patrick and looked worriedly into the rearview mirror. But he had stopped outside and was waiting.

So she stopped her car and got out, then walked back to press the button on the inside of one pillar that permitted the gate to be opened from the inside. The act took on the ludicrous significance of that episode with the luggage at the cabin, with the strong symbolism of the high wrought-iron gate between them.

PATRICK DROVE THROUGH the gate, watching her as she went back to her car. Normally, Meggie was very graceful in her movements, the result, he supposed, of years of ballet lessons she claimed to have hated. But right now, she moved with a slight awkwardness and stiffness, holding her petite, curvy body rigidly. She'd always done that when she was angry.

So maybe he shouldn't have worn the uniform. He could have taken the time to change before he came up here. But he'd worn it deliberately, just as he'd timed his arrival to catch her at Touch of Paradise instead of making a more discreet appearance here.

He'd been thinking about her all week, despite his heavy schedule. She would not appreciate knowing to what lengths he had gone in his effort to understand her attitudes toward him and toward the general.

She undoubtedly chose to believe that she'd been silly and shallow and that she'd been completely under the general's thumb, but Patrick knew better than that. What silliness and shallowness had existed had existed in both of them; they were young and experiencing the first true taste of freedom and adulthood. The strange thing was that what she seemed to be hating in herself she also seemed to cherish in him. She was supposed to mature, while he was expected to remain the same. However, he doubted very much that she would care to have that fact pointed out just now.

As far as her having been under the general's thumb was concerned, that was pure fabrication on her part. A long conversation with the general over dinner this week proved beyond a shadow of a doubt that, if anything, the situation had been exactly the reverse. General Daniels worshiped his daughter, and he had encouraged every move she'd made toward independence, not to mention having given her a few pushes himself. Of course, she wouldn't be exactly pleased to hear that conclusion, either.

Megan had always been passionate, and Patrick now believed that her hatred of the army was nothing more than the safest outlet she could find for her rage over the blow that fate had dealt to her by taking him away from her.

From his point of view, then, all that needed to be done was to convince her that he was indeed back, that she no longer had any reason to hate the army, and that even if they no longer had that giddy love of their youth, they still had something worth keeping.

But he was not about to kid himself into believing that any of this would be easy.

Chapter Nine

Without so much as a glance at Patrick, Megan unlocked her front door and went inside. It was done. He was here in her home and she could not wish him away. But he made the little cottage feel strange, and she finally turned to him with a frown.

He had stopped just inside the door and was looking around with interest. Nothing in this room would be familiar to him. They'd never really owned furniture because their brief married life had been lived in furnished quarters on military bases. Over the past seven years, Megan had expended a great deal of time and money to acquire the things she wanted, choosing each piece with such care that Karen had teased her about suffering from a terminal case of the nesting instinct. It was true. She had spent so much of her life in one temporary home after another that the desire to have something permanent had become an obsession.

She looked back at the living room and dining room, trying to see it as he must be seeing it—all coziness and pastel shades and polished woods. She supposed that he must find it impossibly feminine, but then she hadn't decorated her home with the idea of sharing it with a man.

"This is very nice," he said after a long silence.

"Thank you," she replied formally, her eyes fixed on that offensive uniform. "Now, if you wish any further conversation with me, you can get out of that uniform."

He had started across the living room to examine her stereo system, but at her icy words he stopped and gave her a broad grin.

"Do you really want me to sit around naked?"

She quickly began to fuss with a vase of daffodils that had begun to wilt. His words had evoked the image of his damp nakedness at the cabin, followed by the memory of that much more recent kiss at her office.

"Don't you have any other clothes with you?"

"Yes, they're in the car," he admitted. He straightened up from his examination of the stereo, then about-faced and walked out the door.

Well, she thought with some satisfaction, *I seem to have won another battle. At least the army won't be staring me in the face all evening.*

But she was wrong, as she should have known she would be. The civilian clothes made no difference at all. Major O'Donnell was still very much in evidence. Before long, Patrick would be "the major" just the way her father was always "the general."

She had just brought him a drink when the phone rang.

"Meggie, it's Joel. How are you?"

"Not too well at the moment, thank you," she replied dryly, immediately wondering if their father had put him up to something.

"Want to talk about it?"

"No."

"I was afraid of that," he admitted. "Well, I'll be seeing you next week in any event."

"You're coming home?" she asked eagerly. In spite of his choice of career, Megan loved her brother very much and she hadn't seen him for nearly a year.

"Yes, for the ceremony. That is, if Patrick intends to invite me. I've been trying to catch up with him, but he keeps getting away from me. Do you happen to know where he is?"

"At the moment, he's in my living room," she said, guessing that Joel already knew that. She suspected that Patrick's whereabouts and the status of their marriage were the subject of daily bulletins between a certain Pentagon office and Joel's base in West Germany.

Joel chuckled. "The major must be slipping. If I were in his place right now, I wouldn't be in the living room."

Megan forced a laugh because he was her brother, but she was in no mood for teasing, especially not on that subject.

"I'll let him issue the invitation right now. Hold on."

After she had gotten Patrick to the phone, she went to her bedroom to change. They had her surrounded now—two majors and a general. Duty. Tradition. Army.

It all flashed through her mind in an ever-changing kaleidoscope as she mechanically began to shed her business clothes. The enormous, unyielding bulk of the Pentagon, uniforms, medals and ribbons. Talk of complex weapons systems and manpower strengths. The ever-present threat of their being brought into use that only occasionally troubled most civilians. A world of men, despite the recent changes forced upon them.

She recalled another general, a friend of her father's, saying that the army needed its women officers now, in peacetime. But if it should ever come to war... He hadn't needed to finish the sentence. She knew that women were superfluous to the army's central purpose and probably always would be.

She had forgotten to close the bedroom door, and now, clad only in her lacy teddy, she turned from her closet to find Patrick standing there in the doorway. He was leaning casually against the door frame, giving every impression of doing nothing out of the ordinary.

"So that's what the well-dressed businesswoman wears beneath her suit. I'm afraid that my knowledge of women's lingerie is somewhat dated."

His light, teasing tone and casual stance did nothing at all to dispel the anxiety of the moment. Nothing could have. The silken teddy felt icy cold against her heated skin, and she thought she must be blushing all over. Avoiding his eyes, she hurried into her robe, the first thing she could reach.

How was it that he could be so casual about all this? It had to be an act. And he was obviously making some sort of point, or he would simply have waited for her in the living room.

"Did you invite Joel to the ceremony?" That was a dumb question and she knew it. Of course he had. The long robe slithered over her prickly skin.

"Of course. Do you think that his sister will require an invitation, too?"

"No, I suppose not." She still didn't look at him, pretending instead to be having difficulty with the long zipper of her robe. The real problem was her uncoordinated fingers.

Megan brushed past him as she hurriedly left the bedroom for the relative safety of the living room. She was beginning to realize that while she could still fight the army, she couldn't fight much longer against the liquid warmth his presence produced. She was intensely aware of him, of his every move, of his scent, of those eyes that were always on her.

"I changed clothes, but you're still not very talkative," he observed as he followed her.

"I can't think of much to talk about that won't start an argument." *Or won't send us back into the bedroom,* she added to herself. How long could she postpone the inevitable?

"Okay, let's talk about dinner, then. I've never seen such a bare refrigerator. Are you sure that you really live here?"

"I don't cook. We'll have to go out to dinner."

He chuckled softly, and she felt the little explosions of air against the top of her head as he came up behind her and wrapped his long arms around her, folding them so that his fingertips rested lightly against the sides of her breasts. Fire and ice raced along her spine and the inevitable came seductively closer.

"You're going to make some guy a wonderful wife. You don't talk, you don't cook and you can't even mix a decent drink. Besides, you hang up on a man's superior officer."

She turned around in the small circle of his arms, brushing against far too much of him in the process. "What are you talking about? I didn't hang up on Joel. And besides, he's not your superior officer."

"I didn't mean Joel. I was referring to a very upset four-star down at the Pentagon."

"Good. I'm glad to hear it. Actually, I rather hoped he'd call back so my receptionist could tell him that I wouldn't take the call."

"No doubt that's why he didn't call back," Patrick observed with dry amusement.

"That four-star is one of those subjects we must avoid, Patrick," she said firmly.

"Okay, then, back to the subject of dinner. Where shall we go? I have a whole flotilla of plastic burning a hole in my pocket. You'd be amazed at how fast those things can be taken care of when you're a celebrity."

"And when the Pentagon says 'jump,'" she added with a reluctant grin. It was impossible to remain angry with Patrick when he was in this mood; she knew he knew that.

Patrick saw her smile and took immediate advantage of it, as he had always done. His kiss was gentle and teasing and over quickly, leaving her breathless and wanting more—something else she was sure he knew.

"I think we were discussing dinner," he said with a smile.

The image of a particular restaurant had come into her mind the first time he mentioned that subject. She had tried to ignore it, but it wouldn't go away. Knowing that she was now guilty of hurrying the inevitable, she disentangled herself from Patrick's arms and headed for the phone.

"I know a place. Let me call and see if we can get reservations."

AN HOUR LATER, as they entered the restaurant, Megan told herself that she had made a mistake. On second thought, the inevitable didn't have to be quite so inevitable, after all. She just couldn't afford to let their in-name-only marriage become a marriage in fact.

Still, she kept waiting for Patrick to say something, to indicate that he saw what she had seen the first time she came here. This charming brick-walled restaurant, with its profusion of hanging plants and Tiffany lamps, was an almost exact duplicate of the restaurant near West Point to which Patrick had taken her on their first date.

She had been struck by the resemblance the moment she entered the place some years ago with a date—and she hadn't been back since. That whole evening had been a disaster, because memories of Patrick had immediately flooded in on her, causing her to lose interest in the very nice man who'd brought her there. At one point, she'd even been forced to retreat to the ladies' room to try to get her emotions under control.

It hurt her now to think that Patrick, whose memories had seemed so much sharper than her own, didn't remember. They ordered drinks and discussed the menu, and she kept waiting less and less hopefully for him to say something. It was increasingly difficult for her to refrain from making some remark about the restaurant that might jog his memory. Then he looked up from the menu with a grin.

"Well, at least this time I won't have to worry about doing dishes afterward."

Flushed with warmth, she still frowned as if she didn't understand, and he waved a hand around them.

"Doesn't this remind you of the place we went to on our first date?" Patrick asked.

Later she would decide that inevitability had truly begun with that one remark. She relaxed and nodded and became even warmer.

"Yes, I've been here once before and I saw it immediately."

"And I hope it ruined the whole evening for whoever he was." Patrick grinned.

"It did," she admitted with a smile. That teasing note in his voice told her that they had moved beyond the bitterness that had previously accompanied such talk. A threshold had been crossed.

"You never told me that you couldn't afford that restaurant," she said, recalling his first remark, the one about having to wash dishes.

"Well, I had to do something to impress a general's daughter. So I took up a collection. I told them all that I'd see to it that they all got cushy assignments when he became my father-in-law."

She laughed delightedly, because she could easily imagine his having done just such a thing. "That should have gotten you enough money so that you wouldn't have had to worry."

"You ordered the most expensive thing on the menu... and then wanted a bottle of wine, too."

"Did I really?" she asked, appalled at her thoughtlessness.

"You did indeed. And to add insult to injury, you kept talking about that captain you were dating in Washington and all the expensive places he was taking you."

"Then why on earth did you invite me out again?" she asked, still shocked at her own behavior.

"Well, I had that promise to my buddies to think of. You might say that we had a heavy investment in you."

"I really can't believe I was so horrible," she murmured.

"Oh, it got worse," he responded cheerfully. "You finally invited me down to Washington and then invited the good captain to the cookout your parents gave."

"I did *not* invite him," she replied indignantly. "My father invited him. Doug was one of his aides, and I think Dad wasn't any too sure about you at the time. After all, your reputation at the academy wasn't exactly the best." As she was speaking, she was also recalling the lengthy conversation between Patrick and her father that day, after which any objections the general might have had vanished.

"You talked to the captain most of the time, too," Patrick countered.

"I was trying to make you jealous. You hadn't shown any interest at all in me."

"Some chance I had," he scoffed. "A lowly cadet against a general, a captain and a first lieutenant. Joel was there, too, playing the protective big brother."

Megan smiled, drifting off into her memories. She'd never really thought about how difficult their courtship must have been for Patrick.

"How did we ever manage it?" she said in a wondering tone.

"Manage what?"

"To... fall in love," she said as her eyes slid away from him.

He reached across the small table to take her hand. "We managed it because it was real, Meggie. Because we both knew what we wanted."

She nodded slowly. He was right; they *had* known. But life had been so much simpler then. Love had been all that mattered.

The wine steward appeared just then, breaking into the private space they had created for themselves. As the wine was tasted and poured, Megan continued to think about what Patrick had said. How she wished that they could go back—not so much to the happiness of those days, but more to the certainty, the absolute certainty they'd had then that love could see them through anything.

Dinner was filled with small talk, mostly about Patrick's calls and visits from old West Point friends, and the unhappy news of the divorce of a couple with whom they'd been friendly at Schofield Barracks.

His mention of that divorce was a splash of ice water thrown onto the warmth of the evening. Her happiness evaporated. By the time they were sipping their Irish coffees, she had dragged herself back to reality.

"You've made your decision, haven't you?" she asked.

She'd expected another indefinite response, or at least a hesitation on his part. But he gave her a very level look and nodded. No explanations. No pleas for her understanding. Take it or leave it. The depth of her anguish shocked her, since she'd known all along this would happen. But it hurt, it hurt so bad in so many places and so many ways.

"Why?" she asked, unable to resist the question even when the answer didn't really matter.

This time he *did* hesitate. He leaned back in his chair and regarded her solemnly. The overall impression she received was one of unshakable determination.

"Meggie, I know you think that I've changed, but I haven't, or at least not that much. There were times even before Vietnam when I considered staying in. If I hadn't at least considered making the army my career, I would never have accepted my appointment to West Point."

She made a sound of disgusted disbelief. "Don't try to tell me that, Patrick. All we ever talked about was how wonderful it would be when you were out and we could live in New York. And you were always poking fun at the army."

"I'm not denying that, but I still thought about staying in. I figured I had four years to decide, and besides, it's easy to postpone difficult decisions when you're young."

"But you never even mentioned it," she persisted, as she thought bleakly that she had been right earlier. She'd never really known him.

"Because you wouldn't have wanted to listen," he stated matter-of-factly. "You had our life all mapped out for us, and it didn't include the army."

Megan bristled angrily. "I would never have married you if—"

"Yes, you would have. Because you loved me and because you didn't really dislike the army all that much anyway."

"If I'd wanted to stay in the army, I'd have married some future general-type like Doug, that captain we were talking about."

"No, you wouldn't have. You didn't love him. You loved me. You've got your priorities a little mixed up."

"'Whither thou goest,' et cetera. Is that it?" She glared at him.

"That's not what I meant. I meant that you didn't marry me because you thought I could get you out of the army."

"I got myself out."

"With a vengeance," he agreed. "And you made sure that I saw it straight off, too."

"If I overdid it, it's because of the strain I was under and the fact that I'd just had that argument with the general. Besides, how was I to know you were going to come back feeling differently. I never expected *that* change, Patrick." It was as close to an apology as she intended to come. "Anyway, you haven't answered my question. Why?"

"Because it's where I belong."

There was, she knew, no way she could refute that. He *did* belong to the army; she'd already admitted that to herself. The military demanded a level of commitment far beyond that of most other professions, and Patrick's words had just been a way of stating that fact. She knew far better than most people what those demands were: innate leadership qualities, a sense of duty and the willingness to sacrifice oneself. Patrick had those qualities and, she knew now, had always had them.

When she continued to sit there in silence, he went on. "There are other considerations, too. I'm thirty-five, and so far, all I've known is the army. Other men my age are well up the career ladder by now."

"That's nonsense," she said angrily, not about to let him con her on that point. "You have a West Point education and you're a hero. You could start out where any of them are on the strength of that alone."

"You don't think there would be anything wrong with my parlaying those things into a soft job with some defense contractor?" he asked, challenging her.

Of course she did. But she said, "Why should I? It's done all the time. Everyone accepts it."

"I don't."

There it was, she thought, that unshakable integrity. And it didn't help at all that she completely agreed with him on this matter. She felt totally defenseless. The only possible weapon in her arsenal was their marriage, but the fact that he hadn't bothered to discuss his decision with her first led her to the unwelcome conclusion that that wasn't much of a weapon. If he truly wanted their marriage to continue, wouldn't he at least have talked it over with her?

Megan was silent all the way back to the cottage. She was realizing now that she'd been so busy convincing herself that she didn't love him anymore that she'd neglected to consider just how he felt about her at this point. She had the frightening sensation that the tables might be turning.

If she truly wanted to end things, he had just handed her the perfect reason. Irreconcilable differences. An open-and-shut case. So why did it hurt so much?

Then they were back at the cottage, still locked in a tense silence. Although he'd said nothing about his plans, she assumed that he intended to stay the weekend. While that prospect should have displeased her, it now had the opposite effect. She just didn't want to let him go.

How ironic it was, she thought, that she was the one who had made her decision quickly, even before she had seen him, and now she was the one who was dithering while he appeared to have made up his mind.

"Are there any stores open this late?" he asked, breaking into the charged silence. "I'm going to starve to death tomorrow morning if I have to depend on the contents of your refrigerator."

His tone was teasing, a peace offering. She nodded. "The market where I shop is open twenty-four hours a day."

"Good. Let's go, then."

She followed him back out the door. So they were back to that. Nothing had changed since their days at the cabin. Diversions. Anything to prevent serious talk. But at least she could assume that he did plan to spend the weekend.

IT WAS UNSETTLING, the two of them pushing a shopping cart down the aisles, selecting this and that. Domesticity. She hadn't felt that since he'd shipped out to Vietnam. When she lived with her parents, she'd never set foot in a market, and since then she had tended toward whirlwind shopping trips at irregular intervals, sandwiched in between more important things.

He had stopped to look at something, and as she turned to him she saw his wedding ring, glowing in the reflected store lighting. Her own finger felt bare again. She could have retrieved her ring from the safety deposit box. But she hadn't.

"Have you tried this stuff?" he asked, holding up a container of Häagen Dazs ice cream.

"Yes, many times." She groaned. "It's so rich, it's sinful. But there's a store in Greenwich where we can get it fresh-packed tomorrow."

"Good. I'd like to see more of the area."

Why? she wanted to scream. *Why should you want to see it? You'll never live here. You're going to live where the army tells you to live. You made your choice.*

Then they were back at the cottage again, unpacking more groceries than her kitchen had ever seen at one time and making small talk. Megan was edgy, irritable, waiting for...what? She decided to deal with practical matters.

"When is the ceremony?"

"Next Friday afternoon."

"So soon?" She was surprised. She'd have thought that such a thing would require far more planning.

"You know the Pentagon. Grab it while it's hot. In another few weeks, the public might forget all about me."

Megan understood that. With all the adverse publicity the Pentagon received on a regular basis, they were naturally eager to present to the nation that paid their extravagant bills an example of their best. And Patrick was indeed that, she thought with a bittersweet smile.

"Why didn't you tell me about...all that?" she asked in a tight voice. "Instead, I had to read about it in the papers."

"Did you really want to hear about it?" he asked quietly.

"Yes. Well, maybe. Oh, I don't know." She waved a hand in disgust. "But you must have known I'd find out about it."

She hurried from the kitchen and sank down into her favorite living room chair. She was ashamed of herself, but she didn't want to talk about it. That was a part of Patrick she didn't know and didn't understand—and didn't want to understand, either.

He followed her, kicking off his shoes and sprawling on the sofa, betraying none of the emotions she herself was feeling.

"At the risk of sounding disgustingly humble, I just didn't think that such a big deal would be made of it. I didn't do anything that any good officer wouldn't have done."

"There was a time when you wouldn't have considered yourself to be a good officer," she reminded him.

"That's true enough," he agreed as he lay there watching her. "Meggie, you've got to let go of the past."

She blinked in disbelief at his quietly insistent words. *She* had to let go of the past? What about him? A chill shot through her as she wondered if he might be here because he thought *she* needed *him*.

"It seems to me that we've both been guilty of wallowing in the past," she stated coldly.

"I wouldn't call it wallowing," he gently replied. "It's natural to want to relive happy times. But you have to understand that we can't go back to that."

She couldn't believe this conversation. She'd had it with herself before he returned, and she'd even had it with him in her imagination, with the roles reversed.

"I understand that perfectly well."

"I'm not so sure that you do. I think you still want back that kid who made you laugh and never took anything seriously."

"According to you, he probably never existed in the first place."

"I don't know if he did or not," Patrick said, shrugging. "It was a long time ago, and we all have a tendency to tailor the past to suit our present frame of mind."

She sensed a reproach there. "Are you saying you think that's what I'm doing?"

"Yes."

"You're wrong, Patrick. I remember everything very well and what I remember isn't very flattering to me. So there goes your theory. If I were really tailoring the past to suit my present state of mind, then I wouldn't be remembering what a silly little fool I was then."

"Yes, you would, because the comparison with the present you pleases you."

"And, pray tell, just what is this present me like...from your point of view, that is?" She narrowed her eyes threateningly, but without producing any noticeable effect on him.

"I'm not sure."

He was silent for a long moment, contemplating his stocking-clad feet propped on one arm of the sofa. She fidgeted nervously, not knowing what it was she wanted to hear from him.

"Myths, Meggie. We both created them to make the unbearable a little less so. At least that's what the shrinks tell me."

"Shrinks? You mean the ones who examined you at Clark?" she asked disdainfully.

"Not them." He waved a hand in dismissal of that. "All they cared about was that we weren't committable. No, I mean the ones I talked to this week."

"Why was that necessary?" This whole subject was making her more and more nervous, for reasons she couldn't fully understand.

"I had some questions that needed to be answered," he replied. Then he added, after a long pause, "And some of them concerned you."

"Me?" She stared at him with growing horror. "Me?"

"You and me," he assured her hastily.

Then he sat up suddenly, causing her to draw back more deeply into her chair in an instinctive reaction to the intensity of his gaze.

"Meggie, we both needed our myths in order to survive. That's a healthy, normal reaction to what we both went through. My myth was that I'd come home and find you completely unchanged and waiting for me. I needed to believe that, so I *did* believe it.

"Your myth has been more complicated, because your life has been more complicated. First of all, you needed someone to blame, even though you knew rationally there really wasn't anyone. So you chose the army. No, wait! Let me finish." He interrupted himself as he saw her gearing up for a violent protest.

"The other part of your myth has been this transformation, this going from what you described as a silly little fool to a strong, independent woman. You needed strength to survive, so you created a myth around that strength, sort of a way of patting yourself on the back. You needed that."

She could no longer contain herself and leaped out of the chair to stand before him, her eyes alive with fire. "I've never heard such nonsense in my life. But it's just what I'd expect from a bunch of army shrinks, whose loyalty is to the army first and only secondarily to the truth."

"They weren't army psychiatrists," he said calmly. "They were private psychiatrists who have treated hostages, a specialty that I understand has grown considerably while I was away."

"Then they're still being unethical, making judgments about me when they've never even met me."

"They were only answering my questions. I figured out most of it for myself. I needed to understand, Meggie."

She was so angry that she simply couldn't think of anything to say. But she did hear that quiet plea in his last words. Before she could get her mind working well enough to think about that, he had gone on.

"Why have there been no other men in your life in all this time?"

She was taken aback at what she perceived as a sudden change of subject. "I told you before that I don't know."

"You told me that you'd given up hope after a few years, but you never really did, Meggie. You just buried it so deep that it couldn't hurt you. And the only time it came out was when you met someone you could have become interested in. You said as much yourself when you told me that it was easier to give them up than to face having an affair."

"Do you wish I had?" she asked coldly even as she began a very disquieting mental search. What he said made frightening sense. There were locked doors in there, in her mind. She felt as though he was trying to pry them open, and she didn't want that to happen.

"No, although I know that's a selfish answer. The point I'm trying to make is that you've suffered a lot, and it wasn't over when you thought it was. It just went deeper, that's all. What you really tried to do was to create an entirely new person, one who wouldn't suffer anymore."

She ignored those frightening thoughts and fixed her mind instead on what sounded to her like a repetition of his earlier statement that she hadn't really changed, that this "new person" was a figment of her imagination.

"Patrick, I've heard enough of this. I mean it. If you don't stop right now, one of us is leaving...and this is *my* home!"

He made his point by stretching out on the sofa once more and clasping his hands behind his head—the very picture of relaxation and permanence.

"Okay, if you don't want to talk about where we've been, let's talk about where we're going," he said.

She sank back into her chair, feeling drained and frightened and a few thousand other things that defied description.

"I don't think we should talk about that, either."

"After twelve years of waiting, I'm in no mood to wait much longer, Meggie," he said, his relaxed pose belying the words.

"To wait for what?" she asked nervously.

"For you to decide whether or not you're still married to me."

"You know perfectly well that we're still married."

"Do I? You don't wear my ring, and unless I blanked out somewhere, we've been sleeping in separate beds. I don't even see that wedding picture you loved so much."

"I put those things away a long time ago, and I just haven't gotten them out again, that's all." She ignored the part about separate beds and hoped that he would, too.

"Because you haven't decided whether or not we're married."

"Don't be ridiculous!"

"Do you want *me* to make love to you, or do you still want that kid I was when I left?"

She took a ragged breath. "You were the one who said that we could take these things slowly. It's just taking me a while to get used to all these changes."

"Like hell it is," he said, pronouncing each word very slowly. "I stopped believing that the first time I really kissed you."

She drew in a sharp breath, then forced herself to let it out slowly. That slight harshness in his tone had brought back the differences between this Patrick and the one he referred to as "that kid."

"I just think," she said in a measured voice, "that we shouldn't rush into anything. It isn't as though we have a deadline or anything."

"My patience has a deadline, and it's approaching rapidly."

"Exactly what is it you want from me, Patrick...aside from the obvious, that is?" Her tone was carefully calculated to deny the importance of a topic that she knew was all-important now.

"I want you to be my wife."

She unlocked her gaze from his with considerable difficulty. "You don't even know what you're asking, because you can't accept the person I am now."

"That's because the person you are now is no different from the one you always were."

She exploded from the chair once more and glared at him. "I am successful and independent and I frankly don't give a damn whether you see that or not. You're not going to get back the wife you had, Patrick, because she doesn't exist anymore."

"Yes, she does, and she was always just the way you described her."

"This is some game of yours, isn't it? Something those shrinks recommended?"

"It's no game. It's the truth. Regardless of what happened to me, you would have been successful at whatever you chose to do. And believe me, you were never dependent. There were a few times when I wished that I had a wife like some of the other guys had. The kind who always said 'yes, dear.'"

"It won't work, Patrick. I know what I was."

"You know what you *think* you were, but you're wrong."

Their eyes met and clashed silently. He seemed to be willing her to remember all the things she had forgotten, all the details of their brief marriage. She gnawed at her lower lip nervously.

"I need a drink," she muttered, then quickly headed for the kitchen.

But what she really needed was a few minutes to try to reassemble the jagged pieces of herself that seemed to be lying all over the place. She reached shakily for a bottle of sherry, then had to hold it with both hands to pour some into a glass.

This was some sort of game; it had to be. Those psychiatrists must have suggested it to him as a means of building up her confidence. No doubt Patrick had presented to them the picture of a woman about to fall apart. Why else would he have sought their advice about her in the first place?

"I want you to be my wife." Not "I love you and want you back." There was, in her mind, a very big difference there. Of course he wanted a wife just now; it was part of the image the Pentagon was packaging. All the scattered pieces of herself began to come together and she went back to the living room.

"You're afraid that I'm going to do something to embarrass you, aren't you? And so is my father. That's what's behind all this."

When he just stared at her, she gave him a triumphant look. "You want to make certain that I'll show up at the ceremony and play the role of the adoring wife. Or maybe you think that I'll show up wearing that T-shirt or saying embarrassing things to the press."

She'd expected a denial or a protest of some sort, but what she got instead was laughter. Not just a mild chuckle, but full-blown laughter, of the type that virtually demands a response in kind.

"That could be interesting. I'm told that the president has an exceptionally good sense of humor, though I doubt that the same can be said about the Pentagon brass."

She refused to join in his laughter, but she could not help feeling silly. He knew—and even her father must know—that she'd never do such a thing. She'd told Patrick once how she'd amused herself at pompous official parties and ceremonies by imagining herself doing outrageous things. But he knew her too well to believe that she'd ever actually carry them out.

Well, if she'd been wrong, then what was behind all this? She didn't know what to say next, so she just stood there, near him, nervously sipping at the sherry. Then he reached up and took the glass from her hand and set it on the table. Amusement still twinkled in his eyes as he reached again, for her this time. And she let him draw her down onto his lap.

His lips pressed softly against her temple. "If you don't want to come to the ceremony, then don't. Our private life is no one's business, not even the army's."

"I *do* want to come." She felt herself in danger of breaking into tears. Although she managed to prevent that embarrassment, she couldn't quite keep the catch from her voice.

"I'm very proud of you and I should have told you that. You deserve that medal . . . and a lot more."

He drew her face back against the curve of his neck and she could feel him grin. "Now *that* sounds like a properly adoring wife. The army would be pleased."

Laughter bubbled up and she was helpless against its rise. She wrapped a hand around his neck and hugged him. That sweet warmth was flowing unimpeded through her now. But not even that could prevent her awareness of the impossibility of their situation.

"Oh, Patrick, what are we going to do?"

He chuckled. "I can think of a few things. I've had twelve years of very inventive fantasies."

"That won't solve anything," she protested. But he had already pried open that particular door in her mind, and memories began to flow out, erotic images of two bodies locked in love.

"It won't?" he asked in feigned surprise.

It seemed that she had to play it out, regardless of that delicious melting warmth. "Don't play naive, Patrick. If we . . . make love, then we'll be truly married again."

"I see. That would make it tough for you to dump me, is that it?"

His unexpected bluntness brought a quick return of the image of the officer.

"I'm *not* going back to the army," she stated flatly. "And that shoots your theory that I've been using the army as a scapegoat. If all I had against them was what happened to you, I'd be ready to forgive them, wouldn't I? I don't want that kind of life again, Patrick, always moving around, nothing ever permanent."

"Ah, yes, your terrible childhood and all that." He sighed.

She slid off his lap, moving just a short distance away as she glared at him. "You really find all this very amusing, don't you?"

His look defused her anger quickly, evaporating it in the face of those sensual images. "No, I don't find it amusing at the moment."

Stalemate. Silence. The kind of silence that shatters. Who would fire the next salvo? How would it be countered? And how much longer did they have before all the words ran out and became superfluous in any event?

Finally, he gave her a gentle smile. "Okay. I have a proposal to offer. Let's be lovers. No strings attached. After all, we're not kids anymore, and we can surely handle that."

"If a lover is all you want, you could find that anywhere," she replied, instantly regretting her challenge.

"No, I couldn't. First of all, I spent all those years dreaming about one woman...and that's the woman I want."

He paused and gave her that infectious grin that could still transform his face to semiboyishness. "And second, it just wouldn't do for a hero to disgrace himself by committing adultery, would it?"

A very reluctant smile began to tug at her mouth until she just could not resist the upward pull. It was so like him to say something sweet and wonderful, and then follow it with humor. Very gradually, Megan was seeing the old and the new Patrick blending instead of clashing. And her body was

telling her loud and clear that there were some things she
very definitely liked about that mixture.

"All right. Lovers. With no strings attached."

Chapter Ten

Megan's words had come out with astonishing ease, especially when one considered the agony and anxiety that had preceded them. But they did have a faintly mocking sound to them. Lovers? No strings attached? They'd been married for nearly thirteen years and there were strings aplenty.

But they had to play out their roles, it seemed. He was obviously pretending that being lovers would be some sort of intermediate step, and she was pretending that it would make no difference at all. Both of them knew perfectly well that they were lying.

Patrick stood up and drew her to her feet. She found—not at all to her surprise—that her legs were shaky. Panic temporarily drove down that aching need. What if it didn't work? What if they were no longer right for each other? What if she just *couldn't*?

He took her hand and led her to her bedroom, and the room itself disturbed her. He didn't belong in this room of soft corals and peaches. This was her place, not theirs. Maybe they should go to a hotel.

She stopped and he came to stand behind her. Her dress had a long back zipper; it whispered down as she felt his hair-roughened knuckles against her bare skin. There was no belt, so the dress fell to the floor in a slithery heap, a splash of vibrant red against the pale pinkish-beige carpeting.

The air in the room seemed shiveringly cold, and her bare skin was fevered and hypersensitive. When he cupped his hands around the points of her shoulders, she trembled and then tried to hide it by turning at the same time to face him.

His wide mouth quirked with amusement as he stared down at her. "What do you call these things?"

"Teddies," she replied huskily.

"I approve," he said with a nod, continuing for a moment to hold her only by her upper arms.

Then he slid his hands slowly around to her back, leaving a trail of glowing fire in his wake. He fumbled for the clasp or whatever it was that would release the garment, but was confounded instead of rewarded.

"I think I'm out of practice."

It was only then that his own nervousness managed to communicate itself to her. Until this moment, she had been subconsciously comparing this night to their wedding night, when she had been nervous and he had been calm, patient and very self-assured. The sudden knowledge that he, too, was nervous did nothing at all for her peace of mind. What if they truly couldn't?

Megan brought his hands up to remove the shoulder straps and to Patrick's delight the teddy followed the dress to the floor, another splash of color. Then he was staring at her with a stunned expression.

"A garter belt? What happened to panty hose?"

Embarrassment flooded through her. Surely he could find something to talk about besides her lingerie.

"Nothing happened to panty hose. I usually wear them." Her tone was clipped, if a bit husky, and designed specifically to end the discussion right there.

"But tonight you wore this?"

Obviously, he wasn't getting the message. "Yes."

She didn't want her behavior questioned. She didn't want to think about why she had chosen that restaurant, worn his favorite color and then worn sexy lingerie she'd let Karen talk her into buying but had never worn before. Had her subconscious sneaked in to take control when she wasn't watching? She lowered her head quickly but could not quite suppress a nervous giggle.

He hooked a finger beneath her chin and tilted her face up toward his. "Is it just barely possible that you were planning to seduce me?"

There was laughter in his eyes, and she herself was caught somewhere between embarrassment and mirth.

"S-subconsciously."

"A subconscious seduction," he said, nodding with mock solemnity. "I think it's working."

Seconds ticked away as they stood there, his hands resting lightly against the hollows of her waist and her hands curved around his neck. They leaned slowly, hesitantly, into the next moment.

Her fingers were trembling as she unbuttoned his shirt, and the simple act seemed to take forever. But he was content to stand there quietly, his head slightly angled as he watched her. Finally, she undid the last button and tugged the shirt free of his belt to push it off his shoulders.

Then there was another long moment in which they sensed each other's bareness and vulnerability before coming slowly together to give substance to those feelings.

That blending of skin, of silken softness against hair-roughened hardness, ignited the fires. Abandoning their slowness now, they struggled out of their remaining clothing and then stopped again.

They held hands, standing slightly apart, and remembered other nights long ago in other bedrooms. Fantasies began to sharpen into reality, and there was brief resistance to surrendering those fantasies.

But that resistance was merely a token. Patrick scooped her up and laid her gently on the bed, then stretched out beside her. His mouth reached for hers as their hands began to relearn the shape and feel of each other. It was a far more difficult task for Megan, since his body felt so very different. But Patrick was finding everything just as he remembered, including all those secret places that could bring a shudder of sensuous pleasure.

They both tried for slowness and gentleness and tenderness, certain that it should be this way. But the fires inside consumed all those good intentions. They tried to find words to say what they felt and thought, but words became moans and sighs and sounds of encouragement.

And then they achieved that perfect oneness, that wholeness that had been missing for so long.

He filled that place she had been denying for so long, and she surrounded him with a liquid warmth that was even more beautiful than his fantasies. After so many years apart, they clung desperately to that moment, wanting to hold it forever. Then they discovered that even though the union of bodies could not be maintained, love indeed could.

Patrick propped himself above her, trailing his lips lightly over her throat and down to the soft swell of her breasts.

"I love you, Meggie. I think I forgot to mention that before."

She smiled as she laced her fingers through his springy curls, then traced the outline of that very male mouth. "Yes, you did forget to mention that."

There was a pause of one heartbeat before she whispered huskily, "I love you, too, Patrick."

He kissed the fingertips that continued to toy with his mouth. "And you accept me as I am now."

It was a statement and not a question, so it required no response. That was just as well, because Megan felt a slight chill, a tiny withdrawal, at those words. He might have meant that she accepted the changes in him, and if so, he was right. But if he meant that she accepted his decision . . .

"Even so," he continued with a grin, "I think I might find it necessary to go on proving that to myself. After I get some rest, that is. That's one unfortunate difference between being twenty-two and thirty-five that I hadn't thought about.''

The night became a long, slowly unfolding dream. They slept curled against each other, more amused than disturbed at the strangeness of it after so many years. In the middle of the night—neither of them could recall who had awakened first, although the distinction quickly became immaterial—they lost themselves in love again. Then, in the half-light of early dawn, they began again, exploring each other languorously and thoroughly, taking more time, moving deeper still into intimacy. Past and present had merged and the future was held at bay.

The ringing of the telephone was a shrill, deafening summons to a day neither of them was yet prepared to face. They both stirred, immediately becoming aware of each other, of certain pains and soreness, of the lingering aura of lovemaking in the disheveled bed.

Patrick sat up and frowned at the insistent phone, and Megan turned her head to peer through barely focused eyes at her clock radio.

"It's the general," she said, making no move to pick it up.

"Aren't you going to answer?"

"I thought I'd see just how persistent he is."

Patrick threw her a lazily amused look and reached across her to lift the receiver. She put out a hand to stop him, but she was too late. The cord slithered across her bare skin as he brought the receiver to his mouth.

"Hello?"

A few inches away, Megan nodded with a disgusted sound as she heard the familiar voice boom out of the receiver.

"Yes, she's here, sir." Then a pause, during which Megan wondered just where he'd thought she would be; this was her home. "No, everything's fine." Another pause. Megan decided that he, like Patrick, had probably expected her to bolt. "Do you want to talk to her?" A longer pause, during which Megan made a face and shook her head. "Right. We'll see you then. Goodbye."

She took the receiver as though it were some sort of loathsome insect and dropped it back into its cradle. "I wonder if he knows just how predictable he is."

"He's concerned about you," Patrick said, but with no hint of reproof.

"As well he should be," she replied smugly. "For the first time, he's beginning to see his little girl as a woman."

"Well, if he isn't, I'll be glad to verify it for him." Patrick smiled as he began to trace the outlines of the very womanly curves beside him. "I think he might have been a little surprised to find me here."

"I doubt that," she responded dryly. "I'm sure that top-secret information must have been passed along from West Germany by now."

"Well, then, maybe he was surprised to find that I'm *still* here," Patrick added.

She smiled the smile of a very satisfied woman and reached out to run her fingers across his chest, down over his stomach, and down still farther. "You're very definitely still here, if slightly the worse for wear."

He lay back with a groan as she continued to torment him. "I think I should get some breakfast," he said huskily.

"You have your priorities and I have mine," she teased as she increased her efforts.

"WE HAVEN'T REALLY resolved anything yet, you know." Megan cast a sideways glance at him as they strolled casually around the deserted estate. Everything was soft green, except for the darker evergreens and the splashes of color where the gardeners had set out tulips and daffodils. She was torn between wanting to maintain this idyllic weekend and an ever-present knowledge that their problems would still await them at its end. But it was a measure of her current happiness that she was almost able to believe those problems could be resolved. She smiled sadly to herself as she thought that perhaps they had managed to recapture at least that aspect of their youth.

"I know that," Patrick acknowledged, squeezing her hand gently and sounding as if her comment were unimportant. "But we don't have to resolve everything in one weekend."

She knew that was probably true. But it was also true that the longer they permitted themselves to ignore it, the worse it would be in the end. She said nothing.

"Are you really so sure that we have anything to resolve?"

She stopped and stared at him. "Patrick, in spite of... what's happened, I still refuse to have anything to do with the army, except for the award ceremony, of course." And she was thinking that perhaps even that was a mistake. From such small exceptions grew ever-larger exceptions.

He leaned toward her and kissed the tip of her nose. "You're still the same: outspoken and eager to get on with it. And I guess that I'm just as lazy and content to take things as they come."

"You're not lazy, just easygoing," she stated firmly. "There's a big difference. And I'm not so sure you're that way anymore. If you were, you'd take one of those cushy jobs in a defense industry that we were talking about."

"You never wanted me to take something like that."

She sighed. "No, I didn't. But that's beside the point."

"Maybe that is the point. I really have only two options, Meggie. It's either the army or one of those jobs. I've lost the twelve most important years in a man's career."

"That may be true, but that's not why you're staying in the army," she pointed out. "You're staying because that's where you belong; you said so yourself. And that means only one thing, that you've become army." The final word came out as an ugly epithet.

"Meggie," he pleaded, "can't we leave the army out of this?"

"How can we, when it's going to dominate the rest of your life?" She refused to say "the rest of our lives."

"No, it isn't. And that's the last I intend to say on the subject."

She gave him a triumphant look. "See? That's just what I meant . . . that this-is-an-order tone of voice."

"And you, of course, never use such a tone," he replied dryly.

She started to walk away. "You're right," she said. "We'd better not talk about it. It's been a beautiful day up to now."

And it had been. She'd shown Patrick around the area, extolling its many virtues as if she had some chance of convincing him to change his mind. She knew he'd been impressed and her hopes had raised just a bit higher. Then they'd returned to the cottage with sandwiches from her favorite gourmet deli, and after a lazy, lovely sojourn in bed, had come out to stroll around the grounds.

Each time they made love and she felt the driving force of his need for her, Megan grew more and more confident that she could change his mind. Only now, when they tried to talk about it, did that confidence waver. She knew she shouldn't be kidding herself about her chances, but she did it anyway. Surely he could see as well as she could the specialness of their love, a love reclaimed after twelve years. Surely he wouldn't give that up. Or did he still believe that, aided and abetted by her parents and probably by Joel, too, he could bring her back into the fold?

He was silent all the way back to the cottage, and she hoped that he might be reconsidering his decision. There must be other options for him. Just because she couldn't think of any at the moment didn't mean they didn't exist.

She could easily support them both while he went to graduate school.

But when she turned at the front door of the cottage to look back at him, her hopes faded again. Without that lazy grin he was back to being Major O'Donnell. She could see those damned oak leaves hovering over his broad shoulders and with no effort at all could imagine them being replaced one day by stars.

He must have seen the look on her face, because the smile was suddenly back as he kissed her and gave her a gentle shove toward the bedroom. "Better get packed. The limo will be here in less than an hour."

She balked, frowning. "What packing? What limo?"

"The one I ordered to take us into Manhattan."

"Patrick, I'm not doing anything until you explain yourself." She tried to sound ferocious, but she was already smiling. He'd always loved to surprise her, although he'd rarely gotten away with it because she was nosy by nature—the kind of person who, as a child, had searched the entire house for her Christmas gifts.

"We have a suite at the Plaza awaiting us, and dinner reservations at Windows on the World. Have you been there?"

She shook her head and tried halfheartedly to act annoyed. "Why didn't you tell me about this?"

"Because," he said wickedly, "I had no intention of spending all that money if it wasn't going to be on a second honeymoon."

She dissolved into laughter. "You certainly didn't allow yourself much time for a seduction."

"I didn't really expect to need much," he replied smugly.

An hour later they were leaving Connecticut behind, comfortably ensconced in a long gray limo that was purring its way through the perpetually heavy traffic of I-95, headed south. Megan looked at the limo's glove-soft leather and rich, polished woods and laughed softly.

"I don't believe you...a Rolls, no less. I thought you were planning to spend that back pay on a Porsche."

"Oh, I could still manage that, but I probably won't."

"Why not?" she asked. "You've always wanted one." He certainly couldn't think that he needed to worry about supporting her.

"I still do, but it wouldn't be politic to buy one."

Her gay mood evaporated abruptly. "Damn it, Patrick, do you mean to tell me that you're going to let them dictate what kind of car you should buy?"

"But it just wouldn't be right, honey. It's important to keep the domestic auto industry strong, even from a military standpoint."

She rolled her eyes disgustedly. "Shades of the general again. You sound just the way he sounded when I bought my Subaru. He actually offered to buy me anything I wanted—as long as it was domestic."

Then she waved her hand angrily. "Forget it. I'm sorry that I brought up the subject. I guess I should be grateful that you were willing to rent a Rolls, since I've always wanted to ride in one."

But there was just no way that she could forget it. It might indeed be a minor matter, but the implications were far wider. The army would not only tell him what kind of car he could buy, but also where he could live and for how long, and even where he could travel when he was on leave. She'd seen much of the world, but what she remembered most now were all the places she couldn't go to because of her father's position.

Nevertheless, as they walked up the steps and into the elegant lobby of the Plaza, Megan resolved to forget the army for this evening. She was touched by Patrick's extravagance, chiefly because she knew it was solely to please her. She was also still mindful of that other time—on their first date—when he had done something like this and she had been far from properly appreciative.

Their suite was beautiful and filled with luxurious bouquets sent by the hotel's management, along with a magnum of fine champagne. Patrick seemed rather embarrassed by all the attention, while Megan was quietly amused by his reaction. However, her amusement was short-lived.

"We have reservations for six in about an hour and a half."

"For six?"

He nodded, trying without much success to be casual about it. "My parents and your parents are joining us."

"The general is coming? Oh, Patrick!" There went her evening without the army. "Was that the general's idea?"

"It was my idea, Meggie," he said quietly.

He looked very upset and she promptly felt guilty. "I'm sorry. It *is* a lovely idea, as long as he isn't too obnoxious. But I doubt that he'd risk a scene in public. Are they staying here?"

"Yes. I'll see if they've checked in yet." Patrick went to the phone, obviously relieved.

She watched him with a mixture of exasperation and tenderness. How like him to plan such an evening. His strong sense of family was one of the qualities she had always loved in him. He was an only child and very close to his parents, who were equally devoted to him. It was a closeness that Megan had never achieved with her own parents. Her father had always been busy forging a path to the stars, and her mother had been equally busy promoting the same thing. Family outings had been rare and had always seemed to Megan to be somehow staged, as though her father had penciled them into his busy schedule along with his interminable meetings and inspection tours. And because of their incessant traveling, they had all but lost touch with other family members. Patrick, by contrast, had a whole slew of cousins, aunts and uncles to whom he was very close.

She knew that a repetition of her own life lay ahead for them and their children if Patrick remained in the army. He would deny it, of course, but it would happen anyway. Although Patrick could not be accused of having the driving ambition her father had, he had a quiet determination that she knew would produce the same result—neglect of his family.

But for his sake, because she knew that his motives had been good, she would put the best possible face on this evening. Patrick's wonderful, homey parents could be counted on to lighten the atmosphere, thank heavens. Megan was going to have great difficulty making pleasant conversation with the general at this point, and she knew that her mother would be nervously awaiting an explosion between her husband and her daughter.

Patrick was ready before she was and left the bedroom of the suite as she completed her preparations. A few moments later she heard her father's voice in the sitting room. Why did he always sound as if he were out reviewing the troops? He wasn't loud but he did make his presence felt. The only good thing she could say about him was that he was discreet enough not to wear his uniform on such social occasions. Not that it made much difference, of course.

She had once said to Karen, by way of describing her father, that if one were casting a film part for a general, there could be no one more perfect for the role than Mark Daniels. Joel was a younger version of the same model, and now even Patrick fit that mold. It was enough to make one think that senior officers were being cloned somewhere. Or, more likely, it was a perfect example of what a uniform did to a man. The process had just taken a little longer—and had been infinitely more painful—for Patrick. With a resigned sigh, she went out to greet their guests.

What happened next was something that would forever remain etched in her memory.

The general, who was seated next to her mother on the brocaded sofa, got up and came toward her. Megan stopped and had to restrain herself from taking a backward step. It was a foolish overreaction. Her father, for all his sternness, was certainly not a violent man. But then, neither had he ever been an affectionate one.

His arms came around her with the slight awkwardness of lack of practice and she felt his mouth brush lightly against her hair. Then he disengaged himself with that same clumsiness and looked down at her solemnly.

"Meggie, I . . . I'm sorry if I've upset you. You know I didn't mean to do that."

She stared at him, utterly speechless. Was this some stranger masquerading as her father? Had the enemy sent in a double who didn't quite know his role? Even his voice sounded different. It took a few seconds for her to realize that the words sounded carefully rehearsed. She could manage nothing more than a nod, and then suddenly her mother was kissing her and chattering away and Patrick was pressing a glass of champagne into her hand.

So she sipped the champagne and waited for a return to normalcy as she let the conversation go on around her. The general was himself again and Megan was half inclined to think she must have imagined the whole scene. Her mother was talking about what they should wear to the White House ceremony and Megan was nodding, even though she barely heard any of it. Not even the White House could take precedence over her confused thoughts at the moment.

She was still mostly silent when they departed for the restaurant, once again in the Rolls. Since the restaurant was in lower Manhattan and Patrick's parents lived in Brooklyn, they would all be meeting downtown. She finally fought her way out of her mental fog as they entered the cavernous lobby of the World Trade Center to find Patrick's parents awaiting them.

With the incomparable skyline of Manhattan twinkling around them, the group ate and conversed gaily. The general was relaxed and charming, as Megan knew he could be, and he treated Patrick more like a son than a son-in-law whom he'd actually known for only a short time. Patrick's wry, easygoing father was one of those rare men who is not awed by anyone or anything, and his mother's slight edginess was easily dissipated by Megan's very polished mother.

Megan herself initiated little conversation, but she didn't withdraw from it, either. Nevertheless, a part of her continued to work out possible reasons for her father's unusual behavior. From time to time, she would find herself staring at him, as if the answers were written on that ruggedly handsome face. Once, when he caught her at it, he actually smiled. She was immediately flustered and quickly looked away again. Uncharitably, she wondered if he had practiced that smile, too, just as he surely must have practiced that little speech.

If there was one thing she was not about to do, it was to take all that at face value. Somewhere there had to be a reason, and it came to her far later than it should have.

She knew from Patrick's statements that he and her father had been spending quite a lot of time together this past week, and it finally dawned on her that Patrick must have convinced the general that she was really serious about her feelings toward the army. Since he knew by now that he couldn't order her back, he was just switching tactics. First the apology, then some gentle persuasion, though she found it difficult to believe him capable of that. Maybe he'd turn that part of it over to Joel when he came home and, of course, enlist the aid of her mother.

Furthermore, although she didn't doubt that he truly did want to see her and Patrick together again, there was more at stake than that. What would his cronies at the Pentagon think if he couldn't deliver his own daughter? She knew that bunch all too well.

Damn him, she thought. He had come very close to fooling her with that hug and those so-sincere words. But all he wanted was to guarantee that she came back where he felt she belonged.

Having satisfied herself as to the cause of his strange behavior, Megan relaxed and let herself enjoy the rest of the dinner. But way down deep inside there was a small hurt. Just for once, it would have been nice to know that the general had put something else ahead of the almighty army.

When she, in effect, rejoined the group, she realized quickly that everyone present seemed to be assuming that she and Patrick had put any problems behind them. It was interesting, however, that very little was being said about the future. Two sets of parents beamed happily at their children, apparently with every confidence that things had worked out and would continue to do so.

One of New York's senators was among the restaurant's other guests, and he came to their table to extend his congratulations to Patrick. Megan smiled as, for the first time in her memory, her father took a back seat to someone else.

As word about them passed among the other patrons, they became the center of attention. Patrick continued to act slightly discomfited by all this, but that did not prevent him from lavishing his attention on her. Although he'd always been affectionate toward her in private, he'd generally been more circumspect in public. She didn't know whether the change was due to his nervousness about the attention they were receiving, or was the result of his obvious happiness over the changed status of their relationship. It didn't really matter, though, because in spite of her father's little performance, Megan was happy. She would worry about tomorrow when it came.

Back at the hotel, her parents joined them for a nightcap, and then the general gave an abbreviated repetition of his earlier performance by kissing her good-night. At least she was a little better prepared this time and even responded with a hug of her own that felt as strange as his had.

As soon as her parents had departed to their own suite, Megan made a disgusted sound and twisted her mouth wryly. "Well, he was certainly in top form tonight, wasn't he?"

Patrick tried to look surprised. "I don't know what you see that I don't see, but I thought he was the same as always."

"Including those hugs and kisses and that little speech earlier?" she scoffed. "I can't remember when he's ever hugged or kissed me. Maybe he never has. And apologizing, no less."

"I think that what he was apologizing for was the length of time it has taken him to realize that you've grown up," Patrick said soothingly as he reached for the zipper tab at the back of her dress. She didn't try to stop him, but she couldn't let go of the subject, either.

"He just wants to see me back in the army, that's all."

"Could we forget about the general for a while, hmm?" Patrick ran the zipper down and eased the dress off her shoulders. "I have something else to discuss with you."

"You do?" she asked, not certain whether or not he was serious.

It soon became clear that he was very serious, but that it was going to be a mostly nonverbal discussion. He seized her hand and pressed it against himself. It was a measure of their newfound intimacy that she could accept such gestures without embarrassment. Perhaps there were some advantages to growing older, she thought with a smile as she reacted to that straining hardness with a warm rush.

"It's a very serious matter."

"I can see that it is, but I'm sure that we've had this discussion many times already."

"Not nearly enough times, though," he murmured as he picked her up and started toward the bedroom. "Just think about it. Twelve years. Even at only two or three times a week, that comes to..." He paused as though figuring, then set her down on the bed. "More than I'm capable of, I guess, but I'll do my best."

"I'm sure you will," she said with a laugh, reaching for him.

They lay there for a long time, just holding each other, still half-clothed. Megan had stopped thinking of this big, hard man as an alien body enclosing Patrick, and she had given up any remaining inhibitions. She enjoyed touching him and teasing him and learning more and more about what pleased him most.

Passion built slowly this time but burned just as brightly in the end. By the time Patrick had stripped off her remaining clothes, stroking her and kissing every exposed inch along the way, Megan was eager and wanting.

As soon as she was naked, she raised herself up on her knees and began to pull at his shirt, ignoring his laughing statement that she was going to destroy his new clothes. Then, when his long, very male body lay totally exposed to her, he lifted her onto himself and she took him into that reawakened female core with a strangled moan.

Later, as she waited for sleep with Patrick's slow, deep breaths against her hair, Megan thought about the differences in their lovemaking. Perhaps it was no more than a result of the long years of separation and all those unmet needs, but there was an intensity, a deepening of the passion between them. They were, somehow, both far more aware of each other and yet surprisingly more at ease with each other now.

The best difference, though, was not in their lovemaking itself, but in its foreplay and aftermath. In their younger years, passions had burned explosively, allowing little time for tenderness before and somehow flaming out quickly afterward. Now there was time for all the tenderness and slow warmth and words that would not be spoken at other times.

As she slipped down into sleep, Megan knew that the wait had been worth it and that she would never find this again. For her, love had come early and then, in a miraculous twist of fate, had circled round and come back again.

Chapter Eleven

Megan squinted into the bright Washington sunlight and wished that she'd had the foresight to bring her sunglasses. They had all been standing here, milling around, for close to half an hour now, awaiting the president. The famed Rose Garden did not yet have any roses, but it was resplendent with spring flowers whose delicacy contrasted sharply with all the uniforms and somber, dark suits of the civilians.

She was wearing a bright red linen suit, newly purchased for the occasion. The matching shoes had heels much higher than those she usually wore, and her feet were already suffering. But at least the higher heels gave her enough additional height so that she didn't look like a dwarf next to her tall husband.

At the moment, Patrick was the center of a group of officers that included Megan's father and the army chief of staff. She was trying hard to focus on Patrick and not notice all those other uniforms.

The whole ceremony was making her increasingly nervous, and it had little or nothing to do with the setting. This event was army all the way. The civilians present seemed unimportant, even if their ranks did include the secretary of defense and various members of Congress.

She noted that, as usual, the civilians seemed to be talking just a little too loudly or behaving just a little too self-importantly. It was always that way when they were confronted with too many men in uniform. No doubt they were also standing far more erect than was usual for them. Megan had noticed this behavior long ago, but now, after seven years as a civilian herself, she could sympathize with them. How did civilian men really regard the military, she wondered as she watched them. As a necessary evil? As something akin to the warrior kings of old? As a threat to their own manhood? She suspected that it might be a bit of all three. If it was true that women were attracted to uniforms, it was also true that men were uncomfortable around them, with an awed, respectful sort of discomfort.

There were only three other women present: Megan's mother, Patrick's mother and Patrick's favorite aunt. Megan was standing with them at the moment, temporarily ignoring the conversation that her mother kept flowing smoothly. They were all unimportant, Megan thought disgustedly, herself included. One could almost believe that they had been permitted to join this all-male occasion solely to provide some color amid uniforms and dark suits.

She shot Patrick another glance and felt ashamed of her attitude. This was his day and she was determined that none of her petty grievances would mar it. The army was laying it on for him, and regardless of what she thought of the army, she loved the tall major who was the center of attention.

Despite his busy schedule, Patrick had flown up to Connecticut at midweek, and in a flurry of unaccustomed domesticity, she'd prepared a superb dinner for them. He'd been highly complimentary, although they both knew that a good meal hadn't exactly been his chief reason for coming all that distance.

Megan's hand went to the gold band on her ring finger. It still felt strange, almost constricting. It also felt false. She shouldn't have started to wear it again, even though Patrick had been happy and, she thought, relieved to see it. She had the uncomfortable feeling that she was moving, or being moved, by small increments back to that existence she hated.

Furthermore, Patrick continued to refuse to discuss his future. Each time she tried to bring up the subject, he had deftly changed it. Of course, it wasn't exactly to her credit that she didn't exhibit her usual self-assertiveness by insisting that they discuss it. They were still temporizing, behaving, she thought, like the kids they both insisted they weren't.

A second wave of mild panic overtook her then. The first had come when they alighted from the car that had brought them here and she saw all those other uniforms. Between the other officers and the marine guard at the White House, the place was filled with them. Her aching feet wanted to pick themselves up right now and run out of this place. She had a sudden absurd image of herself fleeing down the driveway, pursued by the marine guards.

A hand curved lightly against her waist and she looked up into Patrick's blue eyes.

"Did I tell you how beautiful you look today?" he asked softly as he drew her slightly apart from the others.

Megan was conscious of all eyes on them and she wondered if Patrick's appearance just then had been more than a coincidence. Had he guessed what she was thinking? It wasn't so farfetched, actually, given her feelings about the army.

"Yes, you did. Several times, as a matter of fact." She smiled at him. Despite his very military demeanor, he was nervous. She could hear it in his voice, a slight change of timbre that she was sure he didn't permit the others to hear. That tiny crack in the army officer image made him all the more real—and dear—to her.

"I'd like to get this over with," he confided in a low tone. "I'm worried about Carson."

Megan followed his glance to the small, nervous man some distance away. Another wave of love washed over her.

This was Patrick's day, but he was obviously thinking of the welfare of others.

"I'm rather surprised that he was allowed to come," she said as she watched the corporal, who was one of the other returnees.

"He wanted to be here, especially when he found out that Jackson was coming. The doctors assured us that he'd be all right, but this waiting is making him nervous."

"Was he like that over there?" she asked, thinking again about all the things Patrick hadn't told her and probably never would.

She watched Sergeant Jackson, the other returnee, hovering protectively near the nervous corporal. She'd spoken to both men earlier, and although they, too, had avoided saying anything specific, Megan had been touched by their respect for Patrick.

"Sometimes he was worse than this," Patrick answered somberly. "At times, he was completely irrational, especially toward the end. I just hope he can be helped."

"Was the decision for him to be here yours to make?"

Patrick nodded. "When the doctors told me he could handle it, I said that I wanted him to be here. We were all in that hell together, Meggie. The medal is as much his and Jackson's as it is mine. In a sense, you could say that he deserves it even more because he's paid a far higher price."

The words of a good man and a good officer, Megan thought, as a gnawing pain grew inside her. How could she even think of ending it? She loved this man so much that it was almost embarrassing. And she admitted for the first time, difficult though it was, that the qualities she loved most in him were the very qualities that made him belong to the army.

There was a sudden stirring along the fringes of the small crowd, and then she saw the tall, familiar figure of the president approaching, surrounded by his own small crowd. At her side, Patrick became very still and even more erect.

Megan would remember the next half hour in snatches, photographic images burned forever into her brain. Their introduction to the president and first lady. The bright sun reflecting off the oak leaves on Patrick's shoulders. The medal itself, much larger and more somber than the other decorations on his chest. Corporal Carson, struggling valiantly to control himself as he met the president. The soft-spoken Sergeant Jackson, whose eyes never strayed far from Carson and whose steadying hand was on the corporal's shoulder when he seemed particularly distraught. Both men telling her again that Patrick was the finest man they'd ever known. A moment when a general and two majors stood together—her father, her brother and her husband. The incessant whir and click of photographic equipment. And the president's words, of course, the recounting of Patrick's heroism as Patrick himself stood erect and still, betraying no emotion. The perfect soldier.

Then, finally, it was over and they were back in the car, headed to her parents' house for a reception. Patrick sank gratefully into a corner of the seat with a relieved sigh. She reached over to touch the medal and examine it more closely.

"It doesn't seem like much, really, in exchange for twelve years of your life." Her voice was choked and the medal was dissolving beyond a veil of tears.

He wrapped an arm about her. "It's enough, Meggie."

You were just doing your duty, she thought, knowing that that was exactly what he meant. Would she ever understand what it was that drove such men? After a lifetime surrounded by them, she was no closer to the answer than she'd ever been.

They were swept up in the gaiety of the reception from the moment of their arrival. People drifted through the spacious house and out onto the large terrace. Food and drink flowed freely, all of it carefully but effortlessly orchestrated by her mother, who still managed to be as relaxed and gracious as always. A lifetime of managing such events guaranteed that.

Nearly all the men present were in uniform, and Megan noted that all the women were turned out with impeccable conservatism. No décolletage, no outrageous fashions. Just classic suits or quiet linen dresses. She didn't think she could have withstood looking in the mirror just now, because she knew she would have seen that same image reflected back at her.

A sense of déjà vu engulfed her and she very nearly cried out in protest. Connecticut was receding into the past, or perhaps it had never really existed. Maybe she'd always been here, playing this role, living out her life in good army tradition, a carbon copy of her mother.

Across the terrace, Patrick was surrounded by a group of senior officers, friends of her father's. There were stars on every set of shoulders but his, and she could easily imagine them there, too. He'd definitely make it to three, and probably to four if he drove himself hard enough and gave up enough. He'd live in a house like this, entertain like this. She turned away, unable to let go of the image, but unwilling to watch that scene any longer.

"Meggie, can we get out of this for a few minutes?" A hand gripped her elbow and began to steer her toward the house.

She didn't protest because she'd seen very little of Joel since his arrival. He led her off to their father's small study.

"I'm so glad you could come home," she said as she hugged her big brother.

"In two months I'll be home for good," he said with a grin.

"You will? You mean to Washington?"

He nodded. "I'm going to be an aide to General Waltham."

Megan knew what that meant—the Pentagon inner circle. In short order, his oak leaves would be replaced by the silver ones of a lieutenant colonel.

"Congratulations, JoJo," she said as she kissed him, using his old pet name to remind him that she didn't care what he was to the army. To her, he was still her big brother. "Dad must be happy."

"He is, although he's probably telling Waltham to be tough as hell on me." He grinned again, then quickly grew serious. "Dad's worried about you, Megan."

She said nothing, but her happiness drained away. She didn't want to spoil this brief time they had together with talk about the general.

"You aren't going to leave Patrick, are you?"

She knew that it needed to be said. The time for equivocating had passed. "Yes. I have no choice."

"You can't. Dammit, you love him and he loves you."

Megan had turned away from Joel and was standing near a window that looked out onto the terrace. Patrick was still there, with the same group of officers.

"I can't come back to the army, either, Joel. When I married Patrick, I never expected him to make it his career. And he knew exactly how I felt when he made his decision."

She paused and drew a shuddering breath as she turned away from the window. "He belongs to the army now. He didn't before, but he does now."

"Megan," Joel said gently, "he always did. Those of us who knew him at West Point knew he'd stay."

"Don't be ridiculous, Joel," she scoffed. "He was the class clown. He was always in trouble with the brass."

Joel heaved a sigh. "Megan, it's hard to explain. You're right, he was always getting himself into trouble of one sort or another. And he was always poking fun at everything. But the brass tolerated it for the same reason the rest of us liked him. He was a safety valve. Whenever a situation got too tense or morale started to drop, you could always count on Patrick to come up with something. And I think he did it consciously, knowing it was needed. Just as he also knew when to be serious. Dad told me once that there's no finer quality an officer can have than to be able to read the minds and hearts of his men.

"You heard Jackson and Carson talking about him. He was just the same over there; easing tensions, building morale and at the same time maintaining the military discipline that kept them functioning and made them remember that they were soldiers."

Megan heard all this with a sinking sensation, because she knew Joel was right. But still she had to protest.

"But he was always saying that he hated all that nonsense. He was still that way when he shipped out to Vietnam."

Joel shrugged. "So he did and still does hate some of it. I do, too. Even Dad has been known to complain occasionally. Most people hate some parts of their jobs, Megan."

"You make me feel as though I never really knew him," she said in a small, choked voice.

"Maybe you didn't," Joel acknowledged quietly. "But you have a chance to make up for that now."

He was watching her with that same grave expression on his face that their father so often wore. Suddenly, she exploded.

"Dammit, Joel, stop looking at me like that. You get more like the general every day."

He smiled. "I could do worse."

"You could do better, too," she snapped, feeling as though she'd lost a lifelong ally. There was a time when Joel had joined her in making jokes about their father.

She had been set adrift, cut off. Her father. Joel. Patrick. None of them was hers, or had ever been hers. She turned back to the window, unwilling to let him see her tears.

"I feel as though I've never known any of you and I never will. You give the army everything, and there's nothing left for anyone else. It isn't just a job."

"No, it isn't," he agreed.

"I won't live the way our mother has and I won't let my children live the way we did . . . dragged all over the world, hardly ever seeing our father, not knowing anyone who wasn't army. I won't give up my own life to follow his."

There was no reply, and she finally turned around to see if he could possibly understand any of this. But instead of one major, she saw two.

Both men were staring at her gravely, with expressions that mixed concern and, she thought, a lack of understanding. Worst of all was the fact that they weren't being deliberately obtuse. They just didn't understand and never would. They'd both long since accepted the demands of their jobs and couldn't understand why anyone should question it. She stared at the two of them, resplendent in their uniforms—the brother and best friend of her childhood and the husband and best friend of her young adulthood. They were two men she loved dearly, and neither of them understood, or would ever understand, the impossible demands they made on that love.

Then some loud laughter from the terrace made her remember the occasion for which they were gathered. She had promised to make this day good for Patrick. But she couldn't bring herself to apologize for speaking the truth. So she moved toward the door, giving them a helpless gesture and a shrug.

"Well, I know when I've been outnumbered, not to mention outranked. So I'll just retreat to play the good officer's wife." She walked out, leaving them to stare helplessly after her.

The problem was that she, too, felt helpless, helpless in her need to explain herself to them. They didn't understand and she lacked the means to make them understand. Worst

of all, they were the two finest men she'd ever known, and
the qualities that she admired most were the very qualities
that she was complaining about. It made no sense. When
she began to think about Patrick's explanation for her
hatred of the army, she knew it was time to rejoin the party.

Patrick and Joel didn't reappear for some time, and when
they did, neither of them made any attempt to approach her.
But whenever her eyes turned in Patrick's direction, she invariably found him watching her.

Time dragged on for Megan until a late arrival caught her
attention. The couple in question were a West Point classmate of Patrick's and his wife. They had been friends at the
academy and had been married at the academy chapel on
the same day. He had long since resigned his commission
and was an executive with a California bank. Megan hadn't
seen them in years, and Patrick, of course, hadn't seen them
since his departure for Vietnam.

She and Patrick converged on the couple and they were
soon mixing reminiscences and news. But when Patrick and
the other man began a discussion of the current state of the
military, the man's wife drew Megan aside.

Megan had learned long ago that when West Pointers left
the military they still always kept up on the news, as though
they just couldn't quite let go.

After some sympathetic questions concerning the shock
Megan must have received, her old friend smiled at her.

"You must be happy that he's decided to stay in the
army."

Megan gave her a surprised look, then realized that the
woman had every reason to think that since Megan was an
army brat. "Actually, no. I'd hoped he'd resign."

"Really?" The woman seemed shocked. "Well, when we
heard about it, I was sure that he would. But Dick said that
he thought Patrick would stay in." She gave her husband a
brief glance, then smiled sadly at Megan.

"I really wish that I hadn't nagged at Dick to resign. I don't think he's been truly happy since. We're certainly much better off financially and he likes his work well enough, but..." She trailed off with a shrug.

In spite of herself, Megan nodded. If she succeeded in persuading Patrick to resign, she, too, might one day be saying that, trying ineffectually to express what it was that was missing from his life and knowing that she was responsible for that loss.

She was still thinking about that as the party gradually drew to a close. Every career officer, and particularly those from the service academies, knew he could do better in civilian life—more money, more regular hours, a choice of where to live. And yet so many—like her father, Joel and Patrick—chose to stay.

She was sick to death of "duty, honor, country," the code on which she had been raised. It was nobility itself, except to those forced to live within its bounds.

What, she asked herself rhetorically, *is so wrong with wanting something for oneself? And what is wrong with wanting a very different sort of life for one's children?*

Nothing is wrong with that, she answered herself. *Except that you can't have that and Patrick, too.*

As she thought about this, while her mother was serving coffee to them, the conversation centered on Joel's imminent return to Washington. She and Joel exchanged knowing winks when their mother began to make plans to introduce Joel into the Pentagon social whirl. Megan didn't doubt for one minute that her mother was already sorting through prospective mates for Joel, who had thus far eluded matrimony. She hoped that Joel found himself a more appropriate wife than Patrick had.

Then they were at the door, taking their leave. They were staying at The Four Seasons, in Georgetown, since Patrick had known without asking that Megan did not want to stay at Fort Meade.

"Are you coming for breakfast before you take off?" Joel asked them.

Megan shot Patrick a questioning look and got a sheepish grin in return. "Uh, yes, if it's going to be fairly early," Patrick said.

There was an awkward moment of silence as Joel and Patrick exchanged glances, and then Patrick chuckled. "I guess I forgot to tell you that it was supposed to be a surprise."

"What's supposed to be a surprise?" Megan asked. The looks she received from the others told her that they were all in on it.

"General Stanton has lent us his sailboat. It's over at the Eastern Shore and I thought we'd cruise the waterway and the Chesapeake for a few days."

Megan felt an enormous tug at her heartstrings, accompanied by a veritable flood of memories. Her happiest days with Patrick had been the week they had sailed off Hawaii, just before he left for Vietnam. Even years later, after she had forgotten so much, those days and nights had remained crystal clear, surrounded by love and laughter and made even more precious by what had come after.

"It's a beautiful boat, Megan. You remember it, don't you?" her father said. He was smiling again, and it still looked strange.

"Yes, of course I remember it." And she did. It was a beautifully maintained old boat, wood-hulled and brass-fitted. "You'll love it, Patrick," she said. "It's something of an antique, as sailboats go."

"It's been recently refurbished," her father put in. "In fact, Jack says he could have bought a new one for the cost of redoing it."

Patrick began to ask her father questions about the boat, and Megan stood there silently. This had all the indications of a conspiracy. It was a safe bet that Patrick hadn't asked General Stanton, one of her father's closest friends, for the use of his beloved boat. And her father knew how very much she had always liked it. She'd even put up with General Stanton's obnoxious son a few times just for the opportunity to sail on it.

But even if this was a conspiracy, she could not become angry over it. It was a wonderful surprise. Long, lazy days gliding over the water sounded very appealing just now.

Then, as they were on their way to the hotel, she suddenly remembered her work and was shocked to think that she had quite forgotten about Touch of Paradise in her enthusiasm over the trip.

"Patrick, I really don't see how I can run off like this, with business booming at Touch of Paradise."

He grinned at her. "Not to worry. We have Karen's blessing. I called her the other day and she's going to bring in that retired woman who helps out. She said I should wrap you in chains and throw you on board forcibly if I had to."

Megan relaxed and was surprised at how easily she could do that. Perhaps, as Karen had often remarked, she did take her work too seriously. But that had been because there was nothing else to take seriously at all, until now, that is.

That thought lingered only as long as it took her to realize that she sounded exactly the way her parents—and Patrick, too, no doubt—wanted her to sound. Nothing else was important. The business she had worked so hard to make successful was secondary.

But somehow she found it very difficult, if not downright impossible, to work up her usual anger over that. The most she could summon up was a vague uneasiness.

They swept into The Four Seasons to the same effusive welcome they had received at the Plaza the weekend before. There was another elegant suite, more flowers and a smiling staff. Megan wandered around their rooms and sighed happily when she saw the oversized bathtub. A long, luxurious sojourn there seemed to her to be the perfect antidote to a party that had been more of a strain than a pleasure. So she announced her intention to Patrick, then left him in the sitting room of the suite.

As soon as he heard the bathroom door close behind her, Patrick went into the bedroom, shucking his uniform jacket as he went. When he hung it up in the closet, he stared at the medal for a moment. Then a grin spread slowly over his face and he shook his head with a low chuckle.

Who would have guessed it? No one who had ever known Patrick O'Donnell would have figured him for hero material. He didn't like to fight, he hated guns and he was all too often inclined to take the easy way out.

Yet here he was, a certified medal-wearing hero and a major in the U.S. army, and generals were already looking at him in that speculative way that Joel called "star measurement": one, two or possibly even four.

He tore his gaze from the medal and let it rest on the closed bathroom door. And in there was someone who was undoubtedly taking her own measurements and might well have reached the same conclusions. He recalled her statement about Joel's being on the fast track to the coveted stars. She knew the game, all right. No way was he going to be able to fool her into believing that he could spend the rest of his career languishing somewhere, then get out in another seven years with a generous pension.

Her silences troubled him because he had absolutely no idea what was going on in her head. He never had, if the truth be known. Megan's moods were mercurial, her thought processes incomprehensible to anyone but her. Maybe if they'd spent the past twelve years together, he'd have figured her out by now, though he somehow doubted that. As it was, all he could do was wait for her to reveal herself in some way and take it from there.

All week long he'd had the uneasy feeling that as soon as the ceremony was over she would declare their marriage to be at an end. He knew she loved him, but that would not prevent her from declaring that she didn't intend to be his wife any longer. She'd lived without love for twelve years, and he suspected that she just might be capable of managing it indefinitely, or at least for long enough to cause them both grief.

He'd known ever since last weekend that not all of her hatred of the army was an irrational reaction to his disappearance. She had some very real concerns; he'd come to see that. He'd almost dealt with them when he'd walked in and found her pouring them out to Joel. But, dammit, he wanted her to admit that nothing was as important as their love.

Major Patrick O'Donnell, U.S. army, hero and survivor of twelve years in hell, knew he had the toughest campaign of his life to fight the next few days. And there was no easy way out, either.

THE HOTEL HAD PROVIDED, among many other amenities, a wonderful jasmine-scented bubble bath, and Megan blithely emptied the entire box into the water. As the big tub quickly began to overflow with shimmering, aromatic bubbles, she climbed in with a luxuriant sigh, ignoring the mess. Self-indulgence beckoned.

She leaned back and inhaled the overpowering fragrance, and was quickly lulled into a soporific state even as she told herself to get to work on some arguments to win Patrick away from the army.

There was the old "if you really love me" argument, but that seemed rather childish. He loved her and he knew she knew it, too.

What about "You wouldn't want our children to grow up as miserably as I did"? That one had distinct possibilities and was perhaps the best she could offer, though it seemed to her that she could use a few others, too.

Well, there was always "What am I supposed to do while you're keeping the world safe for democracy?" Traveling

ravel agents aren't much in demand, after all. Certainly he
idn't expect her to build her life around him.

She was supposed to be serious about this, but it seemed
o her that her thoughts had just a touch too much humor
n them. One did not beat the U.S. army with humor,
hough God knows there was plenty of it to be had there.

It must be the bubbles. Maybe she was getting high on an
verdose of jasmine. She sank deeper into the iridescent
plendor, sending still more froth over the edge of the tub
s she let the water's warmth seep into her. It was very hard
o be serious just now; in fact, it was very hard not to be ri-
iculously happy. Just out there was the man she loved—the
nan she'd thought she lost forever until less than three
veeks ago—and they were about to take off for a wonder-
ul, lazy sailing trip.

Little disconnected thoughts and images bounced through
er head. His nervousness the first time they'd made love
fter his return. A return of that nervousness today before
ne ceremony. That boyish grin that would never change, no
natter how hardened the rest of him had become. The hu-
nan side of the man. The side that belonged to her. Unlike
ne general, Patrick had a human side.

The general. Bubble baths and the general did not go to-
ether, and she didn't want to think about him now, but he
id bear some thinking about. There were those hugs and
isses, and he'd actually remarked proudly to one of his
riends at that afternoon's party that she had "quite a suc-
essful business going up there." What was his game, any-
ay?

She was trawling slowly through her lethargic brain for
ne thread of her earlier thoughts when there was a knock at
ne bathroom door. Before she could think to respond,
atrick came in and promptly began to sneeze.

Warmth and laughter mixed as she saw him standing there
a his briefs and trying to fight off another sneeze.

"I thought the box was meant to be used all at once," she said between giggles by way of apology.

"I think it must have been a week's supply," he replied and sneezed again.

"I'd invite you to join me, but since you seem to be allergic to the bubbles, I guess you'll just have to wait your turn in here." She was beginning to regret her extravagance.

"I'll just suffer noisily," he said, grinning between sniffles as he stripped off his briefs.

A tremor of expectation thrummed through her, not quite driving out her former lassitude, but certainly giving it a new and sensual dimension. The contrast between his very male body and the bubbly, perfumed atmosphere was becoming almost unbearably sexy.

"I'm sure there must be a section somewhere in army rules and regulations about the wearing of jasmine with uniforms," she said, smiling as he stepped gingerly into the tub.

"Section 5248C, subsection 328A," he said with mock solemnity. "Officers shall refrain from taking bubble baths while on duty. However, I am not on duty at the moment, as you may have noticed."

"Well, I *did* think that your summer uniform was just a bit provocative," she replied with a decided leer.

"Only a bit?" He settled down into the tub, sending still more bubbles over the side and onto the floor. "There's no water in here."

"Well, I had to let some out when the bubbles began spilling over."

"The management is not going to welcome us back here."

She shrugged. "So what? We can't afford it, anyway."

Then he stood up suddenly. "The management. That reminds me. Be right back."

She broke into wild giggles as he climbed back out of the tub and started toward the door, trailing bubbles as he went.

Shimmery clumps of them clung to his hard, tanned body, humorously softening those planes and angles.

A moment later he was back, bearing an ice bucket holding a champagne bottle and two glasses. "Compliments of the management. It arrived just after you came in here to make this mess. Good thing they didn't know about it, or they might have sent a chambermaid instead."

She took the glass he offered. "One might be tempted to think that you're someone special."

He frowned at the label. "I think the fame must be wearing off already. The Plaza gave us a better brand. And there weren't as many flowers this time, either. Did you notice that?"

"'*Sic transit gloria mundi,*'" she quoted airily, then lifted the glass to her lips. "It's rather good, though. Bubbly with the bubbles. How appropriate."

"I doubt if the management would agree," he said doubtfully, briefly surveying the mess before rejoining her with his own glass. "I just hope they don't send the Pentagon a bill for cleaning up after us."

"No problem. It'll just get tucked in there with dog boarding and five-hundred-dollar toilet seats. No one will ever notice it."

"I hope not. I'd have a tough time living on a second lieutenant's pay again, after all this."

Champagne called for toasts, so they began to try to outdo each other in proposing them, reaching new heights of silliness and playfulness, amid bubbles and laughter and slippery caresses. The level of liquid in the champagne bottle sank at about the same rate as the bubbles in the tub, until they climbed out and went to the shower stall to rinse off. Just as the bubbles had seemed to induce silliness, so the steam seemed to provoke sensuality, until they had turned the act of drying each other into a worshiping of each other's bodies.

Patrick picked her up to carry her to the bed, then cas
one last doubtful look around the bathroom. "Do you think
I'd be pushing the hero bit too far if I asked for maid ser
vice at this hour?"

Feeling slightly light-headed from the champagne and
more than slightly voluptuous from their activities, Megan
waved a hand airily. "Why not just ask for a different
suite?"

He laughed and kissed her as he dropped her onto the
bed. "Because even for heroes, it is not considered accept
able behavior to be cavorting naked in the hallways."

"That's true," she replied with a hiccup. "The Pentagon
would not be pleased. Major O'Donnell might find himself
facing a board of inquiry."

"Major O'Donnell finds himself facing another problem
right now," he said as he joined her on the bed.

She conjured up a scornful look. "Not *that* again. You
seem to have that problem regularly."

The teasing and joking went on, gradually merging with
passion in a way that had always been unique to them.
Laughter was slowly transformed into the sound of love,
until she drew him to her and his demanding hardness met
her melting softness.

WARM SPRING SUNSHINE bathed the group gathered for a
late breakfast on the Daniels' terrace. A short distance away,
birds provided a cheery serenade as they splashed around in
the big stone birdbath. The soft green of reawakened grass
provided a background for bright beds of spring flowers and
banks of brilliant azaleas.

Megan's gaze wandered over the scene. She was thinking
that wherever in the world the Daniels family had temporarily put down their roots, her mother had instantly created
a garden. This, of course, was her finest, because they had
now lived here for fifteen years.

Was this, she wondered suddenly, her mother's way of coping with the constant changes in her life, this creating of small patches of beauty wherever she went? She looked cross at her mother and very much wanted to ask the question. But she kept her silence because it would seem strange, and perhaps because she didn't really want to know.

Joel and the general were dressed for golf, but neither of them seemed to be in any hurry. Joel gave Megan a grin as their mother once again launched into a mild reproof of Joel's continuing bachelorhood. Megan smiled, thinking that her handsome brother wouldn't last much longer.

Then, abruptly, she thought of Karen. Karen had met Joel and they had seemed to like each other. She toyed a moment with the idea of one-upping her mother, then brought herself up short. How could she be thinking such a thing? Would she really wish on her best friend the life she was trying to avoid herself?

I'm entirely too mellow this morning, she thought disgustedly. *Something is happening here, something very dangerous. It has to stop.* Then she caught Patrick's eye and startlingly clear images of the previous night brought a faint flush to her face before she quickly averted her eyes.

As breakfast and conversation continued, Megan noticed once again the complete absence of any talk about the future as far as she and Patrick were concerned. Her mother was talking about a suitable place for Joel to live, but not about where she and Patrick would be living. They were discussing Joel's next assignment, but not Patrick's.

Patrick himself hadn't said a word about it this weekend. Of course, it was possible that the army hadn't decided what to do with him yet, but it was also possible that everyone at the table except her knew about his next assignment already.

She felt ever more cut out, set adrift, but she still wasn't willing to be a part of any plans that involved the army.

Breakfast drew to a close. Patrick and Joel were deep in a discussion of the current state of affairs in Central America and her mother excused herself to take a phone call. The general seemed to be lost in his own thoughts.

Megan was restless. She got up from the table and wandered out into the large yard, planning to examine the flower beds more closely. She had just paused before a particularly spectacular bed of exotic tulips flanked by brilliant red azaleas when she heard a step behind her. Expecting it to be Patrick, she turned to find her father instead.

She gave him a pleasant, if slightly wary, smile. On such a lovely morning, she was prepared to be charitable even toward the general—within limits, of course.

She commented on the beauty of the flower beds and he responded that her mother had spent quite a lot of time on them, as she always did. That question she hadn't asked before came out now, in the form of a comment.

"I was just thinking earlier that wherever we lived, Mother always created her gardens, even when she knew we might not be there to see them completed."

The general nodded. "It was her way of coping with the constant moves, the impermanence."

Once more, this man she thought she knew had astonished her. She had that uncomfortable, disorienting feeling one gets when the very familiar becomes the very strange. Her father actually thought about such things? Actually admitted that there were shortcomings to the army way of life? She shook her head slightly, as if she doubted her hearing.

He looked at her with that same grave expression for which she had criticized Joel yesterday. "It isn't an easy life, Megan, and I never intended you to think that I believed it was."

"But even so, you want me to stay in it." She spoke mildly because she was still too shocked to be angry.

"Yes. I thought it was what you wanted. I thought you'd made that choice when you married Patrick."

She started to say just what she'd said to Patrick and to Joel, that she'd believed she was marrying a man who had no intention of making the army his career. But the words stuck in her throat because she knew the general had seen from the beginning what she herself hadn't seen—Patrick belonged to the army.

"But I've been living a totally different life for years now," she said finally. "Surely you knew that."

He nodded after a brief hesitation and she suspected that he was agreeing with her only to prevent an argument.

She waved a hand angrily at the flower beds. "I don't want this. I don't want a life of trying to create permanence out of impermanence."

"Do you want Patrick?"

The question startled her, considering the source. Megan met that nearly colorless gaze and knew that equivocating would be wrong.

"Yes, I do," she admitted in a near-whisper. "But I don't want the army."

The general heaved a sigh. "That's our fault, I suppose, your mother's and mine. We tried too hard to give you everything, to make up for your missing a normal childhood. I'm afraid we spoiled you rather badly, Megan, because you seem to think you can have it all."

"No, I don't think I can have it all," she retorted quickly. "But none of you seems to understand what I'd be giving up."

"Or maybe you don't understand what you'd be gaining," he said calmly. "Patrick knows what he's asking of you, just as I knew what I was asking of your mother. But asking a lot means giving a lot in return, too."

Megan started to open her mouth to say that he'd certainly never given much, but she stopped. Maybe he hadn't been there all the times she had wanted him to be, but he had probably been there all the times he *could* be. She recalled his presence at ballet recitals and school plays. And perhaps even more importantly, she thought about her parents' marriage. In recent years her anger with her father had prevented her from seeing what she had always known; they had the happiest marriage she had ever seen. There had to be a reason for that.

They stared at each other in silence. There were questions she wanted to ask of him and of her mother. How do you sustain a marriage under such conditions? Is love really enough? But he was her father and the gap between them prevented those questions from being asked. Still, the moment seemed to call for something.

Before she even quite realized what she was doing, Megan stretched up to kiss him on the cheek. He drew her arm through his and together they started back toward the terrace, oblivious of their audience. And the general was smiling again.

Chapter Twelve

Patrick stood at the helm, his attention focused half on the open water ahead of the sailboat and half on Meggie as she stood below him in the bow. The breeze ruffled her black hair as it glistened in the sun. She was wearing red again, a red windbreaker this time. Red was her color and always had been, not just because it suited her hair and complexion so well, but also because it was like her—bright, bold, full of fire.

But she'd been making him uneasy all day. Meggie was rarely ever quiet and introspective. Action generally followed thought very quickly, and occasionally even preceded it. Not today, however.

Would she actually end it between them, run back to Connecticut and the life she'd made for herself that didn't include him? It was inconceivable, but that, he thought wryly, didn't necessarily mean that it couldn't happen. She could be quicksilver, changing form before his startled eyes; she'd been that way from the beginning.

He thought about the very first time he'd seen her, thirteen years before. A petite splash of red dress and shining black hair amid a sea of cadet gray. The daughter of a general. Everyone knew that her father was headed for the top and that he was an old friend of the superintendent's.

Army gossip reached into even the Gothic fortress on th
Hudson.

For all of ten minutes he'd let the fact that she was
general's daughter keep him away from her. But he'
watched her—oh, he'd definitely watched her. He knew he
date, of course, a hopeless future-general type who wa
making every effort to impress her. He kept watching fo
signs that she accepted this as being her due. But instead, h
thought she seemed faintly amused.

He edged cautiously into the fringes of the group sur
rounding her, still inclined to think she could best be appre
ciated from a distance. But the closer he came, the mor
powerfully he was drawn to her. Still, he listened an
watched, doing nothing to call her attention to him. Whe
their eyes finally met, she was laughing about something
The smile wavered briefly before she put it back on again
and in that instant Patrick knew. No one could ever agai
convince him that love at first sight was impossible.

He'd taken quite a ribbing after that evening. Him, of al
people, presuming to chase after a general's daughter. Th
bets were on that her father would prevent their date for th
following day. So all the way over to the super's house tha
Sunday, he'd prayed that her father hadn't asked about him

When they'd finally escaped the scrutiny of the tw
generals, Meggie had given him a wide-eyed look of grea
seriousness and asked if he was really as bad as she'd heard
He'd firmly denied it, of course, until he saw the laughte
peeking out of those vivid blue eyes.

And that, as they say, had been that. He could barely re
call the rest of that afternoon, but from that moment on h
would have single-handedly fought the entire U.S. army fo
her.

Now he was caught between them, the army and Meggie
He thought about the scene earlier between her and her fa
ther. His hopes had soared when he'd seen her kiss her fa
ther and then stroll back arm-in-arm with him. If she ha

made her peace with the general, then she must have made
with the army, too. Patrick knew that the general was the
army personified for her. But if anything *had* changed, she
wasn't talking about it.

Dammit, why didn't he know what was going on in her
head? He'd had twelve years to figure her out. He seriously
doubted if any woman had ever been thought about as much
as she had. Yet she still eluded him.

He thought about what he hadn't told her yet, and he
thought about those as-yet-unsigned reenlistment papers
back in his quarters. He had his ace in the hole, and yet he
was reluctant to play it because he knew he wanted from her
what he had no right to ask.

Patrick wasn't altogether happy with himself at the moment, either. He understood that her needs were separate
from his and he didn't want to try to deny them. And yet
there was this annoyingly persistent need to force her to
prove her love.

They both seemed to be caught up in this insistence upon
proving things. He belonged to what had to be the most
macho profession in existence, the profession that had virtually defined the male role from the beginning. Years ago,
he'd felt no need to apologize for that or to demonstrate that
he had a gentler side, too. Now, it seemed that he was
constantly aware of having to prove that and of her constant
uncertainty about it.

Surely, though, he *had* proved that. She must know now
that he hadn't really changed all that much and that his decision to remain in the army didn't mean that he'd turned
into some insensitive war machine. But why wasn't he sure
about that, or about anything else?

He'd just about reached the channel of the Inland Waterway when she left the bow and came up to him. She was
smiling, but he thought that the smile didn't quite reach to
her eyes. He drew her to him with one arm while keeping his

other hand on the wheel. Then he bent to brush his mouth against her fragrant, silky hair.

"I love you."

She wrapped an arm about his waist and hugged him as she nestled in the crook of his arm. "I love you, too. And I'm so glad you planned this surprise."

He murmured his agreement, but he was wondering if it had been such a good idea, after all. He'd thought of it because of the voyage they'd taken off Hawaii just before his departure for Vietnam. He'd relived each and every moment of that journey for the past twelve years, until now he wasn't sure how much had been real and how much had veered off into fantasy. And the same had probably happened for her, too.

So here they were, in full agreement that they couldn't afford to linger in the past while doing just that.

"We can't get away from those memories, Patrick," she said suddenly. "And I don't think we should be trying so hard, either."

She saw the surprised and confused look on his face and hurried on. "I know just what you're thinking. You're thinking that if we concentrate on the past, we won't face up to reality."

"That's right, we won't."

"Every couple has problems, you know. Maybe ours just seem worse because we don't have years and years of marriage behind us to help put things in perspective. So maybe we should be putting to good use the memories we do have."

"I'm not sure that I follow you," he said, shaking his head in confusion.

She laughed suddenly. "I'm not so sure that I do, either, but I still mean it. Did the general arrange for this trip?"

Patrick tried to switch gears to keep up with her. "In a way. I told him that I was going to rent a sailboat and take you away for a while, and he asked General Stanton about using this boat."

"But the idea was yours?"

"Of course."

"And already you're thinking that you might have made
mistake?"

"Uh...yes."

"Well, you haven't. I'm going to wallow in nostalgia all
can. I've been trying to face up to reality ever since you
ame back, and it's gotten me nowhere. So I quit."

"I'm not sure how to take that," he said doubtfully.

ATRICK LAY BACK and enjoyed the small ripples of relax-
ag muscles and that unique sense of well-being. Meggie was
urved against him, nestled in the crook of his arm and al-
eady breathing the deep, regular rhythms of sleep.

God, what pleasure she gave him. He wondered how it
ould have gotten so much better for them both when nei-
ner of them had had any practice in all these years. If he'd
ver had any doubts about lovemaking being more than a
hysical act, he certainly didn't have them now.

The difference had to be in their maturity. Before, love-
naking had been all fumbling around and uncontrolled
assion. Now it was more giving and less taking. He'd al-
vays tried to give her pleasure, but he now suspected that he
night not have tried very hard back then.

He ran his fingers softly over her silken flanks as he
hought about this new attitude of hers. What was behind
?? Maybe she did have a point, though. If they'd *really* been
narried for twelve years, a problem like this wouldn't seem
quite so bad, would it? On the other hand...

"Go to sleep, Patrick. I can hear you thinking."

He chuckled and hugged her. "I thought you were al-
eady asleep."

"I was. You think too loud." Then she shivered lightly.
'And it's hard to sleep with someone running sandpaper
over you."

He lifted his hand. "You didn't complain earlier. In fact I had the impression that you might have liked it."

"Now, whatever gave you that idea?" she asked with a yawn.

"It might have been all those yelps and moans and other assorted sounds."

"It's tasteless to remind one of such things," she mumbled sleepily.

He propped himself up on one elbow and stared down at her dark head silhouetted against the pillow. "Does it seem very different for you now, too?"

"Of course it's different. We're older and better and more . . . loving, wouldn't you say?"

"Yes, I would say," he replied as he lowered his mouth to hers, nibbling lightly at her kiss-swollen lips.

She responded, but in a slow, lazy fashion that told him she was about to drift off to sleep again.

"Meggie?" he queried softly, his mouth hovering just above hers.

"Hmm?"

"Did you regret that we hadn't had any children? I mean, after you thought I was dead?"

A long silence followed, and he thought she might have fallen asleep. But then she nodded slowly.

"Yes. I thought about it often."

He dropped back to his pillow, thinking about the children in the village. How many times had he wished that they'd had a child, that he'd left a piece of himself with her? He hadn't been all that eager to have children before he left, because he wanted Meggie all to himself then. Now it was different. Or was he just thinking about it now because a child could hold them together?

"Did you?" asked a soft, sleepy voice out of the darkness.

"Did I what?" he questioned, pulling himself out of his thoughts and assuming that he'd missed something.

"Regret that we didn't have any children."

"Yes," he admitted. "But under the circumstances, it was better we didn't. And I don't know how I'd have felt if I'd come home to find a half-grown son or daughter waiting for me."

She just hugged him to her and said nothing. In a few minutes, he began to drift down into sleep, thinking about the village children, and Meggie's belly swollen with his child, and a house with a swing set in the yard, and . . .

MEGAN FELT GOOD, better than she probably had any right to feel, she thought. After all, if he resisted her plan . . .

He wouldn't. He wouldn't because he couldn't. If he'd had any doubts at all about their love, and she didn't think he did, then these past three days should have swept them away. That's why she'd insisted that they stop struggling against the seductive pull of the past. That past strengthened their love by reminding them both that it was not new. But they'd both been fighting that past and perhaps even fighting their love.

She should have seen this way out of their dilemma earlier and undoubtedly would have if she hadn't been so busy fighting the past and fighting the army. Not that she'd given up her battle with the army, of course. To paraphrase in the words of one famous naval hero, "Surrender, hell! I've just begun to fight."

Megan smiled wickedly. She'd been a rather unwilling student of the army all her life, and she'd definitely learned a thing or three. Although she had scarcely been aware of it at the time, the plan that would save their marriage had begun to take form during the award ceremony and the party at her parents' home afterward. Now all that remained was to convince him.

He'd resist it initially, she thought; in fact, she was quite sure that he would. That's why she was keeping it to herself for the time being.

Patrick was generally a very easygoing person, flexible and always willing to listen to reason. But beneath that laid back manner was an iron will that he rarely asserted. She'd forgotten about it over the years, even though she could now remember several instances when he'd demonstrated that quality. It was as though he'd drawn a very firm line in his mind, and nothing could induce him to cross that line.

Well, he was going to cross it this time if she had to drag him bodily, screaming and protesting all the way. No way was she going to listen to his protests about foolish pride or not taking advantage of the situation.

She opened her eyes as his shadow fell across her sun baked body, then smiled at him as he crouched down beside her chaise. She still couldn't look at him without seeing his younger version hovering somewhere nearby, but the comparisons no longer bothered her. They had become unimportant. There was far too much in this man to love for her to waste time mourning the man she had lost.

She reached up to run a finger along his cheek and jaw, then let it rest in the tiny hollow at the center of his chin. He left it there for a moment, then lifted her hand to his lips and began to run his tongue slowly along her fingertips.

There were many moments like this now, times when words were not only unnecessary, but might even have spoiled things. For a time, they had all but worn each other out with passion, with a powerful need to possess. But by now desire had been sated to the extent that moments like this became just as powerfully erotic and satisfying.

"I've decided to spend the Porsche money on a boat," he said casually. "Of course, it won't be quite like this one, but it'll be a start, anyway."

"From the complaints I've heard from boat owners, that's exactly what it'll be. Someone once described boats as being a hole in the water into which you pour money."

He chuckled, and she managed a smile to go along with her light words. But she sensed a subtle change, a slight shift the atmosphere. It was the first mention he'd made of anything beyond this voyage.

Perhaps he sensed her nervousness, or maybe he regretted his words, because he quickly changed the subject.

"General Stanton's guide to the Chesapeake says there's a great seafood restaurant not far away. I thought we'd go there for dinner. We need to go ashore for supplies anyway."

Where do you plan to keep this boat you intend to buy, Patrick? she asked silently. *You must have given that matter some thought.* "Fine," she said out loud. "I'm already tired of my cooking. You must be, too."

Patrick diplomatically refrained from comment.

An hour later they were drawing up to a well-kept marina, enjoying the envious glances of other boat owners. Wherever they had docked, the graceful wood-hulled sailboat with its gleaming brass fittings had caused a stir. On several occasions, people had asked about its owner, who was, Megan had commented dryly, "rather memorable himself."

They shopped for supplies, and after taking them back to the boat, strolled around town. Here, as in other places they'd visited, people favored Patrick with those haven't-I-seen-you-somewhere looks, but at least no one bothered them.

It felt strange, almost irritating, to be among people again. Megan laughed aloud as she remembered how they'd sought the company of others during those days at the cabin.

When Patrick gave her a quizzical look, she smiled. "I was just thinking about how badly I wanted to be with other people when we were at the cabin, and now I rather wish that they'd all disappear."

He nodded in agreement. "I think that was a disaster that had to happen. Neither one of us was exactly dwelling in the real world then."

"No, we weren't. You came home expecting to pick up where we'd left off, and I went there..." She paused because she realized that she'd never told him what her thoughts had been at that time, although he must surely have guessed. "I went there out of a sense of duty. You were my husband, I had loved you once, and I felt I owed it to you to be there." Just the act of saying that almost made her sick. "God, it sounds so awful now."

Patrick squeezed her hand gently. "No, it doesn't, Meggie. You were actually being a lot more sensible about it than I was, with my wild fantasies."

"It was fear, Patrick. Plain and simple. You were right. Or, rather, those shrinks you talked to were right. I had buried everything so deeply, and I was afraid to let it come out. And I knew you wouldn't be coming back the same person."

She sighed. "It's difficult even now to sort it all out. I didn't really want you to come back the same, because I was afraid that I might fall in love with you all over again. And yet I got mad because you *weren't* the same."

"We were both in a state of shock, Meggie. But we've survived it, and that's all that counts. There was a lot of anger and guilt on both our parts that had to be gotten out. Until we did that, we couldn't find the love."

She thought that, under the circumstances, it was nothing short of a miracle that they *had* found that love again.

They walked on in silence for a few minutes before Patrick broke in with a question that immediately changed the atmosphere between them once more.

"Were the doctors also right about your real reason for hating the army?"

"They were partly right. I did need someone to blame and the army was very convenient. It's such an all-encompassing life, and the army had, in effect, taken care of me all my life. But then, suddenly, it didn't take care of you, and I hated it for that.

"But I also hate it because it demands too much—and gives nothing in return."

"Yes, it does, Meggie," he said firmly. "It gives the satisfaction of knowing that you're doing the most important job in the world, keeping the peace."

An angry response to that was about to leap out of her mouth, but she stopped it, then spoke with deliberate calmness.

"Your satisfaction is not my satisfaction, Patrick, and you ought to be able to see that. You're asking too much of our love."

She was replaying the conversation in the garden with her father. But what her father had asked for—and gotten—from her mother, Patrick should not be asking of her. He had to be made to see that. In fact, he should be able to see it without being told. Before she told him how they were going to resolve their problem, she wanted an admission from him that he truly understood what he was asking of her. That admission constituted an acceptance of her as a separate individual.

To her surprise and dismay, he made no response to her statement. Instead, they wandered through a few antique shops, and to take her mind off his failure to respond, she tried halfheartedly to interest him in the merchandise. He tried just about as hard to appear interested.

When they returned to the boat to change for dinner, each of them heard a forced lightness in the other's conversation and noticed a certain lack of spontaneity in each other's behavior. Megan thought that Patrick was trying too hard to be casual about everything, and he thought that she was concentrating too deeply on the simplest words or actions. Both were waiting.

They agreed that dinner was excellent and thanked General Stanton in absentia for his recommendation, but the meal had passed completely out of their minds by the time they left the restaurant. To make conversation, Me-

gan, who had left their itinerary completely up to him, aske
where they were headed next. Patrick said that he though
they had better be turning back soon. The mood chang
deepened.

Each of them was beginning to sense the dimensions of
momentous clash of wills and, true to their natures, ha
begun to feel around the edges for some sign of weakness
This had, on occasion, happened in the past. What Mega
had determined to be an underlying rigidity in Patrick wa
certainly no less true of her.

The evening had grown surprisingly cool by the time the
returned to the boat, so they went to the comfortable loung
and made some Irish coffee to top off the dinner they'd trie
to enjoy. On other evenings, Megan would have curled up
in Patrick's lap at his eager invitation. Tonight, they sa
across from each other.

"Dinner was very good, wasn't it?" she asked as sh
sipped at the whiskey-laden coffee.

"Yes, it was," he replied, doing likewise.

"But we could have been eating boiled spiders for all th
attention either of us paid to it," she went on.

"That's true," he replied with a smile.

Obviously, he wasn't going to be any help at all, sh
thought irritably. How could she make him understan
something that, by all rights, he should *already* under
stand?

"When I was talking to the general the other day, he sai
that he'd known he was asking a lot of my mother when h
asked her to marry him and accept army life. But he sai
that asking a lot means giving a lot in return, too."

Patrick just nodded, and after she had waited a few sec
onds in vain for more of a response she gave up and wen
on.

"Maybe he has given a lot, although I can't say that I'v
ever seen evidence of it." She shrugged, then added hon
estly, "They do have a happy marriage, though."

Patrick was still sitting there, watching her mutely.

"But they're of a different generation. My mother genuinely believes that her role in life is to provide a comfortable home for my father and promote his career. I'd have to say that she's been highly successful at that."

She stopped again, wondering if all this candor about her parents might not be counterproductive at the moment. He still said nothing.

"I cannot be my mother, Patrick. After that conversation with the general, there were actually a few moments when I wished that I could be. It's all so simple for them, really. And if she hasn't been *my* idea of a successful woman, she has certainly been *her* idea of one.

"What I'm saying is that I'm not going to give up my career to follow you around the world. I love you and I want more than anything for us to be together. But if I try to kid myself into thinking that sharing your life will be enough for me, I'll just end up making us both miserable. Sacrifice like that sounds wonderful in theory, but it's pure hell in practice."

Patrick's gaze slid away from hers and she could feel the tension emanating from him. *He really did believe that he could talk me into it,* she thought disbelievingly. Did he really know so little of her?

In her anguish, there was a brief moment when she wanted to say that she would try. But she held her silence, and he got up to add some more whiskey to his coffee. Then he spoke without turning back to her.

"You're right; it *did* sound good in theory. It seemed like a sort of ultimate test, 'if you love me enough' and all that."

Finally, he turned to face her and she saw the guilt written on his face and the anguish she herself was also feeling.

"I haven't really gotten over my selfishness. Even though I know you love me, I still seem to need that proof. I want to hear you say that you'd give up that life you have that I'm not a part of."

Megan watched him as he came back to sit down. And she had thought he didn't really need her! How very wrong she had been. He needed her badly enough to ask of her something that he had known all along was too much.

"I need you, Meggie," he said slowly and quietly, making no effort to hide his anguish. "I need you so badly. I didn't feel that way...before. Need didn't enter into it back then."

She nodded slowly, tempted to go to him and comfort him but knowing that it was the wrong thing to do. "You needed to know that I would give up my career for you, and I needed to know that you would give up the army for me. It's all those years, Patrick, all those lost years. That's what we both really needed. All those years together would have prevented this."

She was casting around for the words to express what she was feeling when Patrick did it for her.

"I think that love is a whole lot more complex than either of us would have believed back then," he said.

After a long moment of silence, he went on. "I can't give up the army, either, Meggie, any more than you can give up being your own person. But I wasn't any more certain about it than you were, because I haven't signed my reenlistment papers yet."

The clash of wills was over for them both. If neither of them had won, at least they both understood, and that was, for both of them, far more important.

Megan was sure now that he would go along with her plan, although she still expected a token protest. So she forged on, already bracing herself to deal with his stubbornness.

"There is a way out of this, Patrick, a way for us to both have what we need. I should have thought of it sooner, but I guess I was too busy trying to force you to give up the army for me."

She saw the surprised look on his face and raised a hand to silence him. "I want you to hear me out before you start to protest."

He leaned back in his chair with a strange half smile and waited.

"This is what we're going to do. You are going to insist that they give you a permanent assignment at the Pentagon so we can settle down in Washington. Actually, though, we're going to settle down as far away from the Pentagon and its inhabitants as possible, find a neighborhood where there isn't another military couple within miles. Maybe somewhere out near Middleburg. It's a growing area and could be a good place for me to start a new travel agency, too."

She stopped as she saw his smile growing, and she guessed the general direction of his thoughts. "And don't try to tell me that you can't order the Pentagon around, because you can. They want you, Patrick. You're a West Pointer and a hero, and I know that bunch. I watched you with them at the party. You're a definite candidate for stars. As far as duty tours are concerned, you can just remind them that you've had a twelve-year tour, even if it was all in one place.

"Furthermore, if they give you any grief, I know exactly who to go to to arrange for some arm-twisting. I think he'd do anything I ask right now."

He had continued to smile all through this, but she still thought it was a strange sort of smile.

"There's just one problem," he said as he grew serious once more.

"Don't you give me problems, Patrick O'Donnell. It's about time that the army learned a few things, like the fact that they can't expect to continue sending men all over the world without considering their wives' careers."

"Would you let them send us to Boston?"

"Boston?"

"Well, Cambridge, actually. For two or three years."

Megan was confused. "You mean Cambridge as in Harvard?"

"No, I mean Cambridge as in M.I.T. It will take me at least two, and possibly three, years to get a Ph.D. in nuclear physics."

She chewed her lower lip thoughtfully. She should have thought about that. Patrick had talked about a graduate degree years ago, and the army did generally send its top officers on to graduate school.

"I know some people who own a number of travel agencies up there. Maybe I could get a job with one of them," she said, thinking aloud.

"Are you saying that you'll agree to it?" he asked hopefully.

Megan hesitated. If she gave in now, what would be next? On the other hand, Patrick *did* need that degree to succeed, and M.I.T. *was* top of the line.

"But what about after that?"

"After that, we can start to look for that house out in Middleburg and you can set up your business."

"Have they promised you a Pentagon assignment?"

"They have."

"Did you get it in writing?"

"Meggie," he protested, "you don't go asking a four-star to put his promises in writing. General Stanton gave me his word. I'll be assigned to his section."

"Hmm, well, since it's him, I guess we could accept that. After all, he's Dad's best friend and he'd never dare go back on his promise to you."

"Especially since your father knows about it," Patrick added. "I think he's grown rather fond of the idea of having his grandchildren around him."

But Megan was paying only the scantest attention to his last remark. "Are you telling me that you did just what I told you to do?"

He grinned. "That's right, and even before you told me, too. Isn't that amazing?"

"How long have you known about all this?"

"Oh, about as long as you've known about your own plan," he answered tauntingly. "And we both kept quiet for the same reason."

Then, as she nodded sadly, he got up and walked over to extend his hand to her. She took it and let him draw her to her feet and into his arms. He stroked her hair softly, then pressed a kiss against her brow.

"I'm sorry that we can't settle in Washington right away, Meggie. But I really need that degree. I know it's asking a lot for you to give up Touch of Paradise and go to work for someone else for a while. I even thought about the possibility of your staying in Connecticut and my coming there on weekends from Boston. But, dammit, we've been apart for too long. I don't want a weekend marriage."

Megan had been doing some fast thinking and had already considered that possibility. But something he had said earlier changed her mind.

"Neither do I," she said as she stretched up to kiss him. "I'll manage. Besides, it will be a lot easier to work part-time for someone else than to work part-time for myself."

He frowned. "I don't understand."

"Well," she said, leaning back to look up at him with a smile, "it just occurred to me that we could put the time you'll be in graduate school to good use. After all, you'll be home a lot more in the next few years than you will be after that."

He continued to frown for a moment. Then his eyes lit with understanding and he began to grin.

"If you mean what I think you mean..."

"What I mean is that you should be capable of changing diapers with one hand while holding a nuclear physics text in the other."

...d as he swept her into his arms and started to ... bedroom. "I think we'll have a strategic plannin... ...n right now."

Epilogue

When she heard the delighted squeals from the backyard, Megan went to the kitchen window. She smiled, even though she still had some reservations about that new swing set. Mark Patrick O'Donnell, long since dubbed "M.P." by his father, was making a serious attempt to wrap the chains of a swing around the top bar as he pushed himself higher and higher.

His bright red curls caught the sun and his sturdy little legs stretched out before him, straining with effort. Megan felt a powerful tug at her heart as she recalled another little red-haired boy she'd seen once, back when she'd been certain that Patrick was dead. M.P., or "Imp," as she herself had taken to calling him with good reason, was a miracle child—the miracle was that his father had lived to make his existence possible.

She was completing preparations for his third birthday party, to be attended by neighborhood children and all-too-doting relatives, some of whom were already out there, either encouraging him or admonishing him.

Assembling the swing set had been the project of two lieutenant colonels and a retired police captain, all of whom now stood proudly by. The general was expected momentarily. Megan shook her head ruefully. By the time Imp had outgrown that swing set, he would be the son of one general

and the godson of a second, and he was already the grand
son of a third.

Her gaze rested affectionately on the two lieutenant col
onels, both of whom would shortly be exchanging their sil
ver oak leaves for the ''bird'' of a full colonel. The
promotions for both Patrick and Joel were coming fast now.

Then she remembered the latest promotion and left the
kitchen to go to the downstairs family room. The bottles o
champagne sat atop the bar and she put them into the small
refrigerator to chill, smiling to herself.

You've come a long way, old girl, she told herself. *When
you toast the new chief of staff, you can actually mean it.*

The general's final promotion had come through only
few days ago, although it had been expected for months
ever since the present chief had announced his intention to
retire. Megan was actually a little embarrassed at her pride
because she still suffered from occasional twinges of re
sentment toward the army.

But that scene four years ago in her mother's garden had
been a watershed in her often-turbulent relationship with her
father. She was still inclined to fault him as a father,
judgment in which she knew he would concur. However, she
could no longer fault the man. If he hadn't been all that she
had wanted him to be, she knew now that he had been the
best he could be. To reach the very pinnacle of his chosen
profession had required great personal sacrifice, and fam
ily life had been the largest part of that sacrifice.

Back in the kitchen again, she watched Patrick with his
son. She'd made her peace with the army, even if it was
sometimes an uneasy peace. For that, Patrick could take full
credit. Never once had he deviated from his promise that
they would have a life outside the army. Their friends were
drawn from just about every profession except for the mil
itary, and they had successfully stayed on the fringes of the
Pentagon social whirl. As Patrick received promotion after

romotion, that would become ever more difficult, but she
vas sure now that they could manage it.

Only a few weeks ago she learned through Joel that Pat-
ick had turned down flat the offer of a duty tour with the
_atin Command in Panama. This, she knew, was the "hot"
:ommand just now, and aspiring generals were competing
or just such a duty tour. But when she questioned Patrick
_bout it, he had merely shrugged.

"They know the conditions of my remaining in the army,
_nd that hasn't changed. Besides," he added with a flash of
:hat perpetually boyish grin, "I'm rotten at languages and
vould never be able to learn Spanish."

There were times, usually after a particularly trying day,
vhen Patrick brought the Pentagon home with him. But, to
_is credit, it never took more than a mocking salute from her
:o break the authoritative facade of the officer. He might
_ot agree, but she knew that the irreverent cadet was still
:here, hiding just beneath the surface.

She was still at the window, satisfied for the moment to
_e watching the tableau in their yard, when Karen came
_riefly into view as she talked to Joel. After nearly four
_ears, Megan still wasn't sure about the wisdom of having
_eintroduced those two. A definite attraction had been there,
_ut they had soon veered off on separate paths. Karen had
_aid that Joel was "too serious" and Joel had grumbled that
_aren was "too damned stubborn for a woman." But both
_f them had remained unmarried, and a few months ago
:hey had begun to spend time together again.

Karen disappeared from view, then reappeared in the
_itchen doorway just as Megan was putting the finishing
:ouches on the birthday cake.

"I never knew you had it in you," Karen remarked,
_aughing, as she stared appreciatively at the lavishly deco-
:rated cake. "Did you manage to find time to squeeze in a
:ake-decorating course?"

Megan shook her head. "Actually, I bought all these little roses and the letters and the cake came out of a box. Things have been so busy at work that I'm lucky I could take a Saturday off."

"Is that a subtle way of bringing up the subject of my joining Memories-to-Be?" Karen teased.

"You know full well that I'm incapable of subtlety," Megan responded. "And you'd better be prepared for some not-so-subtle remarks from my mother, too."

Karen rolled her eyes. "Joel's threatening me with a tour of duty in the Latin Command now."

"Another example of the family's lack of subtlety," Megan chuckled. "And speaking of that, it looks as if the army has definitely arrived."

Karen joined Megan at the plant-filled window. General and Mrs. Daniels had indeed arrived, with their two ever-present uniformed aides trailing along at a respectful distance. Both women watched as the proud grandfather swept his laughing grandson into his arms, then set him down to begin a close inspection of the assembly work done by the two lieutenant colonels.

Megan shook her head with a wry grin. "He never put a swing set together in his life." Then the two women went out to join the party.

Megan greeted her parents, then impulsively stretched up to kiss her father. "Congratulations, Dad."

The general smiled one of his rare smiles. "I think you really mean that, Megan."

"I do."

Father and daughter exchanged looks that said that while they might never be in total agreement they had at least gained an understanding.

Then Megan turned to see Patrick lifting M.P. to the top of the slide attached to the swing set. She started toward them just as they both noticed her. Identical grins lighted up

heir faces before Patrick released his hold on his son to let
im squeal his way down to the bottom.

The lieutenant colonel looked as if he would have liked to
ry the slide himself.

AUTHOR'S
CHRISTMAS MESSAGE

It has always seemed to me that the Christmas season is far more the season of love than is Valentine's Day— love in the very best sense of the word. For me, the greatest love is that of selfless giving, of acceptance, of understanding. The holiday season seems to bring out that best in all of us, whether or not we accept the religious part of Christmas.

As you steal a few hours from your busy holiday schedule to curl up with this book, I hope that you will also take the time to reflect upon the demands made on all of us in today's difficult world. "Goodwill toward men" is far more than just a phrase in a song. This world has never been more desperately in need of goodwill, of acceptance and of understanding—toward our friends and loved ones and toward our enemies.

The world shrinks and, at the same time, grows ever more complex. The easy answers have been given—only the difficult ones remain. The greatest gift that could be bestowed upon all of us is the gift of tolerance and goodwill. May each of you receive that precious gift in full measure.

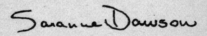

Saranne Dawson

AR 180

Janet Dailey
Americana

Don't miss a single title from this great collection. The first eight titles have already been published. Complete and mail this coupon today to order books you may have missed.

Harlequin Reader Service

In U.S.A.
901 Fuhrmann Blvd.
P.O. Box 1397
Buffalo, N.Y. 14140

In Canada
P.O. Box 2800
Postal Station A
5170 Yonge Street
Willowdale, Ont. M2N 6J3

Please send me the following titles from the Janet Dailey Americana Collection. I am enclosing a check or money order for $2.75 for each book ordered, plus 75¢ for postage and handling.

———	ALABAMA	Dangerous Masquerade
———	ALASKA	Northern Magic
———	ARIZONA	Sonora Sundown
———	ARKANSAS	Valley of the Vapours
———	CALIFORNIA	Fire and Ice
———	COLORADO	After the Storm
———	CONNECTICUT	Difficult Decision
———	DELAWARE	The Matchmakers

Number of titles checked @ $2.75 each = $_____

N.Y. RESIDENTS ADD
   APPROPRIATE SALES TAX $_____

Postage and Handling $_____.75_____

              TOTAL $_____

I enclose _____

(Please send check or money order. We cannot be responsible for cash sent through the mail.)

PLEASE PRINT

NAME _____

ADDRESS _____

CITY _____

STATE/PROV. _____

Take 4 best-selling love stories FREE
Plus get a FREE surprise gift!

A stranger's face.
A stranger's fate.
Or were they her own?

ANDREW NEIDERMAN

REFLECTION

They say everyone has a twin somewhere in time. Cynthia Warner finds hers in a photograph taken thirty years ago. Now she wonders if she will meet the same deadly fate as the woman in the picture...

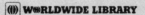